A PARANORMAL BUNDLE

Cover Design and Interior Format

A PARANORMAL PACKAGE

INCLUDES
THREE NOVELLAS
FROM
THREE SEPARATE SERIES

JACKIE IVIE

TABLE OF CONTENTS

THE HUNTED
The Chronicles of the Hunter

TIME TO DIE
Vampire Assassin League

ALLEVIATE
The Portals of Time

THE HUNTED

THE
CHRONICLES
OF THE
HUNTER

JACKIE IVIE

"…THE HUNTED is an exciting suspense/romance that will keep readers at the edge of their seats till the very last page."
~ K. Roma

The Hunted is dedicated to my great friend and fellow writer, Miriam Matthews. Your help and guidance is invaluable to me. Thank you. I couldn't have written LeeAnn and Kane's adventure without you.

CHAPTER ONE

4:57 a.m.
Exactly.

LEEANN GLANCED AT THE DIGITAL read-out on the desk clock. Excellent. Her inner clock was working perfectly. The wake-up call was scheduled for 5:00. Her back-up alarm on her phone for 5:03. She looked toward the window next. She hadn't drawn the room-darkening drapes. That was probably stupid, but she loved things open. Transparent. Open windows. Clear minds. What she didn't like was subterfuge. Cheating. Shady dealings. That's why she'd gone into accounting in the first place. Numbers weren't negotiable. Figures didn't lie. Unless liars did the figuring.

A groan slid past her lips. She glanced toward the clock again. 4:58 now. She was not looking forward to the breakfast meeting with Chad. The man was charming. Good-looking. Single. Smart. But he had a huge problem with integrity. Thank goodness she'd gone with her gut instinct and never had sex with the guy! Talk about adding complication. Then again, LeeAnn wasn't an easy type, like he favored. Nor was she the kind of accountant to overlook accounts that ran through millions of dollars without any source of income. Regardless of how handsome, charming, and debonair her business partner happened to be.

The window drew her gaze next. Again. As if it called to

her. Pre-dawn was just starting outside, highlighting wisps of clouds. Nothing that would bring rain. Not this week. This was just another hot night in a hot week. She was going to be inundated with sunlight. Miami had a lot of that. Especially in the summer. The city was sexy. Sultry. Sticky. She shouldn't have turned the air conditioning down last night. Bed linens clung to her legs as she rolled onto her back.

"Don't. Move."

The words were distinct. Separated. Spoken in a hissed whisper. Carried a lot of threat in a definite bass tone, and resonant with all kinds of masculine vibes. They were accompanied by a long cylindrical item that looked like a rifle barrel. Right above her ribcage.

LeeAnn's heart jumped into her throat, choking her. Her breath caught. Shivers flew down her limbs. Everything went immobile. Deer caught in the headlights. Prey sighted. Spotlighted. Frozen in fear.

Staying still was not going to be a problem.

The rifle shifted farther, elongated. Became a long barrel. Equipped with a large scope. Steadied with his left hand. His other one was on the trigger mechanism. It was attached to a large arm. A really large arm. With a lot of muscle.

Her heart started beating again. Shallow bits of breath were right behind it, followed by mental acuity. She slanted a glance toward him and instantly wished she hadn't. The guy was hooded. His upper face in shadow. But that didn't stop her gasp. Nor the series of shivers that started up.

This was beyond interesting. She must be dreaming here. Nothing else made sense. Bad guys weren't this good-looking. Nor were they sexy as hell. Or ripped. They really weren't supposed to smell nice, either. This was a really great dream.

But what if it wasn't...?

The analyst portion of her psyche kicked in. If this was real, she'd have to file a police report. She needed details. Specifics.

LeeAnn licked her lips. Concentrated.

She couldn't see as much as she wanted. It wasn't light enough yet. He was little more than an amorphous mass in the midst of a lot of black. She could barely make out the tip of his nose down to his shirt collar. A scruff of dark whiskers delineated his jaw. They might match his hair color. He'd dressed in fabric that sucked up light. Everything looked black. No reflection. Not even his gun. The scope was another match. LeeAnn didn't know a lot about rifles, but he wasn't going to hit anything vital in that position. Not on her, anyway.

"You want to live?"

The words were hissed in another whisper. His right arm tensed, putting a lot more forearm definition in her line of sight. She wondered how to describe that to a sketch artist.

"Yes."

"Then, quit moving."

He called this moving? She made a face before replying. "Look. You're in my hotel room. I'm not screaming. I think I'm doing pretty good here. Okay?"

He sighed, sending a slight touch of air across her throat. It lifted all kinds of goose bumps on her skin. She'd selected a peach-colored nightgown last night. It wasn't covering her shoulder area. In fact, it wasn't in evidence at all. The satin felt tangled around her, along with the sheet.

"You should have closed your drapes," he told her.

"Why?"

"Issues."

"With who? Window-washers? I'm on the 29th floor."

"Your levity is out of place."

Levity? What the heck? Who talks like that?

"See that light?"

He gestured with a slight nod. It wasn't necessary. The moment he'd spoken, a long slice of red came through the window, reaching her approximate ankle area. It started moving up from there. She was guessing on its proximity. She didn't check. She'd seen too many suspense movies and crime dramas to be innocent. It looked exactly like she'd seen on a screen.

"Is that a—? No. It can't be. A...*laser sight*?"

The last words were choked. The frozen feeling came back with a vengeance. The guy was completely unaffected. His reply was in the same modulated, calm, deep voice. For some reason, that was even more frightening.

"Yes."

"Well...do something!"

"Have to find him first."

His finger moved, the gun pulsed, giving a slight whisper sound, and the phone rang. Simultaneously. What a time for a perfectly timed wake-up call.

Mister Big-and-Bad had as much strength as it looked. He snagged her about the waist, yanking her and her bedding onto the floor between the bed and wall. That hurt. A thump accompanied her hip hitting the floor, followed by her exclamation. He didn't note it. All kinds of male moved as he reached up and swatted the phone off the nightstand. It landed near her head, sending off a bell tone. A pre-recorded message followed. He settled the handset back onto the phone stopping the noise. LeeAnn wasn't paying much attention. The guy had as much mass as it looked. She was getting squashed. Things were actually going dim.

"I missed."

He sounded surprised. She shoved. He grunted and actually got heavier somehow.

"I can't believe it. I never—"

"You're heavy!" LeeAnn interrupted him.

"Oh."

His rifle made a slight sound as he set it beside her. He pushed up. And nothing had ever felt so sweet! LeeAnn sucked a solid lungful of air, let it out, and grabbed another.

"You hear that?" he asked.

Was he joking? She'd almost suffocated. Loud heartbeats filled her ears along with the sound of her own breathing. LeeAnn inhaled deeply, held the breath, and listened. Heard what sounded like little puffs of air. They were accompanied by smacking sounds as something hit the wall beside him.

She nodded.

"That is the sound of failure."

LeeAnn rolled her head. There was a line of dark spots in the wall that hadn't been there before. Her eyes were wide as she returned them to his face. Or what she could see of it.

"Failure?"

"I never miss."

"Please don't tell me those are bullet holes, okay? Just don't."

"Those are bullet holes."

"I just asked you not to say that."

"Somebody wants you dead. I failed to stop them."

"Oh, come on. This isn't happening."

"You ever been hunted?"

"Hunted? Are you crazy? I'm here to meet with—no. Chad might be laundering money, but—no. He wouldn't hire someone to kill me! This kind of thing does not happen in real life. Okay? It just doesn't."

"We have about three minutes."

"Before what? A room explosion?"

He lowered his chin. She had to imagine the look he was giving her. It was too dark to see in the well of space they occupied, and he was still hooded.

"You said you wanted to live."

"I do."

"Then, follow me. Do exactly as I say. Don't argue. Don't question."

"No way. Do I really look that stupid? And I've got news for you, mister. I'm not leaving without my purse and ID."

"Dead people don't need ID."

"Excuse me?"

"Weren't you listening? I never miss. This is new territory for me, too."

"New territory? Okay. Enough is enough. Who *are* you? Exactly?"

"Guardian angel."

LeeAnn would have laughed, except he was serious as he said it. And everything was just too weird at the moment. As if his occupation was a real possibility. That decided it. She was definitely dreaming.

"I thought guardian angels were old guys...with white beards...you know. Like skinny Santa's. Or, they're beautiful young women. Mostly blondes. And they have wings. Big ones. And...I don't know. This is insane. They don't even exist."

"You ready to try the door?"

"I'm still asleep. That's it, isn't it?"

He might have sighed if the amount of breath touching her neck was an indicator.

"This could be dangerous, LeeAnn."

"How...do you know my name?" Her heart stuttered.

"Later. We have to leave. Now. Right now."

"So, what's stopping us?"

"The door."

"Guardian angels can't get through doors?"

She tried to say it without snickering, but failed. He lowered his chin more, dropping the hood farther, sending a shadow to his mouth. He didn't look remotely angelic. His appearance was pretty damned sinister. And frightening. And he expected her to leave with him?

"Hotels keep their halls brightly lit. Your room is dark. You failed to shut your drapes last night. The moment the door opens, he'll know it."

"You think he's still watching?"

His lips twitched. Her heart leapt. And that was just more weirdness.

"Won't know until we try," he finally replied.

"Give me one good reason why I should trust you. Just one."

"I saved your life."

LeeAnn reached over and ran her finger over one of the holes on the wall. It looked real. It sure felt real. This was starting to get scary.

"We don't have time for this. Hang on."

"To what?"

He didn't give her any time! And the bedding made it easy for him. LeeAnn found herself wrapped in wads of cloth and atop a shoulder, but at least she had a peephole for air. He acted like her bulk was nothing as he squatted at the side of her door.

"We're going to be exposed for a few seconds. You ready?"

"Do I have a choice?"

"Nope," he replied.

A whir of gear noise started up. He swiveled in a sickeningly quick motion. LeeAnn rocked atop his shoulder. Swallowed. A couple of moments later, the noise halted.

"That's my phone!"

He opened the door and slid to the other side, shutting it behind him. She shifted as he resettled her, banging her legs against what was probably his rifle.

"You're not going to let me take it?"

"Dead people don't need phones, either," he informed her and then he started jogging.

CHAPTER TWO

KANE HAD A COMPLICATION. A big one. It grew larger with each passing moment. The rules were clear. Complete the assignment. Clear out. Stay hidden. Whatever happens, do not engage.

Well.

He was pretty engaged now.

The woman watched him unblinkingly from the back passenger seat. She hadn't said anything as he took twenty-nine flights of stairs at a jog – stopping once as a hotel maid entered below them and walked up a flight before exiting. Kane had stepped into the shadows and waited. Watched. Listened. The maid hadn't even looked up. The moment the door closed behind her, he'd continued, taking stair-chewing strides. It hadn't been difficult. A walk in the park compared to ground training and survival skill tests.

The underground parking garage had been deserted. *Good thing.* A hooded man dressed in black, carrying a body-sized bundle over his shoulder, while packing a rifle, would get noticed. Kane crouched down and scanned the area. Nobody was around. No shout rang out as he reached his SUV. Nothing moved. His weapon took some misuse. He dropped the 338 *Lapua* over the backseat into the luggage compartment. The gun gave a slight thud as it landed on the carpet, but it shouldn't be harmed. His sniper rifle should be secured in a case, but he'd had to leave that behind.

He'd left a lot of things behind.

Like his sanity.

His rifle case was now collateral damage. It shouldn't be an issue. That case didn't have any distinguishing marks. It was common back-pack style, PVC construction. Hard to get fingerprints off that material. If any forensic lab managed to pull prints, they'd be smudged. Indistinct. All of that aside, he'd worry about it later.

When they were safe.

Kane had taken a deep breath, lifting her with it, and held it for a full minute. Spent the time scanning the garage again, but he'd mainly used the time to calm down. After-incident jitters could derail any assignment. Aside from the mistake of engaging LeeAnn in the first place, he'd already screwed-up. He hadn't dangled the 'DO NOT DISTURB' sign from her door handle. That would have gained him all kinds of time.

For a man who avoided attention, he was certainly engendering a bunch of it. His mind snapped through scenarios. He had a few hours before a maid would spot the bullet holes in the wall. She'd report it. The authorities would be called. It should be a 'Missing Person' case. There wasn't any blood. No signs of injury. No dead body. But any investigation would probably lead to the room he'd confiscated – unless he was lucky. The room had been unoccupied. They might not use it for days yet.

Kane exhaled slowly. Handled LeeAnn's bulk next. She resembled a mummy bundle, strapped as she was into a lap belt and shoulder harness. He didn't know where her arms were. She hadn't wriggled. She hadn't spoken. She might be in shock. He didn't know and he didn't have time to find out.

Time was passing. Each second upped the risk factor. Kane hadn't gotten a good look at her hunter. It could be anyone. Coming from anywhere. Anytime. If this had been his botched hit, he wouldn't waste time. He'd be right on his flushed quarry's ass.

Black leather sucked him into place in the driver seat. A thumb touch started the engine. His next move shifted gears. Each move was automatic. A well-oiled machine. Auto-piloted. Fastening his safety belt with one hand, he eased the vehicle out of the parking spot, checking constantly for anything that moved, snagged his attention, or looked out-of-place. The place was a mass of polished concrete, lots of lighting, and rows of expensive, well-cared-for vehicles.

Nothing else.

Dawn was progressing, the sun rising, daylight just brushing the tops of buildings. Kane reached for his sunglasses with one hand, while he maneuvered the SUV up the ramp and through the pay lane. He had the glasses in place before he shoved his hood off, settling it on his shoulders. Big, black SUVs like this one caught attention. An anonymous-looking driver wearing a big black hood would collect more of it. He had dark windows throughout the back, but up front, the glass was smoke-tinted. Easy to see through.

That usually kept entanglements to a minimum.

He sent a glance through the rearview mirror toward his passenger. She had one eyebrow lifted, making a slight line on her forehead above it. That was cute. And something more. The expression highlighted her riveting light blue eyes. He was snagged momentarily by her gaze. Caught.

Shit.

That nuance hadn't been in the file. Kane looked back to the street. Even at this hour, Miami was awake. The place was alive with vehicles, noise, and humanity. He cleared his throat.

"You okay back there?" he asked.

She didn't answer. He brought the vehicle to a stop at an intersection and watched pedestrians for a moment. Must be too early for tourists. He scanned the conglomeration of humanity crossing in front of his bumper. Looked like a mix of inebriated ex-party-goers, homeless citizens, city workers, and street vendors. Nothing looked odd. Nobody paid particular attention to him. He looked at her through the mirror again. She had her other eyebrow up now. *Man!* He had to adjust his earlier assessment. She didn't just have riveting light blue eyes. She had really beautiful ones. Clear. Stunning.

He looked back out the front window. Swallowed. Debated donning driving gloves.

"LeeAnn?"

"How do you know my name?"

He flashed another glance at her before the light turned green. She'd narrowed her eyes. Driving claimed his attention for a moment. She waited.

"It came with the assignment."

"I'm an assignment?"

"You want to listen to music?"

The vehicle had a fully equipped stereo, usually set to a special frequency scanning mode. He fiddled with the control switch. Bach's *Suite No 1 in G major* started emanating from the speakers, filling the cabin with mellow strands of a master musician playing the cello.

"I don't want music. I want answers. Okay with you?"

"Yes. And no."

Kane wiped his hand down his thigh before turning the stereo down. He didn't turn it off. Background music helped with a lot of things. Like nervousness.

"No?"

"Didn't you hear me earlier? This is new territory for me."

"Tell me about it," she inserted.

"I'm unsure what to tell you. And how much."

"I'm just supposed to be docile and uninformed?"

"You're alive, aren't you?"

She didn't answer for a bit. Kane checked. She was frowning again. He looked back at the road.

"I want to know how you know my name."

"I'm not...a guardian angel. Exactly."

"Really? Well. I did have that suspicion," she replied.

Kane choked on a chuckle. That was another oddity. He was known as the humorless type. "You could say I'm more of a hunter."

"What do you hunt?"

He sucked in his cheeks, tipped his head, and debated options. When that didn't work, he settled with a shrug that lifted the hood to his ears before it dropped back.

"That's not an answer."

"I know. I'm working on it."

Kane checked her reflection in his rearview mirror again. Her lips twitched. She acted like she caught his glance before turning away, looking out her window. Sunlight was making a dent on the world. Dawn touched her face, highlighting all kinds of things. A slight pout to her full bottom lip. The shadow of long eyelashes. A rose shade that tinted her cheeks.

LeeAnn Schultz was a stunning woman.

Not good.

The complication of keeping her with him multiplied. Kane turned his attention back to the road. They'd reached the Overseas Highway. The freeway merge claimed his attention for a span. Even at this time of morning, there was traffic.

"You're a very careful driver."

"Bad driving can be a deciding factor in any situation. That's how they caught the serial killer, Ted Bundy. And Berkowitz. Nobody caught them with detective work. You sure you don't want to listen to music?"

The opening strains of Chopin's *Nocturne in B-flat minor* had just started up. Kane considered turning it up a little. Chopin was considered an operatic composer. A poet of the piano. This piece was one of his best. It might soothe the dismayed expression she'd just assumed as she'd jerked her head back to look at his reflection. And then she started wriggling about.

"Calm down back there. You're safe with me. I swear it."

"You just compared yourself to...serial killers!"

Her voice was shaking. At a slightly higher pitch than before. For some reason, that affected him.

"See? I have to watch what I tell you. And how much. I bring out that driving issues can change everything and look what happens? You react."

The leather continued to creak as she moved about.

"LeeAnn, listen! I was trying to explain that getting pulled over with a woman strapped into the back seat of my car would not be a good thing at the moment. It would create attention we don't need. Now, stop that. Or, I'll pull over and handle it."

She stilled instantly. Her eyes were huge. Kane cursed silently before looking back to the road. He was doing poorly already, and they had a long drive ahead.

"You need to calm down. Please. You're safe."

"I don't...feel safe."

Her voice shuddered. He sighed heavily. "I belong to an elite group. I can't tell you much, but trust me. I'm one of the good guys."

"Good guys don't break into hotel rooms. Nor do they kidnap people."

"They do if it will save lives. Or are you forgetting that?"

"How can I believe anything you say?"

"My...group monitors chatter. Somebody put out a hit on a LeeAnn Schultz. Arriving on Tuesday. 6 pm. I was given the assignment."

"I arrived on Wednesday morning."

"I know. Your flight was overbooked. You gave up your seat. I've been tracking you since before you landed at Miami/Dade International. I know every place you've been, everything you purchased, and what hotel you were staying at. And when they coded your room key, I even got your room number."

"No way."

"You know that little chip on your credit card? That isn't just for security. It collects and sends data every time you use it."

"You can hack that?"

"Pretty much. Especially since you kept using free Wi-Fi service."

"That's...unnerving. Is that how you got in my room? With a spare room key?"

"Nope. The rooms above yours were vacant. Told you it was a mistake to leave your drapes open."

"You climbed down from a balcony?"

"Three of them."

"At thirty-plus stories above the ground? I can't—no. This is too unbelievable."

"It gets worse."

"How?"

He sent a glance into the mirror toward her. She had her lips pursed. She didn't look frightened anymore. She looked young. Unsure. And cuter than—

He didn't dare quantify it. He could have sworn his heart just skipped a beat. That was illogical and ill-timed.

"Since I missed your would-be assassin, we got problems. I don't know who he is. What he looks like. Or when he'll strike again. All I know for sure is, he will."

The Chopin selection finished. Beethoven's *Symphony No 5* started up. That was a little too lively. Kane reached over and turned the stereo system off. Music hadn't worked at calming him, anyway. That was another oddity. He was unsettled. On edge. Extremely wary.

"Will what?"

"Strike again."

She gasped. He didn't have to see it. He heard it.

"Don't worry. First, he has to find you."

"So...I'm going into hiding?"

"That's the plan."

"Where?"

"The Keys. Safe house."

"Key West?"

"Close."

"Hmm. I've never been to Key West. Is it nice?"

"Yeah."

She was silent for so long, he had to check to see why. The sunlight had moved to his side of the vehicle, putting her in a shadow-land back there. She looked sleepy. She even yawned. His heart skipped another beat.

Uh oh.

This was bad. First he was engaging? And now getting interested?

She looked toward him and caught his glance. Kane immediately shifted it back to the road before realizing that idiocy. He wore dark glasses. She couldn't possibly see through them.

"What's your name?"

Kane sucked in his cheeks and tilted his head. That was a big one. He twisted his lips next. He had his orders. No entanglements. No names. No history. No trail.

"What? Is it a secret?"

"Yes. And no," he answered.

She yawned again. He had a hard time stopping the smile.

"Fine. I'll name you. You look like a Kane."

He wasn't prepared. He jerked slightly and sent a quick glance at her again. She was smiling. Sunlight was just touching her left side. She looked angelic. And wide awake.

"Is that it? Your name is Kane?"

He didn't answer. He'd thought she was sleepy. Another mistake. He was making way too many of those, in a very short time. Kane shrugged again. Toyed with turning the stereo back on. Shifted. His seat creaked in accompaniment. He reached for the climate control switch.

"You okay back there? Not too hot? Cold?"

"I'm fine."

"You thirsty?" he asked.

"Not unless you have coffee."

"Never touch the stuff."

"That figures."

"I've got cold water. Bottled."

"Thanks, but I can't get my hands free to drink it. You know what, Kane? I think I'll just try and take a little snooze back here. Maybe when I wake up, I'll be back in my hotel room, and this will have been a very strange dream. That okay with you?"

"Dream on, baby."

Oh.

Hell.

He did *not* just say that. Not in a thousand years. He wasn't just exhibiting slow wits. They appeared to be missing entirely. Kane's fingers tightened on the steering wheel, making the leather wrap rotate under his palm. Luckily, she didn't respond. A milepost passed. Another one. He sent a peek in the rearview mirror toward her.

She had her head tilted to the side. She looked asleep.

And she was smiling.

CHAPTER THREE

LEEANN WASN'T SLEEPING. ONLY STUPID, insipid individuals would actually sleep at a time like this. She was vulnerable. With a complete stranger. And, even if it did appear as if he'd saved her, she was still at his mercy. Wearing little more than a nightgown. Sans her phone. Identification. Cash. Credit cards. She couldn't even prove who she was. The last thing she needed was to be unaware of her surroundings and how she got there. She'd read this plot too many times. She needed to keep her wits about her. Gain an accurate account of time. Distance. Check when the vehicle changed speeds. Make certain of turns. How many. Which direction.

The rising sun was mostly on the driver side now, so they were definitely heading south. She could just make out the dash clock. His arm blocked it for a moment, as he turned on his stereo again. Classical music surrounded her. She didn't know composers or tunes, but it was strangely soothing. Oddly comforting.

All bad.

And counterintuitive.

She didn't need or want comfort. She was in way over her head here, and didn't like the feeling. Her mind kept sending possible scenarios. Potential plans of action. A lot of truly frightening endings. She really could use some caffeine. She'd even take it cold. With carbonation. And a day's supply of sugar. She peeked occasionally out the window, checking for anything that could be a potential landmark. Looked like a lot of clear blue sky. A lot more ocean. And tons of sunlight. It was going to be a gorgeous hot, sunny day.

The sun sent a lot of warmth with its rays. The heat was like another layer of comfort. Soothing. Reassuring even as it cocooned. LeeAnn mentally shook herself. Slanted a glance toward Kane. She could just make out the back of his neck. She instantly had to stanch a whisper of reaction through her belly.

This wasn't good.

Then again, it couldn't just be her. The guy was beyond good looking...even if a tad overly alpha, a bit too masculine, and entirely too close-lipped and predatory. He was still gorgeous. He had the tall, dark, and handsome monikers covered.

In spades.

Really, LeeAnn. Stop. Just stop.

His jaw was really chiseled. The line was apparent beneath the slight shadow of black whiskers. She knew now that it matched his hair color. She'd been right with that assessment. His hair was definitely dark. More...coal black. Looked straight, but he wore it pulled back, which might exaggerate that quality. She couldn't tell the length. It wasn't short. The start of his queue was just visible before it disappeared beneath his clothing. A few strands slid down his neck.

He had a really thick neck, too.

Another shiver of something unbidden sliced through her, sending a layer of reaction in its wake. Entirely pleasant. And uncalled for. She didn't even like big, muscled guys. Now, that she thought of it, she didn't really know any. Kane looked wrestling-superstar fit. She'd never seen a guy as ripped. He had wide shoulders. Massive arms. The rest of him was probably a match. She didn't know why she even pondered that. He'd jogged down so many flights of stairs, carrying her hundred and thirty pounds that her head had grown dizzy. He hadn't even been breathing hard.

One thing was certain. She wasn't going to be able to fight him. Or outrun him. She'd have to rely on cunning.

Palm trees started showing up in her view. They'd left the highway? When had that happened? The vehicle geared down as he slowed. She heard him flip the turn signal lever.

What?

No.

It couldn't be. She'd actually slept? LeeAnn checked the dash clock. Blinked on the proof before her eyes. Sagged back into her seat with disgust. He made a couple of right turns. Sped up slightly.

Crap.

She was a complete failure at this covert stuff. She didn't know where they were. All she knew was over two hours had elapsed, and that only because of the dash clock. The palm trees gave way to privacy fencing – mostly white stone. Or stucco. She wasn't in the construction business so she didn't know. She'd had construction company clients. She knew their debits and credits. She didn't know a thing about their operations. They'd had a lot of them, actually. Her partner, Chad, was like a magnet when it came to businesses predominantly owned by guys. *Wait.* She needed to call him her ex-partner. It was probably his hand behind her assassination attempt. *Really, LeeAnn...who else could it be?* She didn't even know that much about him...except he was handsome, single, and charming. The background check had been clean. She should have dug deeper. Taken self-defense classes. Joined a gym. Bought a gun and learned how to use it.

All of which was not going to help a thing now.

The fence was connected intermittently with stacks of cemented stones. Very artistic. They were mostly light shades. A few gray ones here and there. Some pinkish toned. The vehicle slowed. Kane signaled. Turned. And stopped before a two-story arched gate. She heard the window retract.

"Leon," he said.

"Kane."

The man's reply sent a flush of pleasure through her. She'd been right on his name! Knowing she'd tagged him correctly almost offset her failure at everything else.

Almost.

They passed beneath a portico. The vehicle darkened. Bright sun flooded in as they came out the other side. And then it grew really dark as the vehicle drove into a cavernous space that might be a garage. They passed vehicle after vehicle, answering that question, before pulling into a spot. Her hands turned into icicles against the sides of her thighs. Alarm bells hit both ears.

He spent a lot of time putting the vehicle into park before turning it off. Unhooking his safety belt. Rearranging the rearview mirror. And then he turned swiftly toward her, surprising her. That wasn't fair. He didn't even take off his sunglasses.

"We're here," he told her.

Her eyes widened. Any words got caught in a ball at her throat.

"You ready?"

"For...what?"

That little, hesitant voice couldn't possibly be hers! *Ugh.* LeeAnn looked away. Checked out the roof of the classy-looking limo just outside her window. She used the time to collect herself mentally, but it was mostly a berating. She didn't have to just be a victim? She had to sound like one, too?

"I'm taking you inside now."

"Inside?" she asked the window glass.

"And you're not going to give me any trouble. We clear on that?"

What a farce. *Trouble?*

Her?

"I know you faked sleeping. You probably think you know exactly where we are. You may already have a plan of escape. I'm not amused. Okay? I'm the good guy here."

She caught the instant smile before looking back at him. He hadn't known she slept? Maybe she wasn't such a failure, after all.

"I've never brought anyone here...especially a woman. It may create some interest."

She choked.

"Actually, it will engender a lot of interest. Conjecture. Nothing I want to address. So, no screaming. No yelling. And no fighting me."

"I'm just supposed to be docile?"

"Would you rather be unconscious?"

One of his brows lifted above the sunglass frame as he asked it. Nothing else moved. On him. Her reaction was the opposite. Her eyes widened. Every limb went ice-cold, her belly dropped nauseatingly. Her heart stopped. And her breathing was right behind it, as if on cue, making an audible gasp.

He smiled. It didn't make him look more approachable.

"That's what I thought."

LeeAnn forced a breath as he just sat there, watching her. There wasn't a descriptor for how these shivers felt as they coursed her skin.

"We good, then?"

He waited for her nod before exiting. The vehicle rocked as he released it from the burden of his weight. Shut his door. It seemed like a moment later her side door opened. He reached across her lap, unfastened her belts, and wrapped an arm about her middle. She was hefted atop his shoulder again. Got a narrow view of polished floor. She didn't fight. She didn't struggle. She didn't make a sound.

He walked through the garage. A whir sounded as a door must have opened. Kane passed through it and she squinted as her vision got overwhelmed with artificial light. The floor turned into a span of light shaded tiles that matched the fence stones outside. Light gray. Off-white. Some pink. The room echoed with his steps. LeeAnn turned her head. Caught a glimpse of stainless steel. A lot of big kettles. Rows of what looked like marine gear. Lifejackets. SCUBA tanks. Spear guns. She couldn't see it all. They entered another space, this one dark. Carpeted. Muted. His steps didn't make much noise. He crossed another portal, and entered a space ablaze with sunlight. LeeAnn narrowed her eyes and tipped her head toward the source, and her jaw dropped. The wall was a solid span of big windows. At least two stories high. They showcased an outside swimming pool that was larger than her entire apartment. It was framed with lounge furniture. Palm trees. Rimmed by more of the privacy wall. And beyond that was a solid horizon of ocean.

Holy crap.

This wasn't a safe house. It was a mansion. The kind featured in stories about the rich and famous. Overpaid celebrities. Rock stars. Billionaires.

He entered an area with a cream colored floor. The walls matched. It was a rotunda. Round. Could be the entranceway. Kane didn't give her any time to decipher it. He was moving so rapidly, she felt queasy. Her head was starting to pound, too. And her abs hurt from contact with his shoulder. They reached a staircase. He began climbing, two steps at a time. Then a voice hailed him, stopping his progress.

"Kane! You're back."

"Rafael."

Kane spun. LeeAnn got a quick panorama of more sunlit windows attached to what looked like a second floor landing, leading to a lot more space. But the way she viewed it was sickening. She wasn't the motion-sick type, but this method of transportation was definitely testing it.

"What you got there?"

"Complication."

"Need any help?"

"No."

He turned back around. LeeAnn's head dropped to the middle of his back. *Leon? And now Rafael?* They had very interesting and unique names in this house. That was one thing she could list for the authorities.

"Wait." Kane spun back as he said it. His back vibrated with the word. LeeAnn swallowed.

"I need women's clothing."

"Any particular size? Type?"

"Just send Jezzie. She'll know."

Jezzie? The relief was palpable. Like a wash of cool water. It didn't help the pounding in LeeAnn's head, but it relieved the anxiety. She wasn't the lone woman here. But then the unseen Rafael had to go and ruin it.

"You sure you want her?"

"Yeah."

Kane spun and started mounting steps again. LeeAnn tried to focus and peek, checking for the man beneath them. It was useless. He was in the shadow thrown by the balustrade and Kane moved too quickly.

"Hope you know what you're doing, big guy."

Kane answered beneath his breath, altering the new-found relief with worry again. LeeAnn's eyes went wide and he probably felt her gasp.

"Me, too."

CHAPTER FOUR

KANE STEPPED OUT OF THE shower, grabbed a towel and ruffled his hair with an efficiency that nearly sent sparks. Dried the rest of his body with the same quick, almost-angered motions. Wrapped the towel about his hips, tying it with a bit more strength than he needed. His movements matched how he felt.

Exactly.

He was in what the others referred to as his black mood. Fighting inner demons. The kind that kept everyone away until it passed. Nobody knew what brought them on. He hadn't either. Before.

This time, he knew the cause.

LeeAnn Schultz.

He was suffering something very close to lust. LeeAnn was at the center of it. Causing heated sensations that sent fire licking at his thighs. Groin. Its heat stirred primal needs. Animalistic wants. His body acted as if a bellows were at work on it, sending oxygen to an already hot fire. Fueling a constant state of arousal. The erection distorting his towel was the proof. Impossible to hide. Readily apparent. The situation was really starting to anger. Frustrate.

Kane slicked his hair back with his hands, finger-combed it back into a tail again, and spent a couple of seconds looking for a strap before letting it go. Steam gradually dissipated, leaving him with a focused view of the room. Him. And his problem.

He snarled at his mirrored image before tipping his head to one side. He concentrated. The bathroom was like a space vacuum. Deathly quiet. No sound came from outside the door, though. No screams. No yelling. No alarms being sounded. LeeAnn must be behaving.

And Jezzie.

The woman's real name was Jezebel. In Hebrew it meant "not exalted." That pretty much explained Jezzie. She wasn't the type to go out of her way for anyone or anything. She liked causing trouble. She'd looked at him with a calculated gaze as he'd explained what he wanted. As if she sensed an attraction he didn't dare acknowledge. Seeing LeeAnn into attractive garments should be right up Jezzie's alley. She could set up a doomed situation and see what developed.

Kane's expression turned into a frown. In retrospect, he should have kept LeeAnn with him, despite how her proximity unsettled, and then challenged. He could have waited to shower. Shave. Change clothes.

Shit.

He was turning into a class-A dimwit here.

One with a testosterone problem.

He really shouldn't have sent for Jezebel, but the tall brunette looked the same size as LeeAnn. She should have something the girl could wear. Kane was guessing on LeeAnn's exact dimensions, but he figured she was about five-and-a-half feet tall. She weighed an easily-portable one-hundred, thirty-five. Maybe less. She was slim. She didn't make an unwieldy bundle even swathed in bedding.

The frown cleared slightly. He was overanalyzing this. Adding issues that might not even happen. Moreover, he wasn't a babysitter. Jezebel might be a manipulative and spite-filled woman, but LeeAnn had proven capable. She dealt with traumatic situations well, followed instructions, and had a quick mind. She could handle Jezzie.

Besides...they were only two doors away. Same floor. Kane leaned toward the mirror. Studied his eyes for several long moments before giving it up. Nothing had changed. And time was wasting. He needed to check on LeeAnn. Make sure she was clothed. Had eaten breakfast.

Kane smirked at his reflection before opening the door. He sure felt like a babysitter.

Air-conditioned air cooled the space immediately. The chill raised goose bumps on his skin and helped with his groin problem. Good thing. He'd set out above-the-knee swim trunks. Jammers. Spandex and PBT construction. They were fit exactly to his proportions. Created less drag...but they had other issues. They were going to show off a lot. He should've chosen loose-fit trunks. Then again...this misguided arousal was one-sided. LeeAnn hadn't acted remotely interested in him.

Kane cinched the waist with more strength than required, and then had to let some of the nylon cord out before stepping into wet-shoes. What the hell was he doing? Thinking? He didn't *want* LeeAnn interested in him! That was just more craziness this situation didn't need.

He grabbed his t-shirt as the phone rang. Land line. Kane yanked the receiver off the cradle with more strength than that required, too. He tightened his hand about it for a second or two before moving it to his ear.

"Kane? You there? It's Leon."

"Yeah."

"We have company."

"Description?"

"Police officers. Two. Unmarked car."

"Anybody have a warrant?"

"No."

"They say what they want?"

"They're saying you dinged a vehicle in a parking garage

in Miami this morning. They have a picture of your front bumper. Mainly the license plate area. From the exit area. Pay stall. It's time stamped at...yep. This morning. A little after five. It's your vehicle, all right."

Oh, shit.

Hindsight was a real bitch. He wasn't just in unfamiliar territory. He was mucking everything up while there. He hadn't hit anything. LeeAnn had some major players on her ass. Moneyed. Connected. Fast. And smart. He should have waited in the parking garage! *Not* been the first vehicle to leave after a botched hit. Talk about painting a target on his back.

"Hit the silent alarm, Leon. Red alert."

"You'll be right down, then? Excellent, my man. We'll just break out the coffee while we wait," Leon replied. "Hey! I hope you two police officers won't mind if I turn my tunes back on, will you?"

Loud strains of rock music came clearly through the telephone receiver. The lights went out, diverting electricity to the perimeter. A humming sound started emanating from deep within the structure as gates went up. Spikes lifted next along the back perimeter walls. Kane tossed the phone onto the bed, along with the t-shirt. Snagged his 9mm from the nightstand drawer. Shoved it into the back of his trunks. Pushed a pair of sunglasses onto his face next. He didn't open his door. He slammed through it. Two doors down looked like a very long way. He smacked into her door with a shoulder, knocking it off hinges, as well. For nothing.

The space was empty.

Just like his head must be.

CHAPTER FIVE

W*OW.*
       This was the life.

Too bad it wasn't hers.

LeeAnn closed her eyes. Soaked up rays. Floated aimlessly. She was out at the pool. She wasn't poolside. She was floating on it, atop an inflated lounger-thing. Sucking up this decadent lifestyle, even it if wasn't hers.

Then again, she could pretend that she belonged. Who would care? Not that Jezzie person. *Oh. Wait.* The woman preferred to be called Jezebel. That was the first thing she'd said after Kane set LeeAnn onto her feet, started unwrapping the sheet from about her, and then left the women together.

Oddly enough, LeeAnn had immediately missed him. Felt vulnerable. Unsure. And really leery. Jezebel wasn't much help. The woman didn't appear to have a bone in her body devoted to altruism or charity. The vibes coming off her had been positively chilly. She hadn't appeared pleased with the summons. Or LeeAnn. It felt weird being around someone who disliked her on sight. Then again, everything about this morning's events had that problem.

Complete weirdness.

Jezebel had the strangest eyes, too. So dark, they were almost black. Soulless-looking. LeeAnn had glanced at her once and then avoided it. Besides, somebody had ordered up a breakfast tray with all kinds of great-smelling and tasty-looking selections. She didn't know who. She didn't even know who'd brought it. And, wonder of wonders! They'd even included a carafe of coffee.

She could definitely get used to this lifestyle.

Some time ago, she and Chad had discussed what it would be like to live in the same manner as some of their clients. Surrounded by luxury. Not having to worry. Someone else around to handle everything. Mortgage issues. Utility payments. Student loan debt. Insurance. Chad had been the instigator of the conversations. He'd done spreadsheets and tacked them onto the office walls, each one devoted to a different strategy toward his goal. There was one for playing the stock market. Another for real estate investment. Another for the pricing structure with their clients. It had been his idea to use a sliding scale. If the client had big bucks, they got charged more.

LeeAnn had ceased arguing over it. Chad had control issues with women. It wasn't worth a blood pressure spike to argue with him. He charmed the socks off everyone he met. Nobody complained about their bill. And – she had to admit – the extra income was useful. She just wished they'd raised rates across the board. Made it fair. She'd thought of discussing that, but Chad was hard to pin down anymore. Come to think of it...they hadn't spoken for some time. She'd had to set up this morning's meeting via email. He'd moved out of Fall River. Given her a PO Box number to use for any business correspondence. She wasn't even sure *where* he lived.

She'd been so naïve!

She should have gone to the authorities the moment she noted the odd account fluctuations. That would have been the intelligent thing to do. But what had she done? Set up a breakfast meeting to discuss the problem. With a man who had this much to lose?

She might have to adjust her thinking here. Naivety was too

nice of a word.

LeeAnn paddled slightly. The pool was immense. Shaped like a big, fat snake, wending its way about the backyard, or whatever they called this area. There was a shallow zone. The rest of the pool was pretty deep. She didn't know how deep, for certain. It wasn't marked on the sides or anything. Beautiful blue water. Perfect temperature. Just cool enough to soothe a sun-warmed body if she dove in. That might prove too much for the bikini Jezebel had brought her, however. LeeAnn might as well be wearing elastic bands. The top was so tight it restricted her breathing.

All of which was her fault.

Jezebel had asked her size while LeeAnn was shoving big bites of ham and cheese omelet into her mouth. The woman sounded snide as she'd correctly pegged LeeAnn as an eight. Stupidity had kicked in. LeeAnn had instantly stated that she wore a size six, thank you very much. This is what she'd reaped: A neon yellow bikini bound to make her skin look sallow, and bonus! Nothing came with a string tie she could let out. Or even a range of adjustments with clasps. She'd never shown off this much skin. But she wasn't letting Jezebel know that it bothered her.

Oh.

No way.

LeeAnn had just gone to the bathroom, tugged the suit on, made a face at her reflection, and then returned. Jezebel hadn't said a word as LeeAnn picked at the rest of her omelet, foregoing even a bite from the display of frosting-covered cinnamon rolls, or the strawberry-glazed crepes, the stack of sausage links. She hadn't touched the mouthwatering pile of bacon. She'd even passed on the perfectly toasted wheat bread.

She probably should have eaten more. Her belly rumbled as she thought it. Breakfast felt like hours ago, but it couldn't be.

This lazy lifestyle altered time or something. Slowed it to

a crawl. Then again, she couldn't be sure. She didn't wear a watch. That's one thing she used her phone for. It couldn't be noon yet. The sun hadn't reached its highest point. Last check of the area revealed small shadows around the lounge furniture and the areas that contained foliage. Heat radiated from the ground, distorting the view slightly. She should probably go sit beside the pool. Find some shade.

And she would.

In a minute.

This just felt so damned sinful. Decadent. She yawned, and then shook herself. She daren't fall asleep! A slight bit of tan was one thing. A full-fledged sunburn something else. Her fingers trailed through the water as if she did this every day. And then an odd buzzing sound caught her attention. LeeAnn looked up, lifted a hand to shade her eyes, and checked. There were two small airborne things just above the palm-tree line. They flew side-by-side. Like little helicopters. And that was just cute.

Somebody played with remote-controlled toys around here?

"LeeAnn! Dive!"

What might be Kane came sprinting from the house. LeeAnn's jaw dropped. He was wearing sunglasses. His hair wasn't bound. It was straight and glossy and black. About mid-back length. She'd guessed he was fit, but she'd been way off. The guy was unbelievably ripped. And wearing way too little. She didn't even know the names of some of the muscles rippling beneath his tanned skin as he raced toward her.

"Get in the water!"

If he wanted to make sense, he needed to put some clothing on. She couldn't think. She couldn't even take it all in. LeeAnn sat up, drenching her butt and thighs as the raft thing bowed in the center. Kane wasn't paying any attention to her. He had a gun in one hand and was shooting toward the toy-things. While running?

The water started jumping as it got pebbled with projectiles. The float took a hit. Started whistling as air escaped. And that's when she knew what was happening. Someone was shooting at her!

With real bullets!

Shock made her clumsy. Shaky. None of which helped in a life-or-death situation. LeeAnn rolled off the deflating float while the water continually erupted about her. One of the helicopters exploded overhead. And then she watched, with wide, unblinking eyes, as Kane launched through the air in a distance-spanning dive.

LeeAnn sucked in a breath just before he slammed into her. His arrival shoved her several feet under the water, beneath the burst of bubbles at his entrance, down to where all kinds of white lines of foam were splicing through water. They were the bullet paths as they lost momentum in the water. For the span of a heartbeat, she watched the scene, recognizing that this looked exactly like what she'd seen in movies.

And then adrenaline kicked in.

She'd been above a deep section. It didn't feel deep enough. LeeAnn dove, steadily swimming down, not stopping until she reached the pool bottom. Kane hadn't followed. His legs were kicking from what looked like a long way above her as he maintained a position. What was he? Returning fire? That was ridiculous. Guns didn't fire underwater.

Did they?

The white foam lines stopped. Disappeared. LeeAnn let an air bubble out. Another followed. She swallowed next, holding air in, trying for time. Her ears popped. Her lungs were starting to burn. She knew she couldn't stay here much longer. And then Kane loomed out of the space at one side, grabbed her, and shot upward. Toward the surface.

And air. Sunlight. Life.

He lifted her above the waterline, and held her there so she could pull in air. As adrenaline waned, weakness took its place. Her arms and legs felt like limp spinach, and emotion sapped what was left of her strength. *Oh. Crap.* She refused to cry. There had to be a better emotion available. Easily grabbed. And there was. Red hot. Heated. Completely illogical.

Anger.

Kane surfaced beside her, sending a wake of water. Wet. Big. Black hair framed his face and shoulders. He was actually still wearing his sunglasses. And that was just full-out ridiculous.

"You okay?"

"No! I am not okay!"

He swam to the side, hauling her along. He might have been gentle. It didn't feel it. Her waist felt like a vise was around it. And then he pivoted, put both hands about her midriff and set her on her butt atop tile so sun-heated, the water off her bottom sizzled. But her only other option was the soles of her feet. LeeAnn jumped up, and started hopping about, trying like hell not to cry. One of the helicopter things had disintegrated, making a trail of blackened pieces about what had been pristine tile. She couldn't spot the other one.

"Now what?"

Kane loomed out of the water, and rose beside her. He didn't have any trouble with hot tile. Because he had wet-shoes on.

"I told you I'm not okay! Didn't you hear me?"

"You're yelling at me," he replied without inflection.

"Yeah? So?"

"You sound like you're fine."

Something exploded behind her, sending a palm frond onto a table. And when that collapsed, the entire thing hit the patio. LeeAnn squealed, leapt, and latched onto Kane's middle with both arms. And just stayed there, hugging him. She hadn't planned it, but her feet ended up atop his, and that was one really nice bonus to this embrace. He also felt pretty good. Stable. Warm. Muscled. Alive.

Correction.

He felt a lot better than just pretty good. Her entire front half was getting a full dose of hard male. Contact with him sent something major. Almost electrical. Her belly constricted. Her thighs tightened. Even her nipples got in on the act. She only hoped he couldn't feel them through this stupid bra top against his chest.

Kane cleared his throat. The sound echoed through his chest. "It's all right, LeeAnn. It's dead."

"What...were those things?"

"Drones."

"Someone is trying to kill me!"

"I know. I told you as much."

She shook her head. Lanky, wet strands of hair slid along her back and arms. "No, Kane! You don't understand! They're really trying to kill me!"

Crap. Crying was going to win the emotion battle after all.

"LeeAnn?"

His voice was low-toned. Softer than she'd ever heard it. Her eyes stung. She blinked rapidly, silently cursing tears that threatened. She held back a sniff, but her voice trembled when she answered.

"Y-yes?"

"You're not going to die. Not on my watch."

Oh, double crap. She'd sniffed.

"We have to leave. You ready?"

She nodded. And sniffed again.

"Oh. Hell."

His curse preceded hauling her atop one shoulder, before he started running. She sent a silent prayer of gratitude that she didn't have to face him! His actions said far more than words. She might be totally turned on by him, but it was obvious the feeling wasn't mutual.

Not by a long shot.

They reached the house, entered the rotunda/foyer area. A strange buzz was radiating throughout the rooms, all of them unoccupied. And every window had a bank of bars on the outside of it now. Those, she knew hadn't been there before. LeeAnn hung from his shoulder and tried to be invisible. Weightless. And if she could wish herself anywhere else, she would have.

It wasn't remotely as comfortable as holding to him, but at least he wouldn't feel the wayward tear she failed to prevent.

CHAPTER SIX

THEY REACHED THE EQUIPMENT ROOM. It was just off the garage, past the kitchens, where a day's catch could be cleaned and packed. A row of generator-fueled, small blue lights delineated the ceiling. Walls. The door leading to the boat ramp. The lights were the extent of visibility. It was more than Kane needed. He bent forward and eased LeeAnn off his shoulder. Set her on her feet. Held her upper arm with one hand while she wobbled. And tried like hell not to notice how little she looked.

Little. Lost. Afraid.

And – heaven help him – she also looked womanly. Really, dream-worthy feminine. Curvy. Soft. Fascinating.

Damn that Jezzie.

No. Wait. This was his fault. He'd sent for the woman so she could clothe LeeAnn. He'd suspected what would happen. But how could he have known how torturous the reality would be? The bathing suit selected for LeeAnn was useless. Absolutely and completely. Especially when wet and under blue lights. He *did not* need the image of her form etched onto his eyeballs. Not right now.

What was he thinking?

This view wasn't ever on his list of needs. He needed to get her into a wetsuit. Covered. Neck-to-ankle.

"You okay?"

He grumbled the phrase. It was the best he could manage. LeeAnn nodded. She was squinting as she looked up at him.

He lifted his hand away and stepped back, watching her waver momentarily. He forced another step away from her.

The woman was industrial-grade magnet.

And he was steel.

Kane snarled before whipping around. Grabbed the handle on a suit locker with a bit too much power. It broke in his hand, but the door had opened a slit. He stuck his fingers in and pulled, bending the metal open. She gasped behind him. Good thing she couldn't see what he did, but the sound was a good indicator. She probably ranked him a step above a Neanderthal. He told himself it didn't matter and reached inside, shuffled through a pile of suits, and chucked several into the room behind him.

"K-Kane?"

If her voice was any gauge, she was still shaky.

"Yeah, babe?"

Shit.

He really needed to cease calling her that.

"Um. How...can you see?" she asked.

"Don't need to. I'm familiar with the room."

The entire house rumbled warningly. The blue lights turned red. Steel doors started slamming into place throughout the home, moving with bone-crunching efficiency. Metallic sounds echoed about them for a moment. Kane's shoulders sagged slightly.

He was out of time. Covering her with a wetsuit just became a waste of precious seconds. He'd have to ignore the fact that she was so womanly and desirable. And then endure it. What a joke. His body was giving him trouble again. He sucked in his abs. Tightened the rest of his frame. Shuddered for a moment.

"What...was that?"

"Lock down."

There were two sets of tanks left in place on the bench, his and Leon's. The tanks were already connected to hoses, and nestled within Integrated Buoyancy Compensator vests. The gear was fitted to his exact specifications. Ready at a moment's notice.

Like now.

Kane sat and donned flippers with angered motions before sliding his arms through the armholes of his vest. A seam ripped somewhere. He stood, grunting slightly at the weight and bulk. His movements were quick. Effective. And harsh. Calming just slightly as he fitted his crotch straps. He maneuvered them between his legs gingerly, going around both sides of his problem, as if framing the area.

He scowled before standing fully upright. He had to stop and physically force a few seconds to pass before securing his gear. Get his emotion in check. His desire for LeeAnn was misplaced. Misguided. Supremely annoying. It messed with his abilities. Made him look and act slow-witted. And had a real impact on his movements. He needed to calm down. Project a certain demeanor. Experienced. Competent. Capable. Even if the situation was dire, he had a novice diver on his hands. The last thing they needed was panic.

The chest fastener pressed into his abs with each breath. The straps were like a caress to his groin. This wasn't normal. Everything felt erotic. He groaned softly. He needed to get into the water and hope the chill put a damper on this. Something needed to.

He took off his sunglasses. Secured them in the little pocket sewn into the waist of the jammers. Grabbed a defogger rag and swiped the inside of his facemask before pulling it on. And then he glanced in her direction. He could swear the floor rocked beneath them as he did so. He moved his gaze before something worse happened.

"I can hardly see you. What are you doing?"

"Getting into SCUBA gear."

"What? Oh, no. You're not—? We're not—? You can't

possibly—? No."

"You still want to live, don't you?"

"Well, yes, but—"

"Then quit arguing."

"Please say you're joking."

"There is only one way out of here, LeeAnn."

"Why can't we take a vehicle?"

"Because we've been flushed."

"What?"

"Haven't you ever hunted?"

"No."

"Well. First you track your prey. And when you find them, you flush them out of hiding. Anything that moves is targeted. We can't take a vehicle. Or a boat."

"But, Kane—?"

"Look. Hon."

Damn his mouth! Another endearment?

He cleared his throat. Spoke at a lower octave. "Uh. The house was already on lock-down. The light change means the perimeter has been breached. Four guesses who it is. And the first three don't count."

"The guy after me?"

"Exactly. And he's good. I've got to give him that."

She moved back from him. What looked like fear stained her expression. He nearly swore aloud.

"I can't do this, Kane."

He took a deep breath. Selected a facemask from the spare rack. Swiped it with the defog rag before pocketing it, too. "Sure, you can."

"No, Kane. Please?"

"LeeAnn. You have somebody with major skills on your ass. He even used a diversionary tactic at the front gate to gain access. The guy is good. I mean, *really* good. That means I have to be a lot better than I have been. Starting now."

"But...this is insane! I didn't do anything. I'm a certified public accountant. I add and subtract numbers! Balance accounts! I live a boring life. In a landlocked state. I've never even been near the ocean until now!"

"You may be a paper-pusher, but you're also really good in a crunch. Calm and focused when you need to be. Extremely level-headed."

"I am?"

"Don't tell me nobody noticed before."

"Um. No." She shook her head.

"You were surrounded by morons. Come on. We're out of time. I'll help you."

Stupid idea, Kane. Really stupid.

He grabbed a set of tanks and approached her, working the IBC vest open as he neared. He stood above her. Inhaled. Then he looked down, trying not to notice she had some really sweet cleavage. The red-toned wash of light caressed one hell of a bosom. And it was right in his line of sight.

"Here." He placed the mask into one of her hands. Waited for her fingers to grasp it. "Put this on. I'll adjust it to your face."

He watched her hands flutter as she took it from him. "But, Kane! You don't know me! I am not calm and focused! I'm going to drown! I'll suck air in the wrong way, and—!"

"You'll be fine. I'll make sure of it. Okay? Now, listen up. The mask covers your nose. The only way to get air is through your mouth. You won't drown, babe."

Damn his mouth. He'd called her an endearment again. Failure made him tense. Edgy. And angered again. None of which helped. He was dealing with real desire here. He'd just have to accept that his body craved hers. Massively. And continually.

Then, he'd have to ignore it.

And not fail at that.

She was shaking. Kane sighed before bending down, leaning the tanks against his leg on the floor. He stood back up. Reached and took the mask from her fingers, and jerked away as the contact zapped. Sent sparks. And singed. He wondered if his hair was smoking. He looked up toward the ceiling, pulled in another deep breath, and dropped his vision back to the top of her head. She didn't balk as he worked the mask over her. Settled it into place. Cinched it tighter. Bent down to check her eyes through the goggles. She was squinting at him.

"Now. Just remember to let the air out completely before pulling another breath in."

"Do what?"

She sounded really cute with her nose pinched. He couldn't help smiling, but sobered almost instantly as her eyes widened. She had some really gorgeous light blue eyes. And he really needed to keep his mind clear. He moved his glance to a wall. Cleared his throat again. It didn't help. Nothing much did.

"We need to focus on the objective here. We're going underwater. It's a whole different realm. You'll need to breathe slowly. Make sure you exhale completely before inhaling again. Your regulator will handle it. I'm putting your tanks on now. You ready?"

"No," she replied.

He smirked, bent to pick her gear up, and got a very good view of her legs while down there. And damn! The woman had some shapely legs, too.

It figured.

Kane stayed bent over for longer than necessary, his hands gripped about the tanks while he struggled with all kinds of things. He was making way too many mistakes already, starting with letting her would-be assassin get this close in the first place. And here he was wasting what precious time they had. But, everything in his body was working against him! He was up against a red-hot feeling of need he'd never felt before. He hadn't even known it existed. Ignoring the sensation wasn't working. Fighting against it was useless. And she was wearing such a tiny, provocative bikini!

The jammers swim trunks weren't going to hide this.

"Um. Kane?"

Her voice was added torment. He tensed. The tanks clanked together in his hands. She sounded more scared than before. That was probably his fault.

What was he thinking?

It *was* his fault.

"Yeah?" Now, he sounded like he was talking around a mouthful of pebbles. This couldn't get much worse. "Just checking the oxygen level." He fiddled with the knob as though adjusting it.

"Is everything...okay?"

"Yeah," he lied.

He stood. Stepped behind her and assisted her into the gear. And had to hold her upright as the weight made her sway.

"K-Kane?"

Great.

She sounded scared. He was going to have to do this in the missionary position.

Worse and worse.

He moved around to face her, holding her upright as he did so. He debated trying to get flippers on her, but she'd probably fall over if he let go. He shook his head. Frowned.

"Looks like we're going to have to do this buddy-style, LeeAnn. You okay with that?"

"How is that?"

Dang! She sounded so cute with her nose pinched! "I'll swim. You hold my vest. It's just like sky-diving the first time."

Her eyes went enormous.

"Don't tell me you never did that, either. Well. You lived a really adventurous life, didn't you?"

She straightened. "I read! A lot. Okay?"

He almost smiled. Not only at the words, but how they sounded with her nasally voice. A large bang against steel came from somewhere in the home. Kane sobered instantly.

"Put your regulator on, sweets. It's time to go!"

"My what?"

He adjusted the hose at her mouth. Waited for her to take a breath. He put his regulator into place. Then he picked her up. She immediately wrapped her legs about his hips, which was perfect for stability and balance, but wreaked hell on concentration. Kane yanked every muscle tight, held her against him with one arm, and started moving, lifting each leg high due to his flippers.

Sunlight bombarded his eyes before they reached the dock. Walked past two speedboats, and a trawler. Nothing with a lot of draft. The big boats were out in deep water. Just out of sight. Within easy underwater swim distance...if he was solo.

He started down the ramp doing his best to ignore the signals firing from his loins. They pulsed down his legs. Through his belly. Into his chest. Down his arms. Existence had become a living hell. Fire. Brimstone. There was too much contact happening. He could swear he felt skin. His every pore was alert. Primed.

And he had to swim this way?

Kane tightened his jaw. Clenched his teeth together. He didn't look down. He didn't dare. He was using every muscle he had to keep from lunging against her.

They were waist deep in ocean water before she reached for his vest.

CHAPTER SEVEN

A N ASSASSIN'S BULLET WASN'T GOING to be the death of her. Embarrassment had first shot. Mortification. LeeAnn tried to keep from looking and acting like they were in a lover's embrace. She did her absolute damnedest. But her body wasn't listening. She had her legs hooked about his waist. His groin pressed to hers. They weren't wearing enough to counteract the sensations as he walked.

And worse.

Or better.

Kane was very well-endowed.

The bright Florida sunshine made her squint. It was exceptionally invasive when coming from a darkened windowless room. Rays caressed and bounced off the span of ocean visible over his shoulder. She kept her gaze glued to that vista. Tried ignoring things. Mentally shifted her focus. Concentrated. Hard.

Harder.

Why...if she was home right now she'd be at the office. Waiting for the coffee to finish brewing another pot. Or, she'd be inputting all kinds of receipts into spreadsheets for clients. She might be scanning the physical receipts Mister Peterson had sent via courier. And that, only *after* he made a photocopy for his records. Martin Peterson wasn't just set in his ways. He was a dinosaur. He refused to scan anything into a program that would send digitally to her. So, she did it for him, without telling him. She didn't even charge him extra...

Cool water lapped at her thighs, taking her back to the present. The chill should have altered things. Stopped this predicament. Helped alleviate things. And...*damn everything!* Her first thought wasn't of an assassin and the threat of death looming over her.

Oh, no.

That would be too sane.

Sensations engulfed her, every one of them linked to the man carrying her. This embrace. How amazing it felt. Thoughts of numbers and coffee and querulous old clients were outgunned. Instantly obliterated. And there wasn't anything she could do to stop it.

Kane wielded massive doses of stimulation. They fired at her with each step he took. She'd never been up against anything like this. It trumped everything she tried. She already had her thigh muscles so taut, the muscles were starting to burn. And that almost didn't work. Every impulse was to move against his hard-on. Rub where she needed it most.

And here she'd thought him cold. Curt.

Completely uninterested.

Water closed over her head. Her initial gasp brought a blast of oxygen. Kane's arm tightened and he moved his head as if to check on her. LeeAnn forced her mind to work again. She wasn't going to be a problem. She refused. She detested people who needed help all the time. What had the instructions been again? Exhale completely before inhaling?

He went deeper. Sunlight glinted on all kinds of things as it diffused. Her ears popped. The water was incredibly blue. Clear. She caught a flash as yards in the distance something moved. Like a fish.

Oh. Sweet.

She was underwater!

She felt faint for a moment. He must have known, for

he'd stopped. Bubbles obscured her vision and her hearing. They didn't come from her. LeeAnn watched them dissipate before she exhaled, listening to the sound of bubbles gurgling. She made certain to empty her lungs before taking another breath. That sound was a hiss. She watched and listened to his bubbles again as he exhaled. Then she heard all kinds of other sounds. Pings. Clicks. Long, drawn-out notes that were almost musical. All kinds of humming sounds that might be from motorized craft. Or pumps. And the occasional splashing of waves.

What was this?

She'd thought the only audible things might be her breathing. Maybe her heartbeat. That was wrong. The ocean was alive with sounds. Sights. Another flash of something occurred in the distance. LeeAnn watched it, wondered at its origin, and didn't even concentrate on exhaling completely. Her next breath was almost natural. She was very proud of herself.

Kane must have sensed it because he started moving again. He stretched out. Released his arm from about her, and then – heaven help her – he started swimming!

Oh.

My.

LeeAnn's eyes widened. Each arm lunge shoved his chest into hers, while his kicking motion did all kinds of destruction everywhere else. His groin grazed against hers repeatedly. Rubbed. All kinds of things happened. No amount of mental concentration worked. His kicks grew stronger. So did his arm motions. LeeAnn eased her ankles apart. Maybe she'd be better off dangling from him, rather than hooked in place, barely suppressing an orgasm.

She let go of him with her legs, and immediately felt the pull on her fingers as water tried to suck them apart. He grabbed her again, handling swimming motions with just one arm. That was her fault. She was already a burden. She needn't handicap him, too. LeeAnn slid her arms into his vest, bringing her a lot closer to his chest, where her nipples got all kinds of stimulation.

Worse and worse.

Or better.

Depended on her viewpoint, but her move must have been the correct one, for he let go of her. Checked his watch, turned slightly to the left, and then started swimming again. Her ears popped again. She looked up, through the water. They must not be deep. Not that she had any clue, but she could easily spot the sun. Looked like it was noon. The sun was directly overhead. She chanced a glance to Kane. He had his cheeks sucked in, but nothing else looked different.

This position was actually manageable. It didn't require much effort on her part, other than ignoring how her nipples itched and irritated. But that was legions better than the full-on male-to-female contact she'd initiated originally.

Besides...

Kane might not be human.

The thought was fantastical. Unbelievable. Insane. But maybe – just maybe – Kane was something like he'd said. He really could be a guardian angel. And they actually came as gorgeous guys. Big. Muscled. Beyond masculine, if there was such a category. All kinds of capable. Why...if Kane hadn't been at her side, she'd have died hours ago. Her life would have been snuffed out. *Finis*. Nothing ahead but a dirt nap.

But...if he was her guardian angel...?

Oh. No. She wasn't really thinking that. *No, LeeAnn.* Impossible.

LeeAnn had no grasp of time, but it felt like they'd been swimming hours, the sun had definitely moved from its zenith, and Kane never seemed to tire. He never even slowed except to check his wristwatch. Kane couldn't possibly be an angelic entity. The man was a machine.

Oh. Wait.

Maybe he was human. He was slowing down. She tipped her head back and looked at why. A span of darkness loomed before them. Any sandy bottom had disappeared. The bottom looked like a big dark abyss. It didn't look like they'd gone much deeper. Her ears hadn't popped but once more, but they were definitely offshore. In really deep water. In the midst of all that darkness was a flashing light. Kane headed for it. As they neared, she got a better view. It was a thick line, dangling down from what looked like the bottom of a large ship. Right above them. Kane had found a ship in the middle of the ocean?

How was that even possible?

Kane grabbed the rope, did something that stopped the flashes and then started climbing. His legs bumped into hers more than once. LeeAnn went with nature and wrapped her legs about him again, only this time it was even more intimate. She didn't pull her forearms out of his vest. She cinched her legs and held on. She couldn't help noticing that any hint of an erection was missing. And she mentally chided herself for even checking. She wasn't just being a burden and a victim here...she had to be a voyeur, too?

Ugh.

She was just adjusting to that bit of embarrassment when he reached a ladder, grabbed the bottom rung and started hauling them up it. His weight. Hers. And their combined SCUBA gear. She didn't know what all of that weighed, but his display of strength was mind-boggling especially when they came out from the water. All kinds of heat, light, and noise assailed her senses. But above all that was the sensation of being attached to Kane as he moved. Muscles rippled beneath skin. Water ran down him in rivulets that glistened. Locks of shiny black hair framed his shoulders. They reached the top of the ladder. Kane flung a leg out and straddled a ledge. It was wooden. Sun-heated. Her butt got a full dose of both as she settled atop it as well. She should let him go. Move back. She knew she should. He plucked his regulator from his mouth with one hand, while the other messed about at his waist. His knuckles touched her inner thigh more than once. More erotic sensations hit her. And with those came the embarrassment again.

He had to be human.

He sure felt it.

He pushed a cheek out with his tongue as he looked down at his hand, unfolded what he'd been after, and then turned away. She watched silently as he pulled the facemask off and put sunglasses on. He'd been after those?

Well.

Maybe he was feeling some of this, too.

Kane turned and caught her looking. Her heart swooped to the pit of her belly. It started pounding from there, sending all kinds of tingling to just about everywhere. He lifted his eyebrows above the lens frame.

"You can take the regulator off now," he said.

CHAPTER EIGHT

K ANE WATCHED LEEANN REMOVE HER mouthpiece. She was quaking. Visibly. He frowned. Reached for the clasp at his chest.

"We have to get out of the open," he informed her.

"O-o-okay."

She was definitely shaking. Despite the sun pumping heat onto the deck. He ripped the fastener open, loosening the crotch straps. The instant release of pressure from between his legs was a welcome change. She didn't move.

"We'll need to get out of our gear first."

She nodded.

Kane unzipped his BCD vest, and would have shrugged everything off except her forearms were still latched in place at his upper abdomen.

"LeeAnn. You're going to have to release me."

"Oh."

She flashed a glance up at him. Sunlight touched the light blue of her eyes for the barest instant. That was enough. The testosterone overload he'd experienced earlier came back with a surge. Intent. Powerful. And visual. It brought something else with it this time. Something that lanced his throat. Speared his chest. Grabbed his heart. Made everything in his chest tight. Pressurized. It was almost painful. His ears even hummed. This was massive. Incredibly special. He'd never felt anything like it.

Ever.

This couldn't possibly be...?

Oh. No way, Kane. Fall back, man. Regroup.

This couldn't be...love? There was no such thing. Love was a fictitious emotion. A wayward fantasy dreamed up by poets. A bit of fluff that marketers used to get advertising dollars. It was an ephemeral spark to passionate encounters.

Nothing more.

If this was love, it wasn't anything like he'd envisioned. Or heard described. He actually felt like he'd been fused to the spot, instantly alert and aware and afire. Fine-tuned to her every nuance. It was too unbelievable.

And wrong.

Love was *not* on the agenda.

Kane watched with wide eyes as she looked away from him, squinting out at the waves. Two spots of color appeared on the tops of her cheeks. She pulled her cheeks in next, which put her lips in a kissable-looking pout. She was pretty damned adorable. He shook his head slightly. He needed to put his gears in neutral. Clear his head. Regain equilibrium.

Nothing worked. If anything, she just looked more endearing. He nearly grinned. *Oh, man.* This was insane. The timing was horrible.

"Um. Sorry."

The mumbled word accompanied her movements. She pulled her arms out first before releasing her legs from about his hips. She probably would have scooted back if she'd had any way to get her feet between them.

"LeeAnn?"

His voice was a croak. He was surprised it worked. He pushed back from her enough he could shrug his tanks and vest off. He slung the bundle down to the deck, making a thud as it settled. Then he reached out to snag her zipper-pull. It slid open down her belly, revealing an itsy-bitsy bikini top and perfect cleavage that looked a little pink, like it might have had a touch too much sun. The vest opened with an erotic gesture. His dick immediately got involved. Kane lifted one leg, shielding his lack of control. And then she glanced up toward him again.

Oh. Man.

Eye contact sent another electrocution-level surge through him. Kane sucked in a big gulp of air, held it for long moments as his heart pounded in heavy beats. His cheeks puffed out as he released the air slowly. He probably glowed. Well. That made it official.

He was hooked.

Caught.

And reeled in.

"Kane?"

"Pull your arms out, babe."

The endearment slid off his tongue automatically. It was instinctive. Perfect. He no longer chided himself. She was his babe. And so much more. And he really needed to get her out of here.

"LeeAnn. Focus, hon. We gotta move. It would normally be safer for you out here. In the sunlight."

"Normally?"

She pulled her arms out. He slung her gear over his shoulder and dropped it beside his. And then he swiveled. Sideways. Her legs fell away. That felt odd. Almost bereft. Kane yanked a flipper off. Then, the other.

"I don't know what kind of resources we're dealing with."

"What?"

He slanted a look toward her. "Hunters do several things if their prey escapes. They hunt it down. Widen the circle. Get it?"

She shook her head.

"We didn't leave any tracks. So...we're either hiding in the house somewhere...or we went underwater. Option two means we'll surface somewhere. Within a certain radius. We already know he has access to drone technology. He might have satellite capability, too. Come on." He stood, shielded his crotch as if adjusting his jammers with one hand, while holding the other out to her.

"Where are we going?"

"Showers. Inside. Salt water dries the skin. It also itches. Come on. Give me your hand, babe."

She gave him her hand. He pulled her to her feet and she instantly hopped atop his discarded flippers. *Oh. Man.* He was lousy at this. He wore wet-shoes. The deck radiated heat. Sun-hot. Burning level. That meant he had to carry her. Again. And why on earth was that bothersome?

She must have sensed his reticence. And misdiagnosed it.

"I...can run. I think. Which way?"

He had her in his arms before she finished. The stupidity of it amazed him. He should have slung her over his shoulder. Like before. Because this move placed her way too close. Right against his abs. Chest. Shoulders. Everything was getting blasted with a series of charges. Carrying heat. Electricity. All kinds of energy. Power.

Kane gritted his teeth. Tightened every muscle. The move lifted her as his arms responded. And then she tucked her nose into the juncture between his shoulder and neck.

Oh. Hell.

Kane moved, charging with swift steps along the bulkhead. Ducked beneath an overhead. Found a hatch. He jostled LeeAnn's knees, using his left hand to lift the handle. Then he spun, bent forward slightly, and hit the hatch with his backside. The door flew open, smacking against an inner bulkhead with a thud that reverberated.

He needed to ease off the throttle here. Get a grip on his emotions rather than just her body.

Oh, man. Bad time to bring that up.

Kane stepped in, turned, and closed the watertight hatch

by dogging it down. Everything was secure again. Except his emotions. LeeAnn didn't seem to be breathing. He made up for it. Kane took another deep breath. Held it for a long moment. And then he started moving again.

They'd entered a large cabin, lined with all kinds of aquatic equipment. Life vests. SCUBA tanks. Buoyancy control devices. Flippers. All of it a reminder. He needed to get their gear off the deck. Out of sight.

"Um. Kane?"

The whisper of her breath was an instant dart heading right for his heart. It affected his balance. Kane stumbled. Caught it before he banged into something. He almost cursed. And finally managed to answer. It was a guttural sound.

"Yeah?"

"I'm not—? I mean, we're not—?"

He entered a passageway. It got lighter. The air grew moist. Warmer. Almost muggy. Dual doors of etched frosted glass came into view. They led to the showers. The doors opened automatically. *Good thing.* He didn't know if he could adjust her weight again to open a door. Not without doing something stupid.

Like kissing her.

A wall of cool air surrounded them. Nothing noticeable. The lights came on next. Motion activated. They were set to a dim level. Cast a muted yellow glow about the area. Everything in this environment was serene. Peaceful. Tranquil. When he needed something intense. Something viciously cold and massively bright. So it could temper some of the nuclear-level fission. Cool things down. He only wished he could set the shower temperature to full-out, icy cold.

But, not here. All he'd get was a pleasantly warm spray of water. Nothing below 79 degrees Fahrenheit. Just like always.

"I mean...um."

Her voice dribbled off. She pushed her forehead farther

into his shoulder, and shook her head, adding to her assault. *It figured*. Maybe she didn't suspect the trouble he had dealing with the touch of breath that accompanied her every word, and that's why she closed in. Not much else made sense.

"You gonna finish that, or leave me guessing?"

He asked it as he smacked the door switch, cancelling power to the portal. It was better than a lock. It would cause delay and give advance warning. They neared the communal showers. Four bays. Separated by frosted glass. Equipped with white painted, wooden stools. They matched the color of pristine cotton towels folded and ready in stacks at the stall edges, as if framing the spaces. Each shower stall held dispensers of potions. Soaps for cleaning. Gels for conditioning. Lotions for lubricating...

Oh. No.

He did *not* just think that! He didn't need images like that in his head! Wasn't the physical reality of holding her enough?

"Am I...showering with you?"

Kane stopped with such a quick motion they rocked forward before he could prevent it. His wet-shoes stuck in place on the tiles, keeping him upright. But nothing stopped the swell of sensation that overtook him. A solid wave of it hit his chest. Belly. And then his groin. He looked down at her head. Back at the shower stalls. And wondered when – exactly – he'd lost control of the situation so completely. He wasn't just dealing with massive lust. Want. Need. And gut-clenching desire.

He was orchestrating it.

In hindsight, he realized he should have set her down already. Ceased physical contact. The moment they'd reached shade. The soles of her feet would've been safe.

So would he.

"Yes. And no," he finally answered.

She lifted her head. She might have glanced toward him. He didn't check. He was in a realm of suspended motion, while pretending to regard the row of stalls facing them. She craned her neck, turning away to look over exactly what he was. And that just put her perfect bosom on display! Despite the idiocy of it, Kane glanced down. One breast was getting smashed and lifted by contact with him. The other was barely held in check by her little bikini bra. As he watched, the pink tone of her skin went darker. She turned back to him, but didn't look up. She was focused on the approximate area of his upper chest.

"Oh. Geez. I am so sorry," she whispered.

"You have to do something for me, LeeAnn. Okay?"

"I don't know what got into me."

"Don't move. Okay? Don't even twitch."

"Kane. Um—."

"I'm about to do something really stupid. Ill-advised. And dangerous."

She lifted her gaze to his. Making eye contact with her was a huge mistake. Even through his dark lenses. The connection sent a swell of sound through his ears while a bolt of electricity shot through him, singeing skin the entire way.

'What?'

Her mouth made the gesture. She may have said it. He didn't hear anything except a long, drawn-out, perfectly pitched note. He couldn't think. He just stood there, vibrating with the effort of keeping everything checked. Held in place. Locked.

Her eyebrow lifted as she waited. And Kane replied with something his mind hadn't cleared.

"I am going to kiss you."

She gasped. Her lips curved slightly in a smile. Despite the hold he exerted everywhere, he almost returned it.

"You are?" she asked.

He licked his lips. "Yeah."

Oh. Shit.
She moved.

CHAPTER NINE

L EEANN LEANED UPWARD WHILE HER thighs tensed against his arm. She'd had one arm about his shoulders. She used it now with debilitating effect. Her fingers tightened on his skin. Her other hand reached up, and, before he could stop her, she pulled his sunglasses off.

That was beyond risky. Kane immediately squinted against the barrage of light.

"Well. That answers *that* question."

She carried TNT with the words. The level of peril was beyond what she'd wielded with every breath. Kane's knees wavered warningly. He wrenched his thigh muscles tighter. Pulled in a breath that shuddered. Prepared an explanation.

"Lee...Ann?"

He said her name. He knew he did. The vibration went through his throat. He didn't hear a damn bit of it.

"You are beyond gorgeous."

Oh.

He heard that.

The awe in her voice triggered all kinds of reaction. As if someone had lit a fuse. He could sense it sizzling somewhere near. He could almost smell the black powder wrapped around the inner string as it burned...nearing combustion.

"I suppose you already know it. That's why you wear these all the time."

She gestured with his glasses and then dropped them. He didn't notice or care. She was too close! Her mouth near his.

The last of her words were whispered against his lips, cursing him with another hint of breath. Kane held his. Her lips touched...

And a shaft of brilliance went through his chest. Sheer blissful pleasure.

And absolute wonder.

If he hadn't recognized what emotion he felt for her already, the kiss would have done it. Kane slammed his eyes shut, barely catching an arc of light that flashed through the showers. He could still see it behind closed lids, though. He could swear he watched it intensify, before spewing a blizzard of sparks that flared and then dissipated.

She moaned. Moved her lips. Each touch carried life. Passionate regeneration. And every kind of intensity. He couldn't get enough, despite trying. Groans erupted from him as he plundered her mouth. Met each and every caress she sent. Throbs of baritone filled the room accompanying her higher-pitched moans. The sounds blended. Became a physical force.

It overwhelmed.

And then it shattered.

There was little means of controlling anything, despite his strength. Not against this much power. Energy. Voracious hunger. And an insatiable level of need.

The shower stalls were cool to the touch. Or he was on fire. Kane's back slammed into one. He heard it crack. It didn't matter, either. Nothing did, except her lips. This kiss. And the amazement of sensation that came with it.

The automatic shower turned on.

The water temperature should be pleasantly warm. It felt anything but. It was hot enough to cause steam and alter reality. Rivulets streamed over his head, across his shoulders, down his back, affecting his ability to breathe. He didn't much miss it. Her kiss was too precious. This connection beyond value. He'd never dealt with anything so wondrous. It was light. Power. Paradise.

It was her move that broke their kiss. LeeAnn pushed from him, arching back to pull in a long breath. That just put her perfect breasts beneath the water. Kane watched, fascinated as the yellow bikini got saturated again. Little nipples from each breast tip puckered the fabric. He turned the spigot toward the wall, and when that didn't feel sufficient, turned sideways in order to block the water with his back. All so he could lift her. Bend forward. Shove material out of his way. Nuzzle her nubs. Lick. And then suckle.

Her flurry of gasps filled his ears. They became cries. Almost screams. Each one sent a flash of something roaring through his veins. It was huge. Heated. And as necessary as air. It was nearly uncontainable. Every limb trembled warningly. Kane lifted away from her bosom and locked his arms before he dropped her. Narrowed his eyes as she looked down at him. Met her gaze. Got struck by something electrifying. And that did it.

He fell.

The stool took the brunt of it, wood creaking ominously as his rear smacked onto the flat surface. His swim trunks flexed, but not enough. His balls got pinched. His erection smashed. Pain got mixed with pleasure as she jolted to a stop atop his bent thighs. And then her breasts *bounced*.

Kane shoved his head back, knocked it against the stall, and sent a roar into the space. He didn't stop until he ran out of air. And then he sucked in another breath and did it again. It didn't help. If anything, it made things worse. He brought his head back down. Glared across at her. Sent harsh breath after harsh breath her way. Her eyes were wide. So was her mouth. He was still blocking most of the water, although some of it splashed off his shoulders and neck and onto her skin. It gathered in little pools so it could drizzle down her perfection. Drip off her nipples. Reach him. And each one felt like it carried fire. Especially when they touched his groin.

'*Wow.*'

She mouthed the word, and then she ran her hands down her torso. To her hips. She linked her thumbs under the sides of her bikini bottoms and ran her hands backward and then forward, reaching the little triangle of fabric covering her front. Her motion sent things from pleasure/pain to an excruciating level. And then made it hover there.

"What do you think? Like what you see?"

Kane's answer was a growl that grew in volume. She flicked her tongue out onto her upper lip. Lifted her eyebrow. And flashed a glance down to where the jammers were contorted and stretched. Back up to his eyes. And then she smiled.

"Want to see more?" she asked.

"*Yeah.*"

He should have growled that reply, too. The guttural word sounded like a beast being tortured. It sent shivers through him. His tone affected her, as well. He watched little bumps form on her skin. Race her body. They tightened her nipples into even tighter, smaller peaks. A tremor shook him next, rattling the stool, and sending all kinds of clacking sounds through the shower stall.

She pushed off him. Stood. He watched with baited breath as she slid the bikini bottoms down her legs, bending forward to free her ankles. Her golden hair was saturated with water, making it an indeterminate dark shade. She didn't wear it much longer than her shoulders. That was way too long at the moment. Kane bit back any reaction at being momentarily blocked from the view. And then she bent her head enough to look across at him. Locked gazes. And winked.

Kane jerked. The stool tipped before re-righting beneath him. And she smiled as if it was funny.

"Well...I want to see more, too," she told him.

His ears got an instantaneous buzzing noise. He shook his head to clear it. She mistook the move. And him. And sounded especially hesitant.

"N-no?"

He shoved upward, sliding his shoulders along the wall, leaning back just enough to get his thumbs beneath his waistband. The move gained shower spray onto his chest and belly that splashed outward, misting the scene. The jammers were doing their job a bit too well. They were supposed to stay in place. Keep drag from slowing him down when he swam. Now, that asset was beyond irritating. It was enraging. He ripped the fly apart. Yanked the waistband open. The damn trunks might as well be glued into place. The material went inside-out as he peeled it down.

And.

Finally.

His erection sprang free.

The relief was palpable. She made a sound. He sent a glance her way. Her hands covered her mouth, and her eyes were especially wide. Intensely blue, even through the haze of vapor between them. He didn't know what her expression meant. She could be awed and impressed.

Or frightened.

Kane looked down to finish disrobing. He shoved the trunks down his thighs with brutal moves. Shimmied them off his knees. They fell to his ankles. A kick sent the garment sailing out into the shower room. And then, he steeled himself. Wrenched every muscle. Shook in place as his body obeyed. All so he could look toward her again. Withstand something beyond containment. Somehow be gentle and lover-like. When everything wanted to pounce. Grab.

Maul.

He probably resembled an enraged beast.

Exactly like he felt.

The shower wall vibrated along with him. He leaned farther into it, making the frosted glass support him. The move put everything on prominent display. As if he did it purposely. And he wasn't a small man. Anywhere.

"Are you...for real?"

The words were barely audible. Kane glanced at her again. Then down.

"Last I checked."

"Oh. Wow."

A portion of him registered that she didn't sound frightened. She sounded pretty damned impressed. He would have grinned, if he wasn't holding so tightly to everything, his body pulled taut like a finely tuned bowstring. Armed and ready to fire.

"Oh. My."

He watched her reach for him. Felt the connection of her fingers with his abs, and despite the impossibility of it, he pulled them tighter. Bowed backward even more. Launched a low-pitched, agonized-sounding reply into the space.

"Sit."

He dropped. It wasn't graceful. It probably should have hurt. The stool shuddered beneath his ass, but held. But he didn't care. Or feel anything attached to his drop. His eyes widened and his mouth followed. Because she lifted a perfectly curved leg and put it over him. Straddling him. Her fingers wrapped about his dick. Positioned him. And then she lowered her body onto his. All while cooing the sweetest sound in existence.

Kane arched backward, lifting to meet her move. Steam-laden water misted the scene. It upped the moist pleasure that belonged just to this. Her body sucked him in. Caressing. Melding. Massaging every inch as she slowly lowered into place. And then she was there! She gave a soft cry as she engulfed him. Joining her body with his. Fully. Completely.

LeeAnn looked toward him. Her eyelids lowered seductively.

That look sent a tremor in its wake. The stool shuddered in concert.

And then she started back up.

Kane grabbed her waist before she got very far. His hands shook as his fingers clamped tight about her. And, he didn't know how he managed it, but somehow he got his fingers to ease up. Changed his grip to one of guidance, rather than direction. Assistance-giving, not control oriented. Helping her strokes...rather than dictating them.

Again.

And again.

Hot, tight coils of pleasure surrounded him. They gripped so tightly, squeezed so pleasurably, held him in a grasp of wet satin. Every move she made toyed and prolonged. And added. No. It multiplied. Her movements sped up. Her breathing became more strident. Kane tightened his grip and used it to pump her. Up. Back down. Each thrust going deeper. Harder. Carrying more power, his efforts assisted and enhanced by the continual shower of water that hit his head and shoulders, and sent droplets spraying from there. Turning the scene into a fantastical vista of glistening perfection.

He helped her lift again.

Thrust back down.

Again.

And again.

And so many times! Her gasps for breath grew heavy with moans. Her skin rosier. The temperature hotter. Steamier. And then she went into a tight series of piston-quick motions atop him. Her breasts bounced in accompaniment. Her screams filled the enclosure.

And Kane lost control of everything.

The stool wasn't constructed for this kind of use. He felt it crack beneath him. An instant later he was on his feet, had her back pressed against the opposite shower wall, his hands cradling her buttocks, and he was thrusting in a non-rhythmic fashion that sent pounding sounds throughout the shower area. Sensation fueled every move. The quest for fulfillment grew fiery hot. Lightning-charged.

Any hint of gentleness got obliterated, overwritten by the need to dominate. Totally. Grunts accompanied each shove, adding to the cacophony of sounds they were making. LeeAnn was at the center of it. She had her legs linked behind him again, and was using the position with vicious efficiency, alternately pushing him away and yanking him back.

Pressure built in his lower back. Slithered through his legs. Grabbed his core. Fused with it. Hovered there, poised in place for an infinitesimal amount of time while his breath caught. His heart lurched. His throat closed off.

And then it detonated.

Kane launched upward, gripping LeeAnn to him as the world exploded, and took him along for the ride. Wonder obliterated reality. Incredulity filled any gap. And absolute bliss permeated everything. His chest took a series of hammer-like blows as his heart tried absorbing this. His eyes watered. His legs locked up. His belly erupted. And his throat tore as a long, agonized-sounding cry burst from him.

And through it all, LeeAnn held on, her limbs locked tightly around him. Her arms hugging him to her. Meshed with him. Linked. Completely and totally.

His cry ended on a sobbed note. He bent his head. Sucked in another breath. Started trembling. The world began reassembling. It wasn't going to be good. His muscles had gone on hiatus somewhere without permission. Or warning. The sounds of water intruded next. It was no longer hot. It wasn't even pleasantly warm. The shower now felt cool. Making his trembling worsen.

"Kane?"

LeeAnn's whisper added to this unbelievable weakness. She

put a hand to his forehead to push a lock of dark hair out of his eyes. Kane squinted as she regarded him. He'd never seen anything as beautiful as the look on her face.

Ever.

"That was pretty...um. Unbelievable."

"Uh..."

His throat was raw. The word sounded like he'd been smoking three packs of cigarettes a day for a half-century.

"What on earth do you do for an encore?"

"Uh..."

He tried again. Got the same result. Her lips curved and that's when Kane started laughing. He couldn't remember the last time he'd laughed. And never with this much abandonment. He should have known what would happen, too. He collapsed into a corner of the shower, and forced the walls to hold them.

CHAPTER TEN

HIS SILENCE WAS BOTHERSOME. AS was the way he shied away from eye contact. She was having trouble getting her arms and legs to work properly, too. She could really use a nap about now. LeeAnn stifled a yawn and went back to drying off. These were really nice towels. Thick. Moisture-sucking. Wet skin didn't have a chance. She bent forward and ruffled one about her hair a few times before wrapping her head, making a large, unwieldy turban the size of a small laundry basket. The weight wasn't balanced properly, either. She tilted her head to one side to keep from toppling. Then, she tipped it the other way. She should probably start over. Do a re-wrap.

Kane was way ahead of her. But he'd cheated. He didn't exactly dry off before moving onto other things. He was already covered and cinching the belt on a thick white, terrycloth robe. It was a match to the one he'd brought out for her.

After he'd quit laughing.

Back in the shower.

LeeAnn looked over at the rather forlorn-looking shower stall. The stool was upside down, one leg a little crooked. There was a big bulls-eye of broken glass in one wall. Cracks radiated outward from it, sending sparkles of color if she moved her head far enough. She sighed softly. It still looked heavenly.

What was she thinking?

It *had* been absolute heaven.

She'd never felt anything like making love with Kane. It wasn't just her body adrift in a perfect blend of satiation and sense of well-being. Her soul felt like it radiated happiness, as well. His laughter had seemed the perfect accompaniment. It had sounded carefree. Infectious. She'd almost joined him. But then he'd just stopped. Without any slow-down of mirth and zero warning. His laughter had ceased. He'd lowered his chin. Narrowed his eyes. Regarded her for long, heart-stopping moments.

And then he'd disengaged her legs from about him and set her onto her feet.

She'd been shaky. Perhaps he'd known. That could have been why he'd taken her arm. Guided her from the shower stall. Grabbed a towel from the stack of them. His gestures had seemed a little brusque. Almost angry. It matched how he'd unfurled the towel and held it out for her.

He'd wrapped the next one about his hips. These towels were large. She still wore the first one. It covered from armpit to knee. Not his. *Oh, no*. On Kane, these towels didn't look remotely bland and innocuous. Or he needed to wear it higher. Chest level. Not low about his hips.

She'd watched him walk from her. Open a tall cupboard. She hadn't noticed it before because it was painted white. LeeAnn had looked about as she realized it. The lighting was really dim. It cast the slightest shade of pale yellow into the area. That didn't do much to alter the impression. Everything was in the same white color. Walls. Floor. Ceiling. Furnishings...

The color was spotless.

Pristine.

Weird.

He'd walked back to her. She watched that, too. It wasn't hard. She could look at him for hours. She didn't want to delve into why. Not just yet. Maybe not ever. It was enough that he was gorgeous. A fantastic lover. His body beyond ripped. And with that white towel barely doing its job, he was showing off a lot of those assets.

That's when he'd brought the white robes. Probably would have handed one to her, except she had her hands full with her hair towel. The garments got set on the floor. And then he'd stood back up and worked his hair into a loose braid of sorts. He had really nice hair. Coal-black. Long. Thick. Shiny. LeeAnn was envious. If she had hair like that, she'd wear it long, too. There was a bonus to watching him. The movements rippled and flexed all kinds of interesting muscles throughout his torso.

Until he'd caught her at it, anyway.

LeeAnn snickered softly at the memory of his expression. It looked like he'd flushed. Been a little self-conscious. But that was just fanciful thinking. Any man that looked like him and had the skills he exhibited, along with the package to back it up...? Well. That man probably had an entire army of women on speed dial.

She'd been easy.

Now, it was her turn to blush. A little late in the day for that. Stupid, besides. So...she'd gone a little sex-starved crazy and practically attacked him. She couldn't be the first woman.

Big fib, LeeAnn.

There was no 'practically' to it. She *had* attacked him. But he'd been a willing participant. She hadn't heard any complaints, anyway.

The lights inset somewhere in the ceiling flickered.

She looked upward. Back down.

"LeeAnn? We need to go. This room...isn't private."

"It's...not?"

Oh. Crap.

She'd been beyond easy. Her voice displayed the mortification. She pegged the emotion easily. Her blush rapidly receded, leaving her feeling a little dizzy.

"Wait. When I muck things up, I sure do it well. I misspoke. This place *was* very private...but that flash is a signal. We've got a new arrival. He'll head for the showers. We need to be gone before that happens."

"Oh."

"You need to don the robe."

"Robe. Yeah. Good plan."

She bent to pick it up and the towel unwound, pulling her hair down as it dropped off her head.

Great.

Now she was clumsy, too. A stab of tears hit her eyes. She was going to cry? Oh. *No. Please, no.* That was too horrid to consider. She blinked rapidly.

"Babe. Please. You are really adorable. But we need to go."

His words sent something sweet flashing through her. It erased everything in its wake. The span of white tile came back into focus. She couldn't do a thing about how her heart seized up. Or the tremor that ran down her back before entering her legs.

"W-what?" she replied.

"Uh...I'd rather not explain the condition of that shower stall. Leon is not stupid."

"Leon?"

"The last hunter. We've been waiting for him."

"We have?"

"I'll explain everything. Well. I'll try to, anyway. The moment we're safe. But, for now, we gotta go. Fair?"

Her answer was halfway between a sniff and a giggle. And then the robe disappeared as he grabbed it up.

"Here. I'll help."

He lifted her to her feet. Stood looking down at her. His eyes were still narrowed. He still looked angered.

"Kane?"

"You need to shed that towel. It's damp. Probably cold."

He shook the proffered robe out. Held it open. The muscles of his jaw clenched. LeeAnn pulled the end of her cover open and dropped it. The robe shook in his hands.

"Oh. *Hell*. You are so beautiful. I am either extremely lucky... or especially cursed. Here. Put this on. Please?"

He was right. The towel had been chilled. The robe's thickness was nice. But it didn't warm her near as much as his words. Or the tone.

"Where are we going?"

She asked it as he stopped at a door, cracked it open, and peered outside. There wasn't much to see. The lighting system out there looked even dimmer than what was in the shower room. But it couldn't be. Or Kane had some real light-sensitive issues. He held her hand with one of his, while the other fished a pair of sunglasses out of his robe pocket. He opened and positioned them onto his face with the same hand. Easily. Almost automatically. The accessory made him look unapproachable. And pretty damned scary.

He looked down at her solemnly for a moment. And then sighed heavily, sending a blast of air that ruffled the dried hairs along her forehead.

"The only place I can think of."

"Is it...private?"

"It's safe."

"But not private? Well. Darn."

She had to hide the smile as he jerked slightly. His fingers tightened about hers.

"LeeAnn—?"

He said her name with an undertone of anxiety. LeeAnn scrunched up her nose and watched her reflection in his black lenses. "Oh, come on, Kane. I was kidding."

"It is not amusing."

She tried to match his attitude. What she could see of his expression. The set look of his shoulders. But she had to factor in the tiredness that dogged her, turning her into the consistency of a leftover limp spaghetti noodle sitting in a cauldron of tepid water. The best she could manage was an eyebrow lift.

"You sure are a serious guy," she remarked finally.

"I have to be."

"I'm beginning to think you're a cyborg, Kane, and I'm not that imaginative. Oh. Wait. I must be. I mean, look at the evidence here. In one day's time I've been shot at. Kidnapped. Almost drowned in a pool. Gone SCUBA diving – without *one* lesson, mind you." Her voice grew louder as she continued. The words came quicker, too. "And then I just had the best um...uh. Well. Sex is not the right word for what happened, is it? I can't even call it a romantic encounter. That was the most amazing session of lovemaking I have ever experienced! Okay? I am still wiped out. And—. Damn it! I can't believe I just said that. This is so not me."

"You're doing fine, babe."

"Fine? Me? Aren't you listening? This is spy stuff! I rarely played video games when I was a kid! I'm a numbers person! I'm considered constant and reliable, not risky and dangerous. You know what I consider adventurous? Adding flavored creamer to my coffee! You wouldn't believe the calories involved!"

His lips twitched. Then, the smile evaporated.

"I've gone from being a successful businesswoman to one without clothing, money, or even identification! I have a deranged killer after me! I'm in the clutches of a sinfully sexy stranger who could be a bad guy for all I know, and oh! You better add in that I have absolutely no idea where I am, either!"

"North, two four. Three zero. Zero seven. West, eight one—"

"What are you doing?"

"Giving you numbers."

"To what?"

"Our location."

"You're giving me longitude and latitude?"

He nodded.

"I was right before. You are not real. Nobody goes around spouting those. Confess. You're a robot. Right?"

He shook his head.

"Then what?"

"I told you. I'll explain later. When we're safe."

"We're on some ship in the Atlantic Ocean somewhere. How can that not be safe?"

He stepped closer. Pushed away an errant lock of hair from where it had fallen across his lenses, making him even more shiver-inducing. "Babe. Please? I lost my head for...a span there. As well as my objective. My focus. And a good chunk of time. I need to check things. Assess. Evaluate."

LeeAnn regarded him for a long moment. Tried not to react. It was really difficult to stay annoyed. "Lost your head, eh? That's what you're calling it?" she finally asked.

"Lee. Ann."

He separated her name into two separate chunks. He might have been trying to sound stern. It didn't work. The man had a voice that matched the view.

"Yes?"

The lights flickered again. That was followed by the sound of the automatic doors opening. Kane pulled her to him. The contact was instantly incendiary. She wondered if he felt any of that.

"We're leaving right now. You ready?"

"Um. Sure. I guess."

"Stay close to the bulkheads."

"What's a bulkhead?"

He swiveled his head, the move cracking something in his neck. And then he looked down at her again.

"Just..." He grunted mid-sentence before finishing it. "Stay close."

He opened the door wide enough to ease through. Pulled her with him. The door shut behind them with a hissing sound that sent a huff of air with it. Any lighting was a joke. She could hardly see. It took several seconds for her eyes to adjust. The halls were beige-toned. The lighting had the same dun quality. The only reason Kane stuck out was his attire. The white of his robe was just a bit lighter than the wall he was flattened against. His arm was crooked about her chest, just above her breasts, sticking her in place alongside him. She didn't have much choice.

But she wouldn't have moved if given one.

CHAPTER ELEVEN

H IS IDEA OF A SAFE place turned out to be his rooms. Or, what he called a cabin. It was located in the middle of a long hallway, above the shower room by at least two floors. Only he called them decks. The flights of stairs were termed ladders. Halls were called passageways. Bulkhead was the name for wall. She knew all that now, because he'd informed her in whispers. Despite telling him she wasn't interested in a career at sea.

Especially not on this vessel.

The entire ship exuded luxury, but it hadn't been put to good use with the color scheme. From the hall of beige-ness, he'd led her up a ladder to a passageway of barely-colored sage green. Then they'd traversed a bluish span of hall that made his skin look sallow. That's when he'd gotten hyper-vigilant. Spent all kinds of time checking the path before proceeding. Continually glanced behind. Always keeping her in his shadow, like an extension of himself. They finally reached these rooms located in a passageway with such a pale pink tone it probably rated 'distinct pallor' in any mime's face-painting box.

And she was lost.

Kane had stopped beside a nondescript pinkish-toned door. Lifted his hand. Placed it flat on the wall at his shoulder level. That was interesting. She could just make out framework around a panel. Her eyebrows rose as a pale light emitted about his hand, apparently scanning his palm. After a distinct click, the door opened inward an inch or so.

Okay, LeeAnn.

This was the stuff of movies.

And pretty darn cool.

Kane pushed against the door, slit it open enough to slither through. Brought her with him. The door closed automatically, barely missing her heels. He turned back, leaned his forehead against the door, and sucked in a large breath. She heard another distinct click of the locking mechanism.

He exhaled. Spine-tingling words came with it. "Oh. Thank heaven. We made it."

"Kane?"

He pulled her into an embrace that sent massive warmth. An unbelievable sense of joy. Exhilaration. His heartbeat was heavy. Full. Easily heard with one ear pressed to his chest. LeeAnn tried to move even closer, loving every second. Being in Kane's arms was paradise. Heaven. Nirvana. All rolled into one. Her earlier claim of tiredness evaporated, leaving awareness. An itch of interest. All kinds of heart-pounding emotion. And Kane just stood there. Looking down at her. He still wore dark glasses. She watched her reflection while the silence grew.

And grew.

She licked her lips. He groaned.

"I broke every rule bringing you here, love. But I didn't know what else to do. I couldn't leave you."

Love?

Her knees quivered and she would have fallen if he hadn't been supporting her. His mouth neared hers. His breath meshed with hers. LeeAnn leaned upward, connected their lips, and held the cry inside. Ecstasy slammed through her. Joy. Happiness. And then he lifted his head. Nuzzled her nose. And sent a shaft of light right through her with his words.

"I love you."

LeeAnn gasped.

He shook his head slowly, back and forth. Several times. "I know it's too soon. I know it's impossible. I know it's a huge mistake. I know all that, and yet it doesn't change anything. I didn't expect this. Don't deserve it. And still can't stop it. I love you. I do. I don't know how it happened...or why. I only know I love you."

This time, his kiss stole her breath. Her sanity. And her heart. They were both shaking when he lifted his head away, and sent a groan so raw it brought tears to her eyes. She held to him until it ended.

"Kane?"

"I just wish love was enough."

She lost her breath. Her heart felt like someone had it in a big fist and was squeezing their fingers about it. "You're joking. Right?"

"I need to set you down."

"Why?"

"And I need you to walk away from me. Understand?"

"No."

"You will."

"But...why, Kane? Why?"

He didn't answer. He set her down with a lurch. His arms fell away. LeeAnn didn't move for long moments while her heart absorbed something heavy. Painful.

He put his hands on her shoulders and turned her around, placing her back against him. And then she lost that contact as he moved away. It took a few moments to see anything. More time passed as she used her sleeve to dab at her eyes, sopping up moisture that shouldn't even be there. She hadn't even known him before 4:58 this morning! She couldn't possibly feel love for him, too. And yet, she knew what he spoke of. It was a physical ache to watch him move farther and farther away from her, until he almost disappeared in the dimly lit, grayish color scheme. The tone seemed appropriate somehow.

It matched how she felt.

Exactly.

LeeAnn faced a sea of grayness. There wasn't one window to break it up. Nothing contrasted. It was difficult to decipher what was furniture and what was floor. There was an old-school phone on a table beside a same-shade gray couch. Kane picked it up. Despite his request, she followed as if there was a rubber-band around them and it had flexed too far. He lifted the receiver.

"Yes. Kane. Yes. One." He hung up. Looked down at where she hovered about six inches away. "LeeAnn, this is too close."

"Give me one good reason why."

He looked over her head as if debating something. She had to guess since he still wore his glasses. And then he looked back down at her.

"I must go. Get dressed."

"You're leaving me?"

"I will return. I promise."

"Look. Kane. Come on. Please? I'm in way over my head here. You can't just announce that you love me and then leave me!"

He'd untied his belt. Walked from her toward a gray-toned door at the back of the room. He pulled an arm free from the robe before turning to face her, and that just made him look like a Grecian statue with a toga draped on it.

"Don't move," he said.

The door shut behind him. Silence descended. It was an eerie silence that lifted goose bumps along her skin. LeeAnn sat on a sofa. What she wouldn't give for a book right now! Something to take her mind off the image of him. Shedding his robe completely. A magazine would even work. Heck, she'd even go for a pamphlet from a doctor's waiting room. Graphic and gory. Anything to take her mind off—

"I'm back."

LeeAnn was slack-jawed as Kane dropped onto the couch opposite her, denting it with his bulk. He'd been gone mere moments. Or she'd lost all concept of time. He was dressed in black again. Black denim. Black t-shirt. Black sunglasses. He had his hair pulled back tightly and secured this time. She'd never seen anything as perfect.

"What?" he asked.

"You."

"What about me?"

"You're...um. Beyond gorgeous. I can't help noticing."

He colored and looked away for a moment. That was cute.

LeeAnn considered him. "Oh, come on, Kane. I can't be the first woman to tell you that. I refuse to believe it. I mean, really. Do I look that gullible?"

"Yes."

"Oh. Great. I look gullible? But that should come as no surprise. I'm here, aren't I?"

She stood. Shoved one side of her robe farther across the other. Yanked her belt tight. Did her best to glare down at him. It didn't help that he was almost her height when sitting. Nor, that he truly was the most handsome thing she'd ever seen. It really didn't help to remember their lovemaking session. And especially his follow-up declaration of love. That alone was guaranteed to soften her glaring ability. LeeAnn sighed.

"Sit down, baby. Please? I am going...to try to explain things. I don't think I can do it with you glowering at me. Please?"

LeeAnn sat. Folded her arms. Did her best to look like a certified public accountant facing an agent from the IRS. At an official audit. "Okay. I'm listening."

"I don't know where to start."

He ran his hands down his thighs. Hugged his knees for a fraction. Slid his fingers back up his legs. It might be a nervous gesture, but it caught her glance. And that sent sparks shooting through her lower belly. She shifted slightly.

"The beginning."

"Which one?" he asked.

"Which one? The first one. How about birthplace. Where were you born?"

"South Carolina."

"Raised?"

"Same."

"Really? I would never have guessed."

"You wouldn't?"

"You haven't got a trace of a southern accent."

"That's because I haven't been there...for a long time. A powerfully long time."

"Okay."

He folded his arms, matching her stance. His move sent all kinds of muscle definition bulging into view. The guy had immense arms. LeeAnn looked there. Suffered a distinct tremor. And somehow managed to move her gaze back to his sunglass lenses.

He uncrossed his arms. Put his hands back atop his thighs. That just moved her attention. He had such massive thighs. And a really nice bulge at his groin. LeeAnn tried her best not to move or act like she'd noticed. She felt the blush burn her cheeks, but otherwise thought it worked.

"I...was the outdoors type. Water sports. Mud-bogging. Hunting. Fishing. Camping. You name it. I was into it."

"Sounds fairly normal so far. I mean, I've never been to South Carolina, but I've seen the ads. Watched documentaries. Been to movies."

LeeAnn slipped a lock of hair over her shoulder. Adjusted the collar of her robe where it had gapped. Decided against re-tying the belt.

"This isn't working. Perhaps you'd better get dressed, too. I can't concentrate."

She looked down at her robe. She was concealed from her

throat almost to her ankles. She looked back up. "How much more do you want me to wear?" she asked.

"A lot."

"Do you have anything in my size?"

"Probably not."

"Well. If you want me to wear one of your shirts...you just let me know. But I have to warn you. That's gonna be very revealing without a bra."

He gulped audibly. LeeAnn nearly laughed. Hearing his declaration of love had altered things considerably. Made this a lot more potent than it might otherwise have been.

"I really wanted to be a SEAL," he blurted out, changing the subject completely.

LeeAnn lifted an eyebrow. "The Navy Special Forces kind of SEAL?"

He nodded.

"Well. That couldn't have been hard. You were probably top man on the recruitment list."

"Took me six years to qualify."

"Six years? You? No way."

"It was a new program. I was young."

"Okay. So. You're a SEAL. That explains a lot."

"No. I'm not a SEAL. I *was* a SEAL."

"Was?"

He nodded.

"Okay. So...what happened? You had an injury that forced your retirement? After which, you joined a group of mercenaries? And now you spend your time hunting bad guys?"

He shook his head.

"You don't look like the kind of guy who'd go psycho and get booted out of the service."

"I'm not."

"I give. Tell me. Why aren't you a SEAL any longer? You're

fit. Young. Extremely capable. And you're...um. Really skilled."

She actually got the words out without stammering. That was a surprise. He took a deep breath. It expanded his t-shirt. LeeAnn's gaze dropped to his chest. She sucked on her bottom lip. She couldn't tell his expression due to the stupid dark lenses, but she definitely heard his groan.

"You need to stop that," he informed her.

"Stop what?" LeeAnn gave him her best innocent look before tipping her head down and adjusting the terrycloth covering her lap. She picked at an imaginary speck as she waited.

"This is not working, either."

"You really know how to beat around a bush, Kane. You know that? Your parents must have pulled their hair out trying to pin down where you'd been when you came home after curfew."

"Did you ever study names?" he asked.

"What?" LeeAnn's head came back up. He looked serious.

"Your birth name. LeeAnn. Do you know what it means?"

She gave him her 'CPA-listening-to-a-lie-from-a-client' smile before replying. "Yes. It means my grand-mother was named LeeAnn. As was her mother before her."

"Lee means 'dweller by the wood'."

"I'll take your word for it. But how do you know?"

"I've had...a lot of time. I met someone named Lee. He has a few strange quirks. I wondered why, so I did some checking. Grew interested. Wondered if a name had any significance. And consequence."

"You have a bookish side? That's—um. Wow. I'm almost speechless here."

He pulled his head back a little. "Are you making fun of me?"

"Oh. Never," she replied.

"I think the name Ann means 'graceful.' Or perhaps it

would be better phrased as 'full of grace'."

"So, my name means I'm a graceful being from the woods. I sound like a fairy. Nice. But not remotely accurate. Look, Kane. You and I are opposites. I'm the indoors-type. Basic hermit version. I've been called a workaholic. And when I'm not working, I'm usually reading. I have a hard time even getting to the gym. That is the farthest thing from a fairy I can imagine."

He sighed heavily. "Can you guess what my name means?"

"Sure. I'll take a stab at it. If it's spelled with a 'C', I'm going to say you were named after the Biblical bad boy, Cain. The slayer of Abel. That Cain. You're not going to tell me you're a descendant, are you? Because I'm not the religious type. I quit going to church in my teens."

"That's the Hebrew origin. It actually means 'spear'."

"Spear. Okay."

"But my name is spelled with a 'K'."

"And that means something different, right?"

"Kane is an Irish name. Celtic. It means 'fighter'."

"Good name. I don't know where we're going with this, but the name definitely fits. Your parents are to be applauded."

"This is not working, either."

"Perhaps you could just give me straight answers?"

"I'm trying, but it's not easy! I told you. This is new territory for me. I've been called cold. Curt. Emotionless. Heartless. Mean. I can go on."

"No? Really?"

"But I've never loved anyone before. I didn't know anything about love. Or how it felt."

Her heart stuttered. Swelled. She didn't know what to reply. Or how.

"I keep thinking of some way to soften this. So you...won't turn from me."

Oh.

She knew how to reply to that.

"Turn from you? Look. Mister. I'm not that faint-hearted. Try just spitting it out. But before you do, I have a confession to make. I'm already...yeah. Let's just say I'm not immune to you, either."

"You aren't?"

"It can't be that big of a surprise. You are extremely easy to fall for. Especially once you dropped the heartless, mean, cold, etcetera veneer."

"Oh. LeeAnn. Love. This is not making it easier."

He had a definite frown now. It sent a line across his forehead.

"Anything I can do to help?"

He lowered his chin. She wasn't certain, but he looked like he was regarding his hands atop his thighs. And that just drew her attention there again. He looked back over at her. She wasn't prepared. He caught her ogling. And that just heightened his color again.

"Do you know where you are?" he finally asked.

"Um. With you?"

"Lee. Ann."

He separated her name like he had before. Probably trying to sound stern again.

"Okay. Yes. As a matter-of-fact, I do. You gave me coordinates. Remember? I am on a boat in the Atlantic Ocean somewhere around the north twenty-fourth parallel. Something like that."

"It's not a boat. It's a ship."

"Oh, brother. Fine. I'm on a *ship* in the Atlantic Ocean somewhere around the north twenty-fourth parallel. You are such a stickler for mariner terms. Must be the SEAL thing."

He slid to the edge of his seat, closing in on the available space and sucking up more than his share of oxygen. It was hard to get a breath. He instantly looked alert. Intense. The hairs on the back of LeeAnn's neck lifted.

"This ship is named *Abaddon*."

"Okay. Interesting name."

"Do you know what it means?"

"I think we've already proved I don't know the meaning behind names. So...no. I don't."

"It means...purgatory."

LeeAnn blinked several times. He looked serious as all get-out. While saying something preposterous. She regarded him for several long moments. "Is that supposed to be funny, Kane? Because...I have to tell you. It's not."

Kane leaned even closer in response. And then he pulled his sunglasses off.

CHAPTER TWELVE

THE LIGHT WAS EXCRUCIATINGLY BRIGHT. At first.

Kane refrained from narrowing his eyes and just accepted the discomfort. LeeAnn had asked about light-sensitivity issues. What he suffered was much worse. It was a mark. And curse. All of them carried it. His eyes were full black, as if the pupils had been medically enlarged and couldn't contract. It was a dull black shade. Light didn't reflect. They appeared bottomless. Empty. Nothing behind them. He knew. He'd studied his reflection often enough over the years.

He thought he'd kept the affliction hidden from her because most light sources were painful. Now, he knew the reason. He loved her. The more that feeling had grown, the longer he'd held back. He hadn't shown her, because he was terrified of her reaction. Literally terrified. His knees shook for the barest instant. His gut churned. The blood in his veins froze. Kane had experienced fear. Every soldier in Vietnam had. He'd always met it head-on. And then conquered it.

Just like he now tried.

But he'd never felt so vulnerable or exposed.

He locked eyes with her, watching for a reaction, even as he tensed in order to withstand it. He didn't blink. She matched that, too, despite her need. He watched her light blue eyes glisten as tears formed atop the surface. His chest felt like a vise had seized him and was clamped in place, winding tighter with each heartbeat. His throat went dry. He tried swallowing anyway. That was stupid. The move scraped and burned. And that was before he tried speaking.

"Lee...Ann?"

"Your eyes are really dark, Kane."

"I know."

"I mean...really dark."

She broke their gaze, and looked down. Hiding from him. He watched her dab at her eyes with the cuffs of material at each wrist. She stood. Kane jerked back so they wouldn't touch, despite how he craved that very thing. She cinched her belt robe tighter about her waist. She was trembling. Her voice reflected how badly.

"I think...I could use a bathroom about now," she informed him.

"Sorry, love. That's a negative."

"Excuse me?"

"There isn't one."

"It's through here. Right?"

She walked to the door to his other room. Pushed it open. He heard her walking about the space. She'd find a closet that held his clothing. A bureau and mirrored dresser that did the same. A platform for him to rest atop. Nothing more.

She came back.

"You don't have a bathroom in there," she informed him.

"I know."

"So...this is like a hostel? The facilities are shared? And out in the hall somewhere?"

"No."

"I mean passageway. Is that the problem here? I'm not speaking mariner lingo? Should I call it a passageway, and the bathroom a 'head'?"

"That's not it, LeeAnn."

This was harder than Vietnam. Worse than when his SEAL Team had hit the wrong village. Killed innocents. And four of his teammates had slaughtered witnesses before Kane could stop the carnage with more of it. That action was what got him sent into this limbo rather than the real hell. Once it was over. And everyone was either dead. Or dying. He still remembered it. Vividly. He'd never forget. He still suffered visions of how every moan from the blood-soaked scene had faded...

And then gone silent.

"Then, what is it, Kane?"

Her voice brought him back to the present with a jolt. It was followed by the sound of the cabin door handle getting joggled. He snapped his head toward the sound. LeeAnn was at the door, working the door handle up and down.

"Babe. Stop. Please."

"Why won't this door open?"

"You don't have my palm marks."

"You have to do that on the inside, too? Well? Come over here and open it for me."

"Why?"

"So I can search out a bathroom!"

"There are no bathrooms out there, either."

"Okay. So where are they located? Near the shower room?"

"No."

"Then where?"

"You are in purgatory, LeeAnn. No one needs them here."

She opened her mouth. Shut it. Put her hands on her hips. Looked really small. Slightly obstinate. Disbelieving. And eternally beloved. If his heart wasn't sending solid shards of pain with every beat, he'd have smiled. The vise about his chest squeezed tighter, nearing crippling capacity. He leaned forward to absorb it.

"Okay. Cut the bullshit, Kane. I wasn't going to do anything other than splash water on my face. Maybe take a sip of water. But now, I'm going to start getting pissed. I don't believe in purgatory. Or—or vampires. Or zombies. Or...any of that crap! Now, get off your ass and help me!"

He sucked in a breath. Stood. It took an act of will to straighten to his full height. And it sent a lot more than pain. He looked down at his chest. Odd. Nothing showed. He should be hemorrhaging from a gaping wound.

Exactly like it felt.

"Now. Get over here and open this door."

"That's not...a good plan."

"It's better than yours."

He walked toward her slowly, wincing once before he caught it. He'd never been in love, so he'd never dealt with rejection of it. He hadn't known it sent physical trauma. And that love, too, had a dark side.

"I've got to get this door open. Find a phone. Or...maybe the lifeboats. That's it! There's got to be a lifeboat station. I can figure out how to lower one. It can't be that hard. There are probably placards. There are signs for everything."

He neared. Each step was agony. She was everything that was light. Warmth. Wonder. He loved her with every fiber of his being. And what had he done?

Brought her into the darkness with him.

The full extent of what he'd done overwhelmed him for a moment. He felt ill. Completely shaken. Tremors ran his frame. Tears stung his eyes. He'd been sent here to earn a place in heaven. Maybe another chance at life. Not blow it this badly.

Kane looked away. Blinked rapidly. Watched a bulkhead blur and mesh into a wash of gray tones. And then he closed his eyes and silently begged for help. Because he had to rectify this. She didn't have anyone else.

"LeeAnn. I'll get you...off the ship. I promise. LeeAnn?"

"What?" She spun, planted her back against the door and looked up at him.

"I can't...let you out there. Not yet."

"Why not?"

"It's...too dangerous."

"That's it! I refuse to believe that there is a hitman out there with the resources to track me underwater to this nightmare, and that he is, right now, hunkered down around a corner, waiting for the perfect shot at me! I refuse! You hear me?"

She was yelling, but the space around them easily absorbed the sound.

"He's not the problem, love."

"Don't call me that! Not right now! Please?"

Her voice broke. And he'd been wrong. The vise-like pain had merely been a prelude. Kane sucked air in so rapidly his teeth iced. Agony roared through him, sending everything to an excruciating level. Fire-hot. Flesh-burning. It didn't seem possible he could absorb it and continue functioning. He slammed his palm onto the wall in order to remain standing.

"Are you all right?"

She sounded truly worried. Her hesitant step toward him matched the impression. As did the touch of her hand where she placed it on his upper arm.

"It's not...your would-be...assassin. It's the...others."

He couldn't even get through a sentence without pausing. That was bad. Her eyes went huge. They drew him, and despite knowing she'd see the emptiness of his soul, he locked gazes with her. She had such beautiful eyes. Perfectly formed. Clear. So full of life. The connection lasted mere seconds. But it sent absolute rapture. Complete bliss. Wonderment beyond imagining. Things he'd never experience again.

And he knew it.

Kane set his jaw and broke away from her gaze. But he couldn't prevent the moan that escaped his lips.

"Kane?"

Her voice was soft as she said his name! So incredibly

beautiful. He wondered if he'd get to keep the memory when he ended up where he was going.

"I have to keep you from...Jezzie. Leon. Rafael. Dozens... more."

"I'm in danger from them?"

He nodded.

"Why?"

"We're in purgatory."

"Give it a rest, Kane. Okay? You're starting to sound crazy."

"Dark angels...normally blend in with humanity. Co-existence is not...a problem. But in purgatory, we revert. Crave...what we do not have. The...human spirit. Light. Life force—"

"Dark *what*?"

"Angels. We're all dark angels."

Her mouth opened. Closed. Opened again. Kane started talking. And it actually got easier. "We're stuck here, hovering between heaven and hell. Purgatory has different names. Different locations. This ship is just one of them."

"What? How?"

"I was pulled from death in 1969, LeeAnn. I've spent the years since trying for redemption. Because the alternative is hell. Literally."

"No way."

"Sometimes...I've heard we can get another chance at life. But I don't know how to—"

She interrupted his explanation. She started gesturing. She got louder and faster as she spoke. As if he wasn't less than a foot from her. Unable to cease listening.

"You know, I always dreamed of meeting a man like you, Kane! Strong. Handsome. Uber-sexy. I'd fall in love! We'd have great sex. A nice wedding. Get a house in the suburbs. Have two-point-eight kids. A family car. We'd live the dream! I wanted to find my soul-mate! Is that so bad?"

She stopped and pulled in a breath.

"I wanted to find the man I could grow old with! But does any of that happen? Oh, *no*. Not to me. I can't be normal! Not LeeAnn Schultz. I have to fall for a guy who says he's already dead! That's what I do!"

"What...did you just say?"

He didn't notice the light outlining his palm, even as it warmed her face. Lit her features. Gave her an ethereal glow.

"You heard me!"

She said it militantly, but then she launched at him, flung her arms about his neck and gave him heaven. Her kiss was pure magic. Filled with healing light. Kane wrapped both arms about her and rocked backward, his fall stopped by the bulkhead.

And then the cabin door clicked open.

CHAPTER THIRTEEN

LEON CAME THROUGH THE PORTAL, pushing the door wide. He had a gun held to his head. It was attached to an arm that turned out to belong to a fellow in black. Approximately Kane's height, but a lot thinner. He pushed Leon into the room. His other hand held another 9mm. He immediately aimed it at toward LeeAnn. Kane shoved her behind him, and held her there with an arm.

"Hi, cupcake," the guy said. "Surprised to see me?"

"What's going on, Leon?" Kane asked.

"Address me, asshole. He's a patsy."

The man shoved Leon away from him. Leon stumbled and caught the door, holding it open as he lurched to a stop. His move kept the door from automatically closing. Kane met Leon's gaze for a moment. Leon smiled. Kane didn't return it.

"You got a name, buddy?" Kane asked conversationally.

"Yeah. Victor. As in…winner. Champion."

"I knew that already, Victor, but thanks for the lesson. So. What can we do for you?"

"You are a hard man to track, pretty boy. Not impossible, but hard. Took every nano-tracker I had."

"You used a nano-tracker?" Kane nodded as if impressed.

"Cute little units. Send a strong signal. Easy to hide anywhere. Real easy to hide in SCUBA gear. You thought you lost me with that little underwater stunt back in the Keys, didn't you?"

"Well. It was a hope."

"Lame. And here I thought you'd be a challenge."

"Likewise," Kane replied.

"So. You know what I want. I suggest you just hand her over."

"That's a negative."

"I'm really not interested in you, bub. Or the little patsy. And I'd really hate to put bullet holes in this ship of yours. But don't tempt me."

"How did you get here, Victor?"

"You had a couple of speedboats at your place. Forget those, did you?"

"Smart. So. You planted a tracking device on Leon's gear, and then you used one of our boats to follow him. And you didn't even get wet. The boat must be close."

"Starboard side. Bottom of the ladder. Enough shit talk. You gonna move, or do you want a bullet?"

"I think you already know the answer, Victor."

"Fair enough."

LeeAnn's hitman was less than a yard away. He lifted the barrel to Kane's chest. Kane narrowed his eyes. Tightened his chest for the impact. Instantly canceled his heartbeat, respiratory functions…determined to live long enough to fulfill his promise to LeeAnn.

"Wait!"

LeeAnn's screech was loud and surprising. Kane embarrassed himself by flinching. Victor's gun didn't even waver.

"Can't we negotiate or something?" she asked from behind him. "I mean, how much is Chad paying you anyway?"

"Chad? I don't know any Chad, lady. And I'm really getting tired of pointless chit-chat."

LeeAnn answered, talking exceptionally fast. "He's my business partner! I'd discovered some high dollar money transfers he needed to explain! I was supposed to meet him over it!"

"Oh. That guy. Shit, lady. He was my first target this morning. Just before I went after you."

"Chad...didn't pay you?"

"He couldn't afford me. Few people can. I work for a family organization. They don't like it when people call them with problems...like a meeting with a suspicious partner. Sounds like Chad didn't have a head for high finance. Well. He won't have to worry about that anymore. And if pretty boy here doesn't move, he's going to have basically the same problem."

Kane caught the vaguest hint of sound out in the passageway. The slightest rumbling noise came through the door. Leon heard it, too. He straightened, making the door waver. Victor didn't seem to notice.

"So. Where do you want it, pretty boy?"

"No!"

LeeAnn stuck her head around his shoulder. Kane swiveled. Victor got off two rounds. One bullet grazed Kane's arm, leaving a gash across his bicep. The wound burned. Immediately started bleeding. LeeAnn screamed. Kane smashed her against his back, preventing her from watching the mass of arms and hands that reached through the open door, grabbed anywhere they could on Victor, and yanked him back out the portal.

Leon surged after him. Kane didn't wait.

He swung LeeAnn to his front, flung her over his shoulder, and leapt the mass of bodies swarming the passageway. He didn't need to see. He knew what they were doing. Victor's screams were bloodcurdling. Loud. And then diminished into strangled-sounding as he got overwhelmed. His life force drained.

And then consumed.

LeeAnn hyperventilated. At least she wasn't screaming. Kane took the ladder with churning steps that echoed. The next one with even more haste. He didn't check for pursuit. He didn't waste the time. The upper deck had never felt so far away. And then they were there.

Kane shoved the handle down and smacked through the hatch, hearing it slam behind him. It didn't immediately reopen. That might mean he'd had a good enough head start. It could also mean they were coming a different way. His luck still held. It was twilight. Millions of stars littered the sky. Nothing bright enough to hamper him. But Victor had been a little off. He hadn't left the boat on the starboard side. Kane couldn't find a mooring ladder anywhere.

"What's the matter?"

Damn everything!

"I can't find the boat."

"What...are we going to do?"

Kane stopped. Approached the side. They were five decks above water. It was going to be a hard landing. But, at least he could see. He pulled LeeAnn into his arms. Hugged her close.

"I'll get you to safety, love. I promise."

"H-h-how?"

"We're not that far from shore. I'll swim it."

"You can't swim that far. Not...with me!"

"I'm going to have to throw you overboard."

"You're coming too, though. Yes?"

"LeeAnn. I didn't know what love meant until now. Right now. I will do whatever it takes to save you. It doesn't matter what happens to me anymore! I give up my hope of heaven! That's how much you mean to me. Don't you get it? I love you!"

Kane caught a glimpse of movement to one side. A second later he was atop the railing. Crouched. Ready to jump.

"Kane! If you're not coming. I don't want to go. You hear me!"

"Quick breath, love."

That was all the warning he had time for. Kane gripped her to his belly and sprang as far away from the ship's side as he could. A long keening cry split the night behind them. From a hunter. Who'd barely missed its prey.

And then they smacked into the water.

CHAPTER FOURTEEN

THE SUN WAS ALREADY PEEKING above the horizon when LeeAnn awoke, signaling another gloriously hot, sunny, Florida day ahead. She nuzzled her nose against Kane's neck. Snuggled closer. They'd run out of gas some time ago. The boat was swaying back and forth as it drifted. Good thing she wasn't the seasick type.

She lifted her head to look up at him. "Kane?"

He grunted a reply. It echoed through where they touched.

"It's...morning."

"Yeah."

"Did you ever find sunglasses?"

"No."

"What are we going to do?"

"It's not a problem, LeeAnn. I know where we are. It's a short swim to the coast."

LeeAnn lifted her head higher and looked over the boat's edge opposite the sunrise. Saw nothing but water. "What coast?"

"Key West. Yonder."

If she squinted, she could just make out a shadow at the edge of the horizon. "I thought you said it was a short swim."

"I'm an ex-SEAL, babe. Give me an hour."

"Better wrap another sock around your arm first. You don't want to tempt any sharks."

He lifted his arm with the bloody sock wrapped about his bicep. Frowned at it.

"What is it?"

"I usually heal quicker than this."

"Why didn't you go while it was still dark?"

"You slept in my arms, LeeAnn. All night long. I...won't get that particular joy again. I wanted to memorize it."

"Don't say that. Please?"

"All right. Then I'll blame it on your attire. Or, lack thereof."

"That's not my fault. The robe weighed me down too much."

"I know. It's not your fault that Victor apparently had the same grasp of nautical terms as you, either. Jerk didn't know starboard from portside. But I did most of the swimming. Admit it."

"True."

"My shirt fits you like a micro-mini-dress, sweetheart. Who could leave? I mean, I may be dead, but I'm not that dead. I think we proved that yesterday. In the showers."

"I love you," she said.

He didn't answer. A glance revealed he was looking out at the waves and blinking rapidly. Each of his breaths shuddered.

"Kane?" she whispered.

"Right with you, love. Just...give me a minute. Fair?"

"Ahoy there! You need help?"

The words carried across the waves. Kane sat up, taking LeeAnn with him. There was a large yacht bearing down on them, the rising sun right behind it. Nicely trimmed. Fancy. Three men and a woman were standing at the foredeck, all waving. The name of the boat was emblazoned on the bow.

Halo Annie.

LeeAnn waved back.

"Well. I guess that settles that."

Kane remarked it when she settled back onto his lap.

"Why so glum? It'll save you a swim."

"We are about to be rescued. That means...my time is

up. The assignment over. Consequences await. You are an amazing woman, LeeAnn. Capable of handling anything that life throws your way. It was an honor...knowing you."

He flashed a glance at her, and then looked away. LeeAnn grabbed his chin and yanked him back to face her. Her eyes were wide at what she'd glimpsed. He had his eyes narrowed to mere slits.

"Open your eyes, Kane."

He shook his head.

"Kane!"

"We did this maneuver already, LeeAnn. I don't think...I can handle a repeat. Not at the moment." His voice broke.

She ran a thumb along his eyelashes. They came away damp.

"Kane! If you don't open your eyes, I'm going to—! Please? I'm begging here. Please?"

He cracked an eye open. Her heart kicked up a notch. She'd been right. Where there had been nothing but black, it was now a warm, golden brown. And his pupils were tiny.

"Your eyes are brown."

His lips thinned. He lifted his brows next. But then he opened his eyes. The longer she looked, the wider his eyes went. His mouth dropped open next. Until he was staring with a wide-eyed shocked expression.

"LeeAnn?"

"Yes?"

"Oh, dearest God. I can see! Do ya' know what this means?" His voice got more excited. And he had a definite drawl starting to come out.

"You don't have to wear sunglasses all the time anymore?"

"I've earned another chance!"

"You mean...you aren't going to leave me?"

"Oh, babe. Oh, joyous morn! You just try to lose me!"

He started laughing. The next moment, he was on his feet with her in his arms, rocking the boat worse as he twirled. And then he sobered. The boat was still swaying wildly beneath them. He didn't have any trouble compensating for it. He looked at her with beautiful warm brown eyes. She wouldn't have moved her gaze for anything.

"I got a question for you, Miss LeeAnn Schultz."

"Yes?"

"Will you marry me?"

"What?"

LeeAnn was stunned.

"I love you. You say you love me. Sounds like we got that part covered. I'm following the list you gave me. Wedding is next. Right?"

"I think we should try out some more of the great sex part first."

She ran a tongue along her upper lip. Raised her eyebrow a couple of times suggestively. Really loved how he stumbled and clumsily dropped onto his backside. The boat rocked wildly several times.

"Lee. Ann. You need to cool your jets. We are about to be rescued."

In answer, she ran a finger along the collar of his shirt, pulling the t-shirt material away from her skin slightly. He growled.

"All right. You asked for it."

And then he rolled backwards and dove into the water with her.

~ ~ ~

THE HUNTED is the debut in my new series *Chronicles of the Hunter* featuring dark angels with a mission! Because I just love a good story where light and dark collide, and humans get in the way…

VAMPIRE ASSASSIN
LEAGUE
TIME TO DIE

Jackie Ivie

CHAPTER ONE

THIS IS IT.
        Steady, Kat.
Steady...

The mountain starling in her lens suddenly spread its wings, ruffling the sooty brown-colored feathers that lined its underbelly. The distinctive black mark on its forehead was glossy and dark. Kat held her breath, while pressing down on the camera's button. The bird settled. She exhaled slowly. The bird wasn't alerted to her. It was simply enjoying the tropical rain.

At least something was enjoying it.

This island chain was known for rainfall. Seeing that in a guidebook, and making massive preparations were not remotely close to the reality of her situation. Kat made a face beneath the mosquito netting that masqueraded as protection against the elements. It was a failure at the latter. She wore mesh headgear that also covered her camera, and a large cape fastened about her neck, mainly for the insect protection and camouflage effects. She'd given up on fighting the rain. She'd been here five days already. She didn't have anything left that wasn't soaked through. Not even her underwear. And those she'd washed and hung in her tent to hopefully dry. She'd packed rain gear. A tarp covering for her campsite. Water-resistant clothing. Supposedly water-tight boots.

Everything was saturated.

She wasn't a beginner. She'd been to some of the world's most isolated places.   That's what you did if you wanted to find and photograph the world's rarest birds. It was her passion. And all she'd ever known. She'd been born into the life. Because it had been her parents' career, and now it was hers. She knew what she was getting into every step of the way. She'd packed so much the float-plane pilot had charged extra. She'd brought enough supplies for seven days, but he should have known most of her cargo weight was drinking water. This was an uncharted island. Nobody ever came here. Nothing could be counted on. Natives didn't even fish the waters. Something about an ancient curse.

The customs fellow had regaled her about it, and then the official who'd come out to the building that doubled as an airport to have a picture taken with her. Everyone she met seemed dedicated to making certain she knew the dangers of this expedition. As if that would stop world renowned nature photographer, Katherine Clark.

Heck, it had taken two days just to reach Micronesia, another day to get her VISA approved, and then she'd spent a day-and-a-half finding a pilot willing to fly her out here and return in a week. And that was only because she had cash. In US denomination.

A lot of it.

The pilot had been named Frank. He'd been un-groomed, uncouth, and uncivilized. Frank's plane was on a par with its owner. But, it got her here. That's what mattered.

The starling continued grooming in the rain, unaware there was an observer about twenty-five yards away, with a scope that brought every detail into perfect focus. A shiver ran Kat's frame more than once as she took photo after photo. These starlings were difficult to see amidst the lush jungle. Their coloring so dark it was almost charcoal. This one had been seen only due to its flight amidst the trees. It had moved like a black arrow shot from a bow, and was nearly as difficult to follow.

Wow.

She was photographing a real *Aprionis pelzeini!* An island mountain starling!

Double wow.

These birds had been listed as extinct until a guide brought a kill into a field office in 1995. Ever since then, they'd been on the critically endangered list. Three previous expeditions had failed to find one. Getting this series of photos was not only going to quiet her sponsors, but it would really bolster her career, especially if she could get them developed and printed in time for her showing.

The bird moved suddenly. Kat followed its flight with her scope up a mass of green. As if a hill all of a sudden sprouted from the jungle floor. Her finger stayed on the filming button, catching the shadow of...was that an arch? Stonework? Maybe even...a man-made structure?

Kat twirled the lens to bring what looked like bricks into focus. Or, they were stones cut to resemble bricks. The top had been assembled into a series of arches. It was jaw-dropping. Unbelievable. This was an uninhabited island. Nothing of import was supposed to be here...certainly not ancient ruins. That didn't change the fact that she was viewing a human-created wall. It stood at least thirty feet high. The top was overgrown and nearly impossible to delineate in spots. The entire structure was covered with moss and decaying foliage, and...

Oh.

Heavens.

There was a nest up there!

She was going to cry. The lens fogged with a hint of tears. Kat pulled it away and swiped the moisture with a thumb. Put it back to her eye. Scanned the wall's height until she found the nest again. The starling she'd found had a mate. Both birds circled and swooped about a mass of foliage that clung to the edge of the wall. They might have eggs. They might even have chicks. What she wouldn't give for a satellite link-up right now! To beam this to the board of directors!

And then, as she watched in a slow-motion sort of horror, a long-shafted spear smacked into the wall she gazed at, just beneath the base of the nest.

A spear!

Shock stilled her for half a second. The other half was filled with anger. The starlings reacted with all kinds of cries and swooping, and flustered flying about their home. Kat's anger rose to rage. If these low-life poachers hurt one feather on either bird, or harmed one egg...

Another spear thudded into the wall as she watched. Kat lowered the camera to the sodden mass of foliage she knelt on. Slid her left hand to her can of pepper spray. These jerks were about to meet a blast that could stop a charging elephant – or so the shop keeper had informed her. She flipped the cap open on the pepper can. At the same time, her right hand was on her blades. She always traveled with knives. It usually made getting through customs a bitch, even with the proper permits, but she wasn't leaving them behind. These blades had saved her more than once. She had a dozen knives, double-sided. Razor sharp. Identical. A finger grip was at one end, exactly six inches of pain beneath that. They were pocketed in two leather straps that crisscrossed her torso. She was an expert with knives. Any knife. Her father had made certain of it. But it might not get to that. She had the element of surprise. With any luck she resembled a swamp creature.

She stood. Turned. And instantly realized her error.

They weren't poachers.

Somebody had the statistics on this island entirely wrong. The place had ancient ruins. It was home to at least one critically endangered bird species. And it wasn't uninhabited, either. Two men faced her, wearing a lot of bright feathers on their heads, a colorful coating of paint, and very little else. And as she watched, two men became four, and then eight, while the damn netting might as well be glued in place, clinging with moisture. She couldn't even get an arm out.

One of them said something. Sounded like an order. He gestured toward her with his spear as if that clarified things. The starlings were still putting up a ruckus above her. The rain was muting the entire episode. All Kat could think was they resembled characters from a cartoon show she used to watch. It was difficult to take these guys seriously. Besides, this was the twenty-first century. She wasn't that far off-grid.

The spear leader guy spoke again. Louder this time, as if that made his gibberish intelligible.   Kat cleared her throat. Lowered her voice to a tenor-range. And yelled back at him.

"You want to try English, buddy?"

Apparently not.

He jabbed his spear into the ground before him, and now he really sounded pissed-off. The feathers atop his head bobbed with his arm gestures. That made it a lot easier to realize he was serious.

But she wasn't a beginner, and she would never make a good victim. Kat pulled a knife from its holder and tucked it into her palm with her little finger. The blade protruded from beneath her hand. She slid out another knife. Tucked it atop the first one, using her ring finger. Blade outward. Got a third one. Held it in place with her middle finger. The effect would look like a spike-tipped fist when she brought it out. She had a fourth blade gripped between her forefinger and thumb when they cheated. At least four of them lifted straw-things and spit darts at her.

Oh, shit!

Oh, shit!

Instinct saved her. And the mosquito netting.

Kat dropped the can of pepper spray to grab a chunk of

covering with her left hand. She started waving. The material spewed droplets and mist into an already wet scene, but it also deflected darts. And she hadn't even known it would work. *Holy crap.* This was escalating rapidly. She faced severely lopsided odds. She didn't know if head-hunters even existed anymore, but she refused to be anyone's dinner. She had three blades ready. That would do for a start.

If she could just get her right hand out from beneath the netting...

A howl erupted from somewhere in the jungle about them, penetrating the scene with menacing tones. It was loud. Deep. And unbelievably eerie. The sound rumbled through the space, reverberating through the wall behind her. She hadn't explored, but she guessed there was enough structure behind the wall it created an echo chamber. Hairs lifted on the back of Kat's neck. The area resounded with another unearthly shriek. Closer this time. Engendering the same resultant reverberation. She'd never heard anything like it.

She didn't know about the natives' knowledge, but the howl had stopped their attack. They assembled into a tight group, butts touching, their knees slightly bent. Their spears were thrust outward, but mainly pointing up. Toward the treetops.

Despite every instinct against it, Kat took her eyes off the natives and craned her neck to look, too. The view was a blur. A lot of green set against a grayish sky. There were really tall trees about her, with some dense tops. Not enough to block rainfall, unfortunately. The scene was viewed through a deluge that created a tunnel effect. But there wasn't anything abnormal up there.

Darn.

It sure would be nice if Tarzan was swinging through the trees. Having a ripped guy in a loincloth dive out of the trees to save her right now would be nice. But it wasn't happening, so Kat dropped her eyes back to the indigenous guys. They weren't paying attention to her. She finished pulling another blade with her right hand. With her left, she lifted the netting high enough she could toss. She steeled herself for the worst. She might have to take a life here. And why? Because men were a notoriously chauvinistic sex...especially if they were in a group. Very few would accept having to negotiate with a female.

Unless they were forced to it.

She shoved her fist up and rotated it, making sure they could see the blades. "Well, guys. What do you think? Shall we call it a draw?"

They looked back down to her. Kat nailed the ground with her blades, skimming toes. It took a second and a half. Maybe two. She chucked like a machine, one-after-the-other. The reaction was immediate. Involuntary. And highly enjoyable. The group jerked backward. It wasn't a massive move, but it happened. Kat had two more blades ready, and was sliding the third before anyone had time to blink. And while it was foolhardy, she continued announcing terms in English.

"So. Here's the deal. You quit shooting at the birds up there, and I'll go back to my camp. Nobody wins. Nobody loses. But I am obviously not going to sleep much from here on out. Well? What do you say? We have a deal?"

Her answer was immediate. And negative. Blow-guns got lifted before she'd even finished. Kat tossed her two knives, aiming for throats, before spinning sideways, pulling the net over her at the same time. Any moment, she expected darts to hit. Pierce her flesh. Send poison through her veins. She dropped to her knees. Huddled in a small ball. Scrunched her eyes shut. But she knew it wouldn't work. Her flesh itched in preparation. She was going to die a miserable death.

All alone.

Like always.

She heard thudding sounds. Sensed darts hitting flesh. But

couldn't feel anything. A cry sounded next. It was cut off. Muffled gasps followed. Some gargling sounds ensued. Then all she could hear was the continual sound of rain. Drops were still peppering the area. Running water could be heard in the distance. Trickles of rainwater sluiced off things. Trees. The ancient wall. Her. All of it added wetness to an already saturated environment. It created a layer of moisture near the ground. Kat turned her head and peeked, but couldn't see much through the mist, and the two saplings that blocked her view.

Wait a minute...

There hadn't been any trees there. Kat focused on what looked like a man's lower legs. He was standing about a foot in front of her. He had some really nice legs. Toned. Bare.

Kat scanned upward.

Yep.

They were definitely legs. And male. And really muscled. His thighs were just more proof. One of them sported a large tribal tattoo in a blood-red color. Kat blinked slowly.

Blinked again.

And a third time.

Nothing altered. That meant, despite the absurdity of it, there really was a near-naked man standing in front of her. He was crouched slightly, facing her adversaries as if to take any projectiles sent at her. He was large, even from this perspective. And really well-defined. He had some shapely glutes above his thighs, too. Kat couldn't help noticing. He was wearing a really small loin cloth.

Oh. Brother.

It was insane. But that didn't make him disappear.

Kat looked back down, checked out the scene from between his legs. There were bodies on the ground. She couldn't tell how many for certain, but nobody was still upright, ready to attack. Her blade was sticking out of one corpse's neck. She couldn't tell if she'd hit the other man. She couldn't see the other knife hilt.

Mister Loincloth's legs moved, swiveling at the waist to look down at her. Kat glanced up. And lost her breath.

Oh.

No way.

Mister Loincloth didn't just have a body so perfect it wasn't real, his face was beyond belief, too. Guys did not come this gorgeous. Not without a lot of photo-shopping. He had perfect features. A strong chin. A lot of dark hair stuck to his head with rain. A nice tan. That coloring really made his neon blue eyes stand out.

"Were you hit?"

What the heck? He spoke English?

That's when Kat knew this wasn't real. She'd obviously been hit by a dart. Lost consciousness – maybe even her life – and this was the result. She was dead. But death really should be worse than this. Shouldn't it?

"Well?"

His query carried something that could be worry. He had a supremely deep voice. Massive. Resonant. With an edgy quality she couldn't peg at the moment. It commanded attention. She immediately knew it been his hollering she'd heard moments earlier.

"What?" she finally asked.

"They used poisoned darts."

Says the man with fifty or so stuck in him.

She didn't say it but her brows rose. The darts couldn't possibly be poisonous. From this angle, she couldn't help noticing a plethora of dart ends protruding from him. He looked like a pincushion.

"One scratch and you will die," he informed her. And then he started brushing projectiles from him as if they were insects. They didn't make much sound as they landed at his feet.

Kat nearly giggled. "Oh. Really?"

Everything about Mister Loincloth altered at her tone. *Wait, Kat.* She should probably drop the 'Mister' title when referring to him. It didn't fit. Right now, he looked pretty damned primitive. His entire frame tensed, bunching muscles that didn't need the definition. His nostrils flared with the strength of each breath. And then his eyes narrowed. That last part took him beyond overkill. With his eye color, it was like getting zapped with flashes of intense blue light as he glared at her.

Great.

Just great.

In what appeared to be her afterlife, she had to deal with a primordial male? One with a shitload of testosterone and zero ability to control body language? The guy exuded arrogance. Power. Domination. It was obvious what he considered to be gender roles. She didn't even need to ask.

"Come with me."

He stuck out a hand, palm upward. Kat glanced from it back to his face. It hadn't sounded like a request. It didn't look like one, either. She slowly rose to her feet. She'd been right on his size. He stood a good six inches taller than she did. He was broader, too. And she was even covered in mosquito netting that hung off the headdress like a cloak.

"I think we need some ground rules set first," Kat informed him.

His jaw worked as if he bit his tongue. And then he just plucked her up, chucked her across his shoulder, held her legs in place, took a step, and leapt upward, clearing the ancient wall with room to spare.

Oh. No way, Kat.

That wall was thirty feet tall. At least.

It was impossible. That didn't change it. The rain wasn't much of an issue for him, either. They were moving so rapidly, raindrops looked like a tunnel from this perspective, too. Kat watched the wall grow small and then disappear amidst tree branches and leaves as he soared upward. Her heart jumped into her throat and lodged there, choking off breath. Any screams. Not that she'd have sounded them. Kat was not the panicky type. She dealt with facts. Every situation could be handled if you kept your objective in mind. Emotions at bay.

She usually listed possible methods of response.

If she had enough time, she'd write them down.

Then she'd systematically go through them until something worked.

The view changed as he took her even higher. Somehow moving right above the tree line! There wasn't anything beneath them except a long freefall. Even the treetops began to look minuscule.

And that's when she panicked.

CHAPTER TWO

THE WOMAN NEEDED TO CEASE fighting him. She expended energy with every lunge and kick, but at least she was no longer screaming. All of it was ineffectual. Her efforts hadn't done much except get her limbs held tightly to him. The netting she wore scratched his skin. That was an irritant. As were her struggles. They didn't gain her much. Perhaps he should have enthralled her before snatching her. So she could conserve her energy. She was going to need it.

By the gods!

He had a mate...and he'd found her!

At the thought, Tane grinned. He couldn't help it.

It was just like he'd been told when he'd become one of the un-dead. Vampirism didn't equal eternal life. It was an existence of animated death. Emotionless. Passionless. Endless. There was only one thing that altered it. If Tane was supremely lucky, and chances of this happening were astronomical, his mate would enter his sphere, and just like that...everything would regenerate.

He hadn't received a hint of warning. No time to prepare. He was in luck it was the midst of the wet season. He hadn't taken time to shower. Groom. Select appropriate garments. He'd been awake, checking email and debating assignments when his heart had given a shudder. Tane had first felt denial. Then shock. And then absolute astonishment.

He remembered it perfectly. Exactly. And he still felt the same incredulity.

It felt like hours had passed, but they couldn't have. He'd shot from a tunnel. Gone airborne. Searched. Locating her hadn't been difficult. That area of the island had seemed aglow. Her voice had even been a beacon. The alarm tingeing her words was a direct catalyst. It sent speed to his flight while his heart had seized up with a completely foreign sensation. His shrieks had carried the level of it. And he'd finally spotted her.

She'd looked so small.

Vulnerable...

And under such threat!

He still didn't know what his mate looked like – nor did it matter – but he knew one thing. She was extraordinarily brave. She'd been facing a group of headhunters as if she had a chance. She'd managed to stick knives into two of them before Tane reached her, using a burst of speed that surprised even him. He'd rocketed into the scene, completely annihilated her assailants. Without pause. Or care.

It felt like a fuse had been lit somewhere in his body. It had been on a slow burn-level until he'd touched her. Then things had turned really chaotic. The return of sensation had gone massive. It was a supreme force. His body had reacted without any instruction from him. He'd grown hard. Ready.

Oh!

This was extremely enjoyable. These were signals he had no trouble reading. This was beyond wonder. It was perfection. He'd been particularly virile when alive—with compliments to prove it from many an appreciative woman. Finding his mate sent everything about that time right back to him.

Everything.

He had to get her home. Hold her close. Demonstrate what she meant to him. Somehow keep from frightening her when the combination of want and need he suffered just kept ratcheting higher. His body was near pain with the level of it. His gut coiled with something that flicked tendrils of fire through him. His groin was heavy. Throbbing with ache.

It was too much to fathom.

Tane shoved his head back and sent a triumphal bellow into the rain-filled day. He didn't cease until his breath ran out. And then he did it again. His lungs burned as they expanded and contracted. His abs joined the fray, tightening until they were ablaze with heat. That's when he started laughing. Because he could do all of that!

He was even *breathing!*

His cry of jubilation was ill-timed. Completely stupid. It disturbed more than one jungle creature and it altered his ability. His flight slowed, then ceased altogether, and that's when they plummeted. Tane gripped her legs tighter to him with one arm. The other hand held her in place atop his shoulder as they fell. He spun and rotated, taking the brunt as wet leaves smacked at them, grunting more than once as he careened off something. Broke off a branch.

Thank the gods!

One of his platforms loomed into view. Tane released her shoulder, grabbed a tree limb, and swung through the entryway. The door had been fashioned from ropes entwined about rough-hewn boards. It didn't slow him. The door swung upward and smacked into the ceiling as he vaulted through it. The center tree stopped him. Tane slammed into it, cracking his back with the force. The entire structure shuddered about them. Planks jolted beneath his feet. He grabbed for an upper limb on the support tree, held his breath, and finally the platform ceased swaying. He waited. Listened for cracking. Anything that might portend disaster.

Good.

The integrity of the structure hadn't failed.

That was satisfying. He'd built these platforms because he liked inventing and constructing. It helped pass time, and he'd had a lot of that. He'd also had all manner of building material and nothing much else to do. These structures were one level. Some were plumbed with running water. They were situated all over the island, mostly high in the trees. Sturdy. Hidden. He used them for many things. To hide from sunlight. Watch interlopers on the island. Endure the passing of hours.

This was the first time he'd considered using one for mating.

Tane released his pent breath with a sigh that should have contained worry, and it would have if he wasn't so beset with physical craving. He sent a swift glance about. This particular structure had some furnishings. A collection of old travel trunks were placed along one wall. They looked like ones he'd pulled from a shipwreck, a century ago. Maybe longer. Before air travel was invented. Back then, ships had sailed these waters fairly frequently, and they'd carried cargo.

Cargo.

Yes!

That was it! Stacks of still-tied bundles were piled haphazardly atop the trunks, covered with layers of fallen leaves intermixed with dust. More than one industrious spider had woven its web atop the area as well. He'd have to knock everything aside. Dig through the piles. Perhaps rifle through trunks. There should be something he could use for a bed...

A tremor ran through him. Tane clenched muscles against it. This mating thing was large. Almost overwhelmingly so.

He quickly moved his gaze to the far corner, and stared at a partition for a bit before he recognized it. *Ah.* He'd somehow reached one of his platforms with running water. While that wasn't of any use at the moment, it might be later. Above the partition he could see the large bowl he'd poked holes in to make a shower head. There would be a large clamshell beneath it for use as a basin. The plumbing he'd designed was working. He could see water dripping from the shower as well as hear trickling sounds. That would be overflow from the system of rain barrels he'd designed. Sounded functional.

Unclogged.

But there was nothing in that area to assist him right now. Tane swiveled his head to view the other half of the room. A large mass of rope was fastened above where he still held to the support tree. The hemp poured downward from there, making a large pile on the floor.

Ah.

Interest sparked instantly, but just as rapidly waned. The rope was a hammock. One end should be affixed to the far wall. But a hammock would be too difficult. Tane smirked. He'd be better off making a pallet of some kind on the floor.

Then again...

Despite the time involved, he could always take her airborne again. They weren't that far from his home. Half an hour. Maybe less. It was located deep in the mountain. He had all sorts of amenities there. Volcano-fueled heat. Running water. Electrical power. Some really large beds...

"All right. That's it."

His mental planning halted at the words. She possessed a stirring voice. It lifted goosebumps on his skin, even with the acidic tone she used. She didn't sound like a smitten woman. Or even one who was interested.

This could be trouble.

"Put. Me. Down."

She separated the words. Used a low tone. Tane cocked his head as if considering her command. There wasn't any reason to deny it. She couldn't go far. And he wanted her down. Unwrapped. And naked. In his arms. Her legs wrapped about him...

"I know you understand me. Okay?"

Her words stopped his thought process, as well as gave him a swift dose of annoyance. Because he was the one who'd given her his knowledge of English. But he hadn't known she'd use it against him! *Uh.* The annoyance worked well for something, however. It took the edge off his ardor. Not enough, but some.

Tane finally bent forward, lowered her to her feet, and then released her. The sense of loss was instantaneous, as if she was the lone source of heat and the room held a sudden chill. He almost grabbed her again. Before that could happen, Tane moved, sliding around the support tree to the opposite side. He was in luck again. If he crouched slightly, the hammock ropes reached high enough it concealed his hips. He was primed and ready to mate. It was obvious. The last thing he wished to do was frighten her.

She was still shrouded in a mass of net but it wasn't an issue. He could see beyond each strand. Discern her shape. She was shapely. Feminine. He couldn't see her face, however. She wore a short brimmed hat that held the mesh off her face, and her head was lowered. He couldn't tell her hair color, either. She had it tied back or kept it short. No hair rested on her shoulders. She wore a jacket with two bands that crossed in front. Loose-fitting khaki-colored slacks below that. Rugged boots were on her feet. She was extremely wet. She dripped on the floor beneath her, making a dark spot. It grew larger as he watched.

She flashed a glance toward him and quickly looked down again. It hadn't been long enough to catch much. But she had dark eyes. Darker lashes. And a really lush, red mouth. Tane narrowed his eyes, lowered his chin, and waited. The netting waved about her as she lifted a hand and gestured toward him with her index finger.

"Look. I don't know who you are. Or...what, for that matter. But this has gone on long enough. Okay?"

"Tane," he offered.

"Tane? What the heck is that?"

"My name," he informed her.

"Oh. Fine. In that event, I'm Kat."

Tane frowned slightly. "You are named for a...feline? Is there some meaning?" *Perhaps she resembles one?*

"Not that I know of. Look. Not every name has to have a meaning."

"Mine does."

She gave a heavy sigh. "I'm almost afraid to ask what it is. I suppose you're going to tell me anyway, though?"

"It means 'god of the forests'."

"Oh. Brother."

Her tone was sarcastic. As was the way she folded her arms beneath the netting. It had to be uncomfortable under there. Inside this platform, with the walls latched down, it would soon grow hot and humid as well. He was experiencing the start of it. He could actually feel his skin grow moist.

He could sweat?

Tane nearly crowed with the delight. But instinctively knew it would be a poor move. And this was definitely the wrong time.

"I really should have seen *that* answer coming," she finished.

"Are you attempting to anger me?"

"Not hardly. I'm trying to figure out what's going on. And...I admit. I'm not exactly succeeding."

He considered her for a long moment. He couldn't enthrall without direct eye contact. But he might be able to do it verbally. When he spoke, the deep tone vibrated through the enclosure.

"Take your netting off."

"Oh. I don't think so."

What was this? She wasn't affected by his powers? Tane straightened. That was foolish. Every second in her proximity sent blood pounding through him, all aimed for one region: his groin. He immediately crouched back down again. Modified his voice. Tried speaking in a softer tone. It wasn't successful. His question sounded like another command.

"Why not?"

"Because this feels a lot safer to me."

"You do not feel safe?" He was surprised. His voice reflected it.

"I know. Hard to believe."

"Yes. It is," he agreed.

She looked up and regarded him for several moments. Tane instantly felt a rush of goose bumps all along his skin. He couldn't tell her exact eye color, but they were dark. He tried to lock glances with her. To mesmerize. It didn't work, either.

"Are you for real?" she finally asked him.

"Yes."

She snorted. "Okay. I'll try another angle. Sounds like I'll need to be...a bit blunter than my usual. And I'll use smaller words."

She was trying to be insulting. Raise his ire. That was not remotely near what he wanted. Needed. Craved. Tane's canine teeth tingled warningly, however.

"So. I'll start. Why am I here?"

"I brought you."

She sighed heavily. It wasn't only audible, but her head moved, and the netting bobbed with it. Tane almost smiled again.

"You're an 'absolute' kind of guy, aren't you?"

He didn't know what to answer, so he settled for a grunt.

"That means you like absolutes. Nothing hidden beneath the surface..."

She had no idea how accurate that statement was at the moment. Tane couldn't prevent the smile. He looked down for a moment while she continued.

"...can handle that. It makes things easier. So. We'll deal in the facts. I'm definitely here because you brought me. That is true."

Tane looked back up at her. Directly at her. "Yes."

"And that means you want something from me. Am I right?"

"Yes," he replied again.

"Well? What is it?"

"I want...your netting...*off*." He spaced the words subconsciously. The last word was hissed. It came through set teeth. Even to his ears, he sounded threatening. This was not going well.

"If I decline?"

"What if I say 'please'?" he offered.

She snorted as if he'd said something amusing. He didn't respond although everything in his frame gave a distinct twitch of irritation.

"Look. Tane. Let's get past the stupid net already."

"You'll take it off?"

He got another heavy sigh from her. She was mystifying. And that was starting to frustrate.

"Nope."

Tane growled. He couldn't help it. He remained crouched down, as though coiled and ready to spring. Every muscle was wrenched to tightness. He'd done it to prevent movement. He'd locked his jaw against fang growth. And now he was breathing hard. His chest lifted and fell with each one. He probably looked as bestial as he felt. She couldn't fail to notice.

"Well. That response? Right there. Is exactly why I don't feel safe," she finally replied.

Tane slapped his fists to his chest, shoved his head back, and roared the reaction at the ceiling. The sound reverberated like a pressure wave. The rushes that formed his ceiling rustled. Timbers all about them rattled. The water in his clamshell basin even sounded like it had become a stream before settling back to trickling. She hadn't moved when he'd finished although she'd pulled something metallic and sharp from her chest band. He recognized it.

She was preparing to use her knives?

Against him?

Her mate?

"I'm not real good with...non-verbal communication, Tane. You want to put that in words?" she asked next.

No.

He didn't.

Tane lifted his chin to glare at a ceiling joist above her head. A red glaze had attached itself to his vision. It intensified with every heartbeat. And then it grew hot. He'd never been so close to completely losing control. Ever.

But he'd never faced anything this immense.

She was maybe four feet away from him. Within easy grabbing distance. The netting about her would be a minor obstacle. The knives she threatened him with, even less. He could force her. Satisfy the need that was already massive, and just kept growing. It was at a crushing level. Devastating. Almost overpowering.

But he wanted her willing.

Loving.

Open.

Her cavern moist and warm...

Tane slammed his eyes shut, and fought the instant images as well as the fire of desire that shot through him. The need to mate with her was powerful. He needed to be more so. He yanked every cell in his body tight. Demanded submission. Control. He shook with the effort. The floor shuddered beneath them in concert.

"T-T-Tane?"

She stuttered on his name. He heard the fear in her voice. Both sent a cooling sensation, like a sprinkling of drops from his shower. It wasn't much. A bit of wet against a bonfire. But it helped. Tane's canines started to recede. He licked his lips, watched the red haze soften to pink. And then he lowered his chin to face her again.

CHAPTER THREE

SHE NEEDED TO DO SOMETHING drastic. Kat knew she was female, but she'd never experienced this kind of reaction to a man. Her hormones were on hyper-sensitivity mode or something. She was feeling sensations she didn't dare examine. She was alert, aware, and totally receptive.

Oh. Heavens.

She was getting turned on?

She needed to take a huge mental step back. List potential strategies. Work through them, eliminating and modifying as needed. And it shouldn't be that damned difficult. She'd already noted his handsomeness, but she'd been around beautiful men before. She'd dated some. Looking at a handsome man used to tie her tongue and render her witless. She'd found out how narcissistic it made some guys. She'd been disillusioned. Then cured. Most super-good-looking men took way too much time to groom, they worried almost incessantly about every aspect of their appearance, and they had a limited conversation range that mainly revolved around them. She'd felt like a minion. They needed someone to bestow constant attention and that had decided her. Handsome men were high maintenance. Some other woman could have them.

She'd also been exposed to sexy men. Her social network feed was filled with them. Advertisers knew to put lots of skin on display. They usually possessed washboard abs. Large biceps. Defined obliques that led down to hidden things. The models knew their stuff, too. They could portray looks that sizzled.

She'd even been around guys who exuded sex appeal. It was like they'd been born with something indefinable. Extremely captivating. Truly basic. It got them noticed by just about everyone – especially women. Testosterone radiated off of them or something. Like a non-verbal promise of sexual satiation – and lots of it. That was probably what male fragrance companies were trying to copy and market.

She'd never thought through this stuff. There hadn't been a reason. Until right now. Because she'd never come up against anything like Tane.

Holy crap.

The guy was indescribable. Even the word gorgeous failed. His face was a photographer's dream. She'd studied symmetry and Tane's every feature was perfect. He had the smoldering thing locked in, too. Especially with his chin lowered and his eyes narrowed. His eyes were really amazing. The vivid blue was impossible to look at for any length of time. She tried meeting his gaze with an assertive one, but all kinds of buzzing had started up in her ears, and she could swear she'd heard someone whispering. She had to move her glance somewhere else. Anywhere. But nowhere on him was safe. Maybe if he was balding. Wore long trousers. A shirt. Had a raging case of psoriasis.

Something.

Anything.

This was insane. And it had to stop. The entire world may have gone crazy this morning, but she was still Katherine Clark. Organized. Grounded. Completely sane. And Tane wasn't that special. He was the X-Y chromosome combination. So what? He was just a man.

But what a man.

Kat nearly ground her teeth at the instant thought. There

was no excuse for this. She was in his control. That made things unequal. And that made everything about Tane off-limits. Even if he was sending off male vibes that almost visually radiated from him, making every inch of her body react. Shivers continually flew along her skin. Her nipples had puckered more than once. Her knees had wavered. Her lower belly had quivered.

And then he'd given that primal yell!

Wow.

She was lucky her mental faculties were still working, but she could probably thank her prior experiences with handsome guys for that. She needed to get outside. Inhale some fresh air. Clear her senses.

"Look. Um. Tane. Thank you for rescuing me. And… whatever. But I really should…be l-l-leaving."

Kat's voice wavered as she headed for the door. That was unfortunate. Tane didn't reply. Nor did he stop her. She shoved against the wood and rope structure with her free hand. That was dumb. The door smacked her on the head as she rushed beneath it. The resultant stumble probably looked as awkward as it felt. She didn't fall, however. That was a minor victory. Kat took a deep breath, straightened her shoulders, looked about, and couldn't see much except tree limbs.

Some gray sky.

And a lot of dark mosquito netting.

She could really start to hate the stuff. It was uncomfortable. Hot. She was already rain-soaked. Soon she'd be sweaty. That was going to be miserable.

What was she thinking?

It was already miserable. And if he hadn't been so adamant about the netting's presence, she'd have chucked it already.

Stupid male.

His deck wasn't large. An instant dose of rainforest hit her. The scent of greenery. Damp wood. The buzzing of insects.

The chatter of monkeys. Exotic bird calls. The rustling of leaves as raindrops continued hitting them. The deck had an overhang, protecting it from some of the elements. The only section dark with dampness was near the edge. Kat slid her knife back into its holder, and stepped forward, peeked over the side, and almost fell again with her move backward.

Holy shit!

They were a half mile in the air. At least. She wasn't afraid of heights, but that drop could start a good case of acrophobia. She cleared her throat and tried to sound assertive as she called to him over her shoulder.

"All right. Um. Tane?"

"Yes."

His answer came from inside the structure. Didn't sound like he'd moved.

"I need you to come out here and show me the stairs. Or ladder. Or...whatever you use."

"There is no ladder. Or stairs."

"A vine?" she asked hopefully.

"There are no vines."

"Then...how do you get down?"

"I jump."

That was impossible. As such, it didn't even warrant an answer. There had to be a way down.

Period.

Kat went to her knees. Crawled toward the edge, and peered over. The forest floor was obscured by mist, and it was a long way down. It looked surreal. That helped. She leaned out a smidge further and bent forward, to look beneath his tree house. There was a branch about a dozen feet below her. The next one down was twice that distance and on the other side of the tree. The limbs looked large enough to handle a jump onto them, especially if one stayed near the trunk, but it was beyond risky. He had to be joking.

There had to be another way.

The next scan of the area proved just as futile as before. There wasn't anything resembling a rope. Or a ladder. There weren't any vines hanging about either. And she was growing dizzy with this perspective.

Kat pulled up and shimmied backward until the faintness ebbed and she could stand. There was nothing for it. Her options were limited. Stay out here. Or go back in. She was dusting her hands when she pushed on one side of the door. It swayed open with a whisper of sound. Swung back into place. It was darker inside than before. Tane hadn't moved. His eyes gleamed neon blue with what light there was. He had them narrowed. Exactly like a predator.

Kat looked at him, then away. She couldn't hold his gaze. Worse things than before happened, and they came with even more direct consequences. A tremor ran her entire body. Her legs went crazily weak. Her breath caught. Her heart skipped a beat. A sliver of sensation shot through her lower belly. It wasn't fear that caused any of it, either. And that was really scary.

"O-o-okay." *Damn it*. She'd stuttered. And she was trying to be assertive here! Kat cleared her throat before continuing. "You win."

She glanced toward him again. It was involuntary. Magnetic. His eyes flashed strangely, looking like almond-shaped blue laser lights. Kat eased her pent breath through her lips. Quivered as she inhaled another one.

"What have I won?" he asked.

"Um. I'm here. I can't leave."

"I already had that."

Great. She had to deal with stubbornness, too? *Men*. "What do you want from me, Tane?" she asked.

"I told you already. I want the netting off."

Kat looked toward him. Got hooked. Tried to stare until

her eyes burned, before ripping her gaze away. He hadn't blinked once. She should feel angered. Annoyed. Perhaps even defeated.

She didn't.

Kat felt a vast amount of something really frightening. Despite the absurdity, she knew exactly what it was, too. She was experiencing excitement. As if she faced a terrifying thrill-ride at an amusement park. It made her clumsy. She had a hard time grasping the bottom edge of her covering. Even more trouble controlling her breathing.

And for some reason, it sounded like each of his short breaths matched hers.

CHAPTER FOUR

STUNNED, TANE COULDN'T SEEM TO move, not even when he tried to force himself to look away. Not only at her beauty – although she definitely possessed that – but at the amount of sensation that accompanied looking at her. He felt every speck of her emotions, from the hint of apprehension she felt first, to a pulse-pounding sense of excitement and anticipation. That realization almost sent him reeling.

It was incredible.

The reactions had been tamped down to a controllable level while she'd been outside. He hadn't followed her. No need. He'd known exactly where she was and what she'd been doing as if he'd been beside her, watching. He'd even felt dizzy as she'd bent over his deck. It hadn't faded until she regained her feet. He seemed to match her every physiological response to a level that was unfathomable. He didn't know how it worked. He only knew that it did.

Years ago, when he'd been told of mating it had been a spark of hope. A bit of bright at the end of a dismal existence. *Well.* He should have gotten a massive warning, too.

Direct sight came with an even bigger effect, akin to dumping fuel on a fire. Her eyes were a brown shade, but not as dark as he'd suspected. There were golden flecks within them, giving off hints of glimmer. Despite the idiocy, Tane locked gazes with her. A swell of music hit his ears to a deafening level, while his heartbeat quickened. His knees wavered. And then his fangs reacted. They erupted into long spikes. Razor sharp. He locked his lips shut. Took small breaths that matched hers. Watched as two dark spots of color appeared on her cheeks.

By every god!

Tane yanked his gaze away with a rapidness that made him light-headed. The move dulled the symphony in his ears. Strengthened his legs. Didn't do much for how rapidly his heart was beating. Or the fangs that bit into his inner lower lip. This was unbelievable. He was supremely lucky. His mate wasn't just here...but she was so beautiful! She was small. Trim. Extremely womanly. Her curves were apparent even dressed in loose-fitting safari-inspired clothing. She had sun-kissed, tawny-colored hair. It was a beautiful shade, not unlike a lion mane. It was perfectly complimented by skin slightly lighter than his. Akin to liquid caramel. Engendering a voracious need to touch it. And taste. Her lips were red-hued. Lush. Large.

Her hair was secured in a bun at the back of her head but tendrils had come undone when she'd pulled off the hat. They slid like trickles of water over a shoulder and to a breast pocket of her shirt.

Damn it!

Why had he looked there? She had little nipples. And they were erect. Tane yanked his muscles to a painful level. Made fists with his hands and then shoved them into his chest. It was almost working when she spoke.

"Well?"

He was beside her instantly. He didn't even know how. He looked down at her. She glanced up toward him and then back down. Her blush appeared again, darker this time. Her every breath was panted, as were his. He lifted a lock of hair with a hand that shook.

"Um. Listen...uh..."

He brought her hair to his nose and inhaled. She smelled

so fresh. So...young! He thought he detected the aroma of wildflowers. A hint of honey.

"I...don't—. I'm not—. This is—."

She ended sentences abruptly, leaving a major portion unsaid but he knew just what she meant. She spiked a glance toward him again. This time she didn't move away. Her eyes were incredibly warm. Golden-flecked. Mesmeric...

"I don't understand any of this, Tane."

He grunted something low. Deep. She expected him to make sense? *Now?*

"I mean...you're so—uh. And this is so—. And I'm feeling so—."

"I am going to kiss you," he answered.

She gasped. Tane lowered his head...and the shrill call of a Micronesian Megapode erupted between them.

Kat cried out and jumped backward, her motion sending her toward the center tree. It kept her from falling. Tane's reaction was much more visceral. He sprang so quickly, his head smacked through the ceiling rushes, dislodging several bits of dried grass that floated down. The bird's distinctive call came again, louder this time as usually happened in nature. And that's when it hit him.

He'd programmed that sound into his satellite phone.

He had a call.

Tane dropped onto the floor and yanked the phone from where he'd shoved it beneath the material at his hip before it rang again. He had his teeth gritted as he clicked the connect button. His fangs sliced into his lower lip. Blood immediately welled in his mouth. His heart pounded in heavy thumps that almost hurt. He glared at the ceiling. Everything else was in an agony of tautness, holding back a mass of emotions he couldn't even name, let alone place. He lifted the phone to his ear. The combination of responses accompanied his greeting. He couldn't prevent it.

"What!"

Bits of old grass filtered down onto his head. He brushed his free hand at his hair, dislodging debris that was now wet, since he'd punched a hole in his roof. He narrowed his eyes at the opening and barely kept the groan unvoiced.

"Whoa. Jungle man. Calm down. It's me. Nigel Beethan. You know...the debonair, eternally youthful, entirely fascinating and—."

"Nigel!" The name was hissed through Tane's teeth. That was a new sensation.

"Well, yeah. I told you already. It's Nigel. I'm calling you because we have an assign—"

"Your timing is horrid." Tane interrupted again, putting all his frustration into the words.

"Oh. Right. *My* timing is horrid. You live on a deserted island surrounded by surf and sand, with nothing to do but watch time pass...and now – all of a sudden – you're busy?"

Tane growled the reply.

"Look. It's an easy hit."

"No."

"What? This is too weird. You called me last week, practically begging for something to do, and—wait a sec. I have another call. I'll be right back. *Yeah? What is it? Oh. Hi there, Takeshi. How's it hanging?*"

Tane listened in disbelief as Nigel just started ignoring him. He chanced a glance across to where Kat stood. She had her arms folded and was watching him without one expression on her face. He should have tried harder to enthrall her. And this was a stupid time to think that. Tane had to look away.

"You've named your triplets? That's cool. About time. I was beginning to think they'd be Baby Number One. Baby Number Two. Baby Number...oh. That isn't funny? Sorry."

Tane's canines started to retract, pulling free of his flesh as they resumed normal size and length. He sucked on the wounds while he waited. He didn't dare look toward his mate again. He wondered what the penalty was for disconnecting the call and how quickly it would happen. Nigel was the second-in-command of the Vampire Assassin League. Akron's chosen protégée. Akron wasn't a vampire Tane wanted to cross. Then again, it might not be a severe infraction to hang up on the kid. If it was, Tane could always say a blip in the environment must have caused a disruption in satellite service. It wasn't unreasonable. They were experiencing a supremely wet rainy season. Tane was still debating it as Nigel started speaking to his caller again.

"*Wait. What? You're naming your third-born after me? Oh. Takki! I can't even. You're going to make me sob like a baby here. Wow. I am so honored. Look! Gotta run before I need tissues! Oh, Takki. You—! Uh. 'Bye, man.*"

Tane heard what sounded suspiciously like a sniff, and then Nigel spoke to him again.

"Um. Tane? You still there?"

"Yeah," Tane replied.

"I can't even remember why I called. Whatever it was, I'll handle it. So...you have a good day, okay? Adios."

The connection went dead. Tane pulled the phone from his ear and looked at it in disbelief.

"You have a phone?"

Kat's voice was even. Calm. Tane glanced over at her. Looked back at the phone. It was useless to deny. Just as it was useless to pretend the call hadn't happened. And at the worst possible time! They'd been about to kiss!

That had certainly changed. The entire mood had been altered. Tane focused on the plank floor beneath him. It looked hard. Dirty. Whatever had filmed the floor was turning to mud as the wood got sprinkled with raindrops. His tree house wasn't even dry anymore. But his mate hadn't sounded upset. Or Angered. Or confrontational. Then again, Tane didn't know her that well. How was he supposed to know?

"Uh..." He didn't really have a reply. His answer dribbled off into nothing.

"All right. I'll phrase it differently. Who are you? And just what the hell is going on?"

"I can explain." he offered.

"Oh, really? This should be good. And I can't wait to hear it."

Tane pulled in a breath. Opened his mouth. Shut it again. How should he start? Should he tell her about vampires? Tane glanced toward her again. She had an eyebrow raised now, as well as her arms folded. She was projecting stern body language with that pose. He looked back at the phone in his hand. He eased out the breath he'd inhaled.

She didn't look receptive to hearing about vampirism, not at present anyway. Maybe he should tell her about his past – the mortal one. Describe how a large ship called a caravel from the Colonial Spanish Empire had been shipwrecked on one of the islands. His father found more dead than alive. Brought back to health by a cadre of women who had become something like a harem.

Tane opened his mouth again. Shut it.

It would be hard to explain any of that without bringing up his age. And immortality. Perhaps he should start with mating. Describe what her arrival had done to him. Tell her why he'd responded as he had. That he suffered a level of want and need and desire that wasn't going to go away.

Ever.

"I'm waiting."

Her words decided him. He couldn't explain much of anything. Mating wasn't something he could speak of. He needed to show her. But, not here. And definitely not now. She no longer sounded noncommittal. Her voice had projected something close to how she looked. Skeptical. Annoyed.

No.

He had the wrong word. She sounded irritated. That was probably worse. She didn't even sound angered....maybe because he didn't mean much to her.

Tane snarled at the thought and squeezed his fingers about the phone, crushing it. When he opened his hand and tipped it, only bits and pieces fell out. He heard her gasp. That's when he turned his head and gazed directly at her. Something must have warned her because her eyes went wide and she lurched backward, stopped by the center tree directly behind her.

"You know...I was a little hasty. Explanations...can um. Wait. It's been nice meeting you, Tane, but...I should be going now. I...just need a little help to get down, and—ah!"

Tane leapt across the space, grabbed her to him, and shot up through the hole in the roof. It stopped her words. Her scream wasn't loud, nor were the gasps for breath that followed it. She needed to calm her breathing. He was matching her, and that affected his ability to move. And that altered the length of time to his home. But he didn't dare let her finish her words. He wasn't remotely going to acquiesce to her request.

But she might have already guessed that.

CHAPTER FIVE

O*KAY, KAT.*
    This was going beyond scary.

And it just kept getting worse.

The fear wasn't because she was in a strange man's control, essentially being kidnapped. It wasn't due to how they moved, as if jetting forward by some unseen propellant. She wasn't even worried by his power, demonstrated when he'd crushed a phone as if it was an eggshell. If her fright was attached to any of that, it would have made sense.

Kat had a pragmatic disposition. That was her base. Her modus operandi. How she viewed the world and reacted to it. She rarely smiled. Hardly ever cried. Her last boyfriend had called her a cyborg. The moniker hadn't bothered her. She'd secretly been pleased with it. But even her parents had worried. They'd taken her to specialists when she'd been young to see if she had autism or some other spectrum of the disorder. Negative. She was just firmly rooted in the physical world. She wasn't fond of fantasy. Everyone had just gotten used to it. To her, anything that could be encompassed beneath the umbrella of paranormal was fictitious. She didn't go to movies. She didn't read fiction books. If something occurred that wasn't explainable, she disregarded it. She didn't even care to waste the time to figure out what. Or why. Or how. Someone else could have that responsibility.

Most of this morning's events weren't remotely explainable, which meant they could be disregarded.

Fair enough.

If only that was the issue.

Something really strange was happening to her in the physical realm. She was experiencing something truly unbelievable. It felt as basic as breathing. As vital as air.   Smashed against his side, her crossed knife-holder-straps biting into her chest, her feet sodden and uncomfortable in wet boots and socks, while her hair streamed loose from the bun...well. She should be planning her next move. She needed to think through strategies. Craft arguments to use. Decide potential methods of attack.

But was any of that happening?

No.

All she could do was experience a continual wave of shivers. Tremble with a tingling that brought a sensation of heat with it. Find each breath difficult to gain due to the pressure within her chest. Was this passion? Could this be what writers meant when they spoke of that thing called lust?

Oh, shit.

That was terrifying.

Katherine Clark had never experienced anything like this. It felt like every cell on her body had just come into existence. It hadn't been a slow awakening, either. It had been raw. Heated. Massive. Like she'd been flung from slumber and given a massive dose of Turkish coffee via intravenous injection, but nobody had given her any time to assimilate her surroundings and circumstances first. The feeling enlarged with every thump of her heart. Every breath. Her pulse joined in. She could hear how rapid it was if she listened hard enough. Even the strands of hair that skimmed her cheeks whenever his speed altered felt like a caress.

She'd never felt so alert. Ready. Desirous. Available.

And Katherine Clark wasn't any of those things. She wasn't easy. She could prove it. She was armed. She should have stuck one of her blades in him.

Wait a minute here...

He'd been riddled with darts. Even if they hadn't been poisonous, they should have left marks. Puncture wounds. Red spots. That was odd. She hadn't noticed anything about Tane's torso except a lot of tanned skin.

Some really ripped abs.

Hard pecs...

Argh.

Kat gritted her teeth. This continual listing of masculine attributes was almost insidious. Utter nonsense. And it was stopping. She may be plastered to his side, her legs wrapped about one of his, her chin against his shoulder, her arms linked about his waist as though she wanted this contact, but that didn't mean anything other than she was afraid of falling. And she was going to prove it. Kat moved her chin. Looked over at his chest. And actually sighed aloud before she could stop it.

Shit.

He grunted. She looked up and caught a flash of neon blue from his eyes as he looked away quickly before their gazes connected. Her ability to breathe got suspended. Her belly flipped. Her heart dropped. And none of that was physically possible.

Was it?

He put his free hand against her head. Kat would have fought it if trees hadn't instantly surrounded them. He tipped forward and swooped through the mass of foliage. The world went dark. Cavernous. Sounds of dripping water and something that hummed echoed around her, giving her some idea of space. His speed increased, adding a windy sound to the mix. None of this was possible.

It wasn't easily disregarded, either.

They entered a chamber with a lot of light. And warmth. Tane slowed, then swiveled her to his front. All so he could set her atop a structure. He released his grip about her waist, and stepped back, his hands held high. He took another step back. Kat sat up. Looked around. The entire time, he was breathing just as hard as she was. It wasn't possible to disregard it. His chest was rising and falling with the force of the motion.

"Um. Where...um...are we?" Kat's attempt at pragmatism failed. The words trembled.

"My home."

He only said two words, but in this place it was amazing! The words had a growl to them. It was really deep. It sought out the corners of the room and bounced back. It lifted goose bumps. Kat twisted. Looked about. She was atop a really large surface. It had a bit of spongy feel to it.

"Um...what is this?" She put a hand to what felt like velvet beneath her. No. It was more the texture of suede. The structure had stone pillars at all four sides, and...

She narrowed her eyes.

Were those pillows?

"An altar."

Altar?

Kat folded her arms. The structure shimmied beneath her. "It looks like a bed," she informed him.

He grinned.

Crap.

The guy had a killer smile. Her heart did the down-elevator thing again. He sobered instantly as if he felt it, too. That was just more ridiculousness she needed to disregard. And she would, if that element of her personality was available and working. She didn't know what had happened. She'd been jettisoned into a realm of physical sensation outside her experience and Tane wasn't remotely helping. Any amusement he might have projected disappeared. He looked directly across at her, and the vivid blue of his eyes altered. They looked more yellow. Then orange. Then red. And they glowed. Humming filled her ears. Flashes of light lit the area about him. His lips were full. Almost feminine. Totally kissable. And she'd never had that thought of any man in her entire lifetime.

Kat licked her lower lip. Tane rocked backward. She pulled in a breath and yanked her gaze away.

This was the strangest day of her life.

And Tane was at the center of it.

She didn't dare look toward him again. She scanned the chamber instead. The longer she kept from glancing toward him, the easier it became. The humming sound slowly faded to the barest whisper of sound while the flashes turned out to be torches. It looked like he had hundreds of them. All lit. Flickering. Occasionally hissing. They sent illumination throughout the rock-hewn area, but surprisingly little smoke.

"Do you value your clothing, Kat?"

Her clothing?

"Um...maybe you should call me Katherine." She spoke to one of the torches. She needed to make this impersonal. Focus on something inanimate. And fast.

"Katherine. I like that."

Oh my!

She'd never heard her name in such a tone! It brought images of dark chocolate pouring out of a fountain onto a bed of ripe strawberries...or maybe it was closer to a trail of warm candle-wax strewn with red rose petals...or something equally as decadent. And she'd never seen or imagined either one of those things until right now. A sliver of heat went through her, melting through all kinds of things. Sanity. Normalcy.

Resistance.

"Do you value your clothing, Katherine?" he repeated.

"W-Why?"

"I am wondering how much care to take while removing it."

"Doing what?"

"Removing it."

She swallowed. Hard. "Why...um...would you want that?" Erotic images filled her head. Naked flesh matched to the same. Her breasts pressed to those hard pecs. His thighs between hers, ankles linked behind him, locking him to her...

"You are on my altar, Katherine."

The way he said her name should be illegal. The rest of his sentence just added reaction she didn't need and had no idea how to deal with. The words alone should have alarmed, but his tone cancelled out everything except want. Enticement. Thrill.

"You don't...um...practice sacrifice, do you?"

"Not with you."

"With me?"

"You are on my altar, Katherine...so I can worship."

"Worship?"

Focusing on the cavern wasn't working. His words and tone were impossible to disregard. They invoked all kinds of erotic images that came in flashes. Learning the muscles beneath his skin as her fingers grazed his skin. The touch of his lips to her throat. His strength pressing against her softness. She barely stopped a writhing motion before she came to her senses.

Oh! This was horrid.

And pretty darned wondrous.

No.

Wondrous hadn't even been a word in her vocabulary. That's when she decided she'd be better off looking at him. Kat turned her head and immediately got snagged by his gaze. He'd lowered his jaw and narrowed his eyes, and was regarding her through his lashes. The only hint that he possessed blue eyes was the color at the center of a lot of red. It was like staring into the center of a flame. He looked like he'd enlarged, too. Become much more male. And turned extremely predatory.

His stance should have produced instant fear and a lot of

it. Perhaps anger. Definitely adrenaline as a fight-or-flight response kicked in. It did neither. Instead, she got a huge dose of feminine-tinged excitement. Her nipples tightened beneath her garments, and then rubbed against material, engendering even more reaction. Her belly got hit with all kinds of flame-tipped tingling. Her loins grew moist. Inflamed. Heated. Everything felt restrictive. This was insane, but it was insanely exciting at the same time.

Her fingers moved without thought. Or attention. She didn't break the magnetic quality of his gaze. He didn't blink. She matched it, for as long as she was able. Each blink took a micro-second of time and she didn't want to spend even that amount of time disconnected to him. She didn't question why. She was caught up in a fantasy for the first time in her life.

And it was breath-taking.

The knife-holder complete with all her blades came off first. It fell off once she'd unlatched it, making the slightest thudding noise as it landed on the altar behind her. Her fingers flew through the buttons of her shirt. The material was damp. Clingy. Kat opened it and struggled to get it off her shoulders and down her arms. So it could join the knives.

Tane didn't move. Well. Parts of him didn't. Every muscle was sculpted with how tightly he must be holding himself but the front of his loincloth was lifted with his size. It was impressive. Even more so as the leather bobbed occasionally. It figured he would be as well-formed there as everywhere else, and that there wouldn't be any way to avoid noticing. Her peripheral vision was functioning too well. Or something else was at play. Her entire focus was filled with male. Perfectly formed. Intense. And barely held in check.

She didn't need to ask.

The shoelaces on her boots were stiff with water. They should have required attention. Kat's fingers unfastened them and then slid the boots off without moving her eyes. The socks were peeled inside-out as she pulled them off next. She pushed them off the edge of the bed. There was a solid thump as they landed somewhere between the bed platform and where Tane stood. Just watching. Twitching once or twice. He resembled a large cat-creature ready to spring...eyeing its prey. Waiting for the perfect moment.

And that was even more exciting.

Kat had to stretch back and suck in her belly to get her belt undone. Her fingers flew through the fastening of her trousers. She didn't need to check anything. She'd dressed and undressed in the dark often. But never had she been so aware of it! Every inch of skin she revealed instantly responded. The air felt like a touch. The whisper of material sliding across skin resembled a caress. There was something at work here she didn't comprehend...and worse. She didn't remotely want to. She was down to her granny-panties and sports bra. Kat stopped. Looked down at herself. *Odd.* This attire didn't fit in with the siren she'd been envisioning. She almost frowned. A growling sound started emanating from where Tane stood.

Kat glanced back up and had barely enough time to gasp before he reached her.

CHAPTER SIX

HIS MATE WAS INTENTLY FASCINATING. Watching her disrobe turned into an unbelievably poignant experience. Fraught with frustration. Alive with ache. Tane pulled every muscle taut as he watched, welcoming the edge of pain. It heightened his desire ten-fold even as it ate away at his control. He'd kept his jaw lowered to hide his fangs, shook in place as he somehow kept from lunging at her. But he hadn't had any control over his loins. He hadn't even tried.

And when she'd gotten down to the last lacy bits of material covering her, she'd pulled from eye contact, looked down at herself, and demurred?

His growl had contained his agony and something else - loss of restraint. He flew at her, landed on the bed beside her with a bounce that sent her attire into the air. Tane swatted at it with one hand while the other grabbed for her. Yanked her into contact with him. Somehow kept the joy from sending them both airborne. A purring sound emitted from him as he lowered his mouth to her throat. Lapped at the skin with his tongue. Slid his fangs along her vein...

And stabbed.

Liquid ecstasy filled his mouth, rocketed through his veins, slammed into his groin. His mate pulsed against him, latched her hands about his waist, and sent a cry into the air. It sounded of energy. Power. Rapture. Their hearts beat as one, each thump coming quicker. Stronger. More strident.

His pulse turned into a rapacious hum. Intense pleasure sent him soaring. And then his head smacked into the top of the cavern.

The blow unlatched his fangs. The instant flash of anger was immediately replaced with relief. She was panting, her flesh slightly clammy to the touch, her heart pulling his into a slow pace. He'd almost gone too far. Tane licked at the dual puncture wounds, sealing them before lifting his head. Meeting her gaze. She had such perfect eyes. It was especially noticeable with how wide open she had them, while her pupils were enormous. Tane sliced a cut open in his lower lip, waiting for the fluid to well, and then lowered his mouth to hers. And instantly experienced even more euphoria.

The exchange of life fluid was unbelievable. He instinctively knew physical mating would be more so. Intense. Powerful. Massive. Tane rotated, placing her above him, so when they dropped, he took the brunt of the landing. He grunted at the impact. The entire time she lapped at his lips. Sucked at his mouth. Moaned. And writhed against him. Tane shoved his loincloth aside. Gripped the backs of her garments and shredded fabric. He'd glimpsed her breasts already, noted the tiny nubs of her nipples. Now he got to feel and experience them as she shoved them into his pecs. Twin mounds of softness smashed against him, engendering infinite sweetness. Boundless pleasure.

Her moans galvanized. Skin-to-skin contact electrified. Her every move contained a strength that incited. Her hands molded to his pecs. Shoulders. Her touch moved down his arms, skimming flesh as she caressed. His fingers slid down her belly, found her center, moist, tight, and hot. Eternally perfect. She gasped as his fingers learned her body, and she went rigid for a moment as his thumb found her nub, and started vibrating. Each motion quested. Going faster. More strident. And he matched her breath-to-breath as she pulled from the kiss, arched her back, and sent the sweetest feminine cry into the atmosphere about them.

And that's when the world went crazed.

Torches flared about the cavern sending acres of light and mountains of heat. The air had a sensation to it. Pressured. Moist. It shoved against everything in its path, melding them even closer. Tane grabbed her to him and spun, putting her beneath him. Her legs gripped tightly about his hips. Her arms enwrapped his chest. Everything stimulated. Roused. Her throat sending a litany of sound into existence, all encompassed with one word.

"Yes! Yes! Yes!"

Tane slammed into her haven. She screamed, and when her breath ran out, she sucked in more air, and used it to scream again. Tane shook throughout the length of her cries, struggling to keep connected while staying still. Unmoving so she could absorb his size. Length. Soft, moist coil-like pressure engulfed him. Massaging. Accommodating his size. Length. Width. The experience was beyond scope. It wasn't possible to stay still. His shuddering moved them along the bed. And just as he gave up, she started the movements.

Fireworks exploded somewhere. Lightning shot through the chamber. The bed platform was in full accompaniment. Tane lifted. He needed the range. The position. So he could move. Stroke. Dominate. Match the rhythm she'd initiated and then seize it. Her body sucked at him each time he pulled out. She was awaiting his every thrust back in. Again. More.

The room about them became its own entity. A myriad of sighs. A plethora of whispers. Thumps of heartbeats that resembled drums. The tapping of raindrops. Dripping of water. The buzzing of jungle life. It surrounded the platform, adding impetus to his strokes. Power to his motions. He thrust wildly. Pulled back out. Shoved back in. Her breaths increased in stridency, pulling his into cadence. Each one began with the slightest sigh of sound, before turning into a whiff of air. Her legs flexed about him, helping. Guiding. Again. And again.

He pumped into her.

Over.

And over.

Deeper. Harder. Faster.

The bed platform joined in, adding a creaking to the mix of sound. His every stroke got faster. More intense. Substantially more powerful. Beyond scope. Or experience. Beyond even description. Katherine was gasping for air, taking his ability to breathe with her. And still he pumped. Again. Faster. Harder. Her legs locked about him, her entire body gave a tremor that leached into his very being, and then she started a long scream again.

And Tane erupted.

A sledgehammer of pleasure slammed into him, ecstasy on its heels. The force sent them skyward. He scrunched his eyes shut and flung his head back, giving vent to a jubilant howl. It combined with her cries, filling the room with an unworldly sound that muted everything else. His world spun off its axis. Re-righted. Started twirling the opposite way. His body pulsed in a frenzy without coherency or order to it. A fist grabbed for his heart. Held it. And then it started squeezing.

His head smacked against something with a jolt. It felt and sounded like he'd hit glass, shattering it on impact. Tane cracked his eyes open, saw his beloved, and was instantly smitten. Katherine's eyes were wide, as was her mouth. She looked as stunned as he felt. Tane had never seen anything so exquisite. He couldn't move his gaze despite the shards of crystal showering down in multi-colored hues all around them.

She blinked. The physical realm intruded. With it, a measure of sanity. That was lucky. It prevented him from falling. Tane held her close and glided back down to the altar. His movement matched how the bliss that still radiated through him had begun to fade. It left emotion in its wake. His throat closed off. His eyes stung. His belly burned. None of it was remotely familiar. They were almost back to the bed when she spoke.

"Oh. My."

The words were a whisper of sound. Then she smiled. They dropped the last few inches. The platform shimmied. Somehow, Tane kept from crushing her. He didn't know how.

He was totally surprised that he hadn't wept.

CHAPTER SEVEN

HAVING THE MOST INTENSE, AMAZING sexual encounter of her life was one thing. Having it happen while being immersed in a paranormal environment was quite another. That part needed to cease. Or at least, withdraw a little. So she could think. Ponder. Plan. Reality was in here somewhere, and - while it would be a pure shame – she needed to figure out where it was hiding. And then expose it.

Kat turned her head and looked over at Tane. He was on his side, his head resting atop an upraised arm. He could be sleeping. He might not be. How was she supposed to know? She'd never studied any of her partners when they slept, and she didn't even know Tane.

She hadn't been mistaken at any point about him. The guy was gorgeous. He had a mass of dark hair. Strands of it were caught on his lashes. His eyes were closed. He looked like a statue of Hercules with a touch of life to it. *No.* That was wrong. He wasn't that hulky. His physique was beautifully defined even in repose. Maybe she should compare him to another Greek god or one of the heroes...maybe the guy who'd poisoned the lady with all the snakes on her head. Or maybe he'd beheaded her and taken her scales for a trophy. *No.* That wasn't right. He'd taken her head for some reason... *oh!* What did she even care? She hadn't paid much attention to Greek mythology or any ancient folklore for that matter. In her opinion, they were far too ridiculous for anyone to actually believe.

But that still left her situation; lying naked beside a male who was in some version of repose. She had to factor in all kinds of sensations, too. Tingling. Warmth. Even shivers as his breath touched her skin.

Wait just a minute.

He was breathing in tandem with her. She watched and counted. He matched all of her breaths. Inhalations. Exhalations. All of it. Exactly. That was odd.

She lifted her head. Looked down at herself. Her neck felt sore. Kat touched a hand to the spot. Pressed. When she moved it back, she didn't imagine the two small dark smears on her fingertips.

Was that...*blood?*

No.

Impossible.

That couldn't be blood. She'd have known if he'd hurt her. It had to be something else, but until she needed to figure it out, she did what she usually did - sent it to her subconscious. So it could be ignored. She had larger things to assimilate. Like her incredible vision. All-of-a-sudden she had sight equivalent to her 5x camera lens?

Kat blinked several times. That didn't work. She closed her eyes and counted to ten before reopening them. The view still didn't change, nor did her ability to see it. It was a fact that she was atop a stretched piece of something. On her back. Without a scrap of clothing. With a strange male. That should have been chilly, except Tane had one arm across her ribcage and a crooked leg atop her thighs, as if to lock her to him. The weight of his limbs was substantial. But it felt so nice. Secure.

That was pretty scary.

And really hard to disregard.

Kat lowered her head and turned to look over her surroundings. They were in a cave of some kind. The torches were still sputtering in spots, illuminating black rock walls, while light reflected off multi-hued sparkling pieces scattered about the floor. It looked like a night sky had been turned upside down, strewing stars beneath, rather than above. And that was way too imaginative for Kat. She narrowed her eyes. The pieces actually looked like...crystals?

Where had he gotten those?

She followed a far wall upward, passed by something that looked suspiciously like a carved face, until she was looking straight up. The ceiling was at least fifty feet above them. There were stalactites pock-marking the entire field of view. But there was something that looked like the remnants of a crystal chandelier.

In a cave?

In the middle of an uninhabited island?

She blew a sigh of disbelief. Tane's breath hitched beside her. Kat moved her head slowly back to face him. He hadn't moved much except his eyes were open. The neon blue had warmed markedly to a sky blue shade. Her heart immediately gave a lurch. And he smiled as if he knew it!

"You do not rest?"

"Um. I need to know what is going on," she informed him. *Crap.* She sounded unsure. She needed to project the demeanor she was known for. Assertive. Confident. Anything except uncertain. And a little hesitant.

"I do not think you are ready."

If he'd wanted to alter the hazy warm afterglow she'd been experiencing, he was doing a fine job. She actually felt a flash of irritation. It sent a cooling sensation as if cold water had been dripped on her. But that was way too imaginative.

She stiffened before replying. "I don't think that's your call."

"You will not believe me."

"Oh. Try me."

"I am a vampire. And you are my mate."

Her face fell.

"You see? You do not believe me."

"I want the truth, Tane."

"You do not have an open mind. You will not accept it."

"I don't think you know me that well," she replied. *And just how the hell would you know that, anyway?* She added silently.

"You are already giving me a skeptical look...and I just told you. I know it because you are my mate."

Kat's eyes widened. Her jaw dropped. His features didn't change, although he matched her gasp.

"Oh. I am very favored," he told her.

"I...need to...um. Get dressed. And...figure some things out. Go. Yeah. That's it. I should leave. Tane. It's been...really nice, um...meeting you."

He turned his head away and laughed heartily. But the sound ended on a howl. The same one she'd heard just before she'd first seen him. In the jungle it had been unearthly. In here it bounced off the walls, reverberating around the chamber, and then it felt like it wrapped about her. Like a presence. That should have scared the hell out of her. It didn't. It felt like every cell in her body had just been nudged. Primed. And gone on alert. She was trying to decipher that when he turned back to her. His eyes were riveting, especially with a hint of gloss atop the blue.

"You are delightful. Do you know that?"

"Um. Look. This is just a little too weird for me. Okay?"

"That's why I said you weren't ready."

"To hear that you're a vampire? Is there a readiness level for that?"

He grinned. He had beautifully white teeth, but his canines had elongated and looked exceptionally sharp. Fangs? *Oh shit!* The guy had grown fangs? She tried ignoring them. Disregarding. It didn't work.

"Um. Tane?"

"Yes?"

"Will you...let me up?"

He sobered, a move that hid the spikes in his mouth – that couldn't possibly be fangs – and then he just gazed at her for several heart-stopping moments. Kat didn't have to question the last part. Her heart was giving her all kinds of trouble. It felt like she was flirting with arrhythmia before he lifted his arm. A moment later he removed his leg from where it rested atop her thighs. The instant loss of heat was palpable. It sent a large dose of loss. She was just ignoring and compartmentalizing that emotion when he sat without appearing to expend a hint of effort, and then he turned to regard her from over his shoulder. The look he sent restarted her heart with a shockwave. And his lip quirked up as if he knew of it.

"There. You are free to get up."

Kat also sat, using some method that didn't use any muscles. As if she'd miraculously gained a nice set of abs. She'd never been able to do a decent sit-up.

Until now.

Disregard it, Kat. You have bigger issues. She needed to find out where she was. Get directions back to the ancient ruins. Snag her camera. Slink back to her base camp. Hide. Go into survival mode until the pilot returned. She took a breath.

"Okay. So. Where are we? Um...exactly?"

"You wish to know of me now, do you?"

"Uh. Yeah. That works."

He smirked. "You are incredibly easy to comprehend, *il mio amore.*"

"You speak Italian?"

"You know the language?"

"Um. No. But I know that phrase. And I really hope you're not calling me 'your love'."

"Your hope is in vain. You are *il mio amore. Il mio compagno.*

And *il mio donna.*"

"I don't know what all that means."

"My love. My mate. My woman."

"Oh, boy. This is getting really complicated."

"What can I do to help?"

She swallowed heavily. It looked and sounded like he did the exact same thing. This was ridiculous.

"Why don't you try explaining some things, okay? And use...facts, not fictional means. Can you do that?"

"Go on," he prompted.

"Why do you know Italian? Never mind that. Why do you know English?"

"I know many languages, *benin kadinim.*"

"What language is that and what does it mean?"

"It's Turkish. For...'my woman'."

Kat sighed heavily. He matched it. She narrowed her eyes. "I need you to stop that, too."

"What?"

"Breathing with me. Like...exactly with me."

He laughed again, more heartily than before. Only he didn't stick a howling sound at the end of it. The place was cavernous. It sounded like an audience of amused people cackled at her expense before the sound died away.

"I am afraid I cannot accede to that wish, *mi amor.*"

"You have a really large vocabulary."

"As do you," he replied.

"Well. Yeah. I should. I've done secondary education to the point it almost bankrupted me."

"You are telling me you went to college?" he asked.

"Yes. I am. And I did. Three of them. To get degrees. I have two Bachelors of Science. And a PhD."

"I see." He smiled.

"And...so will you now explain why you speak so well?"

"I too, have been to college. Ah. I see you do not believe

me."

"What?"

"You have a skeptical look again."

He could read expressions? And listen in on her thoughts? *Great. Just great.*

"Perhaps I should call it a 'Does Not Compute' sort of expression," he added.

"Go back to the college thing. Explain it. You've attended a university?"

"I have attended many universities, *mein gebliebte.* Well... those that offered night classes. And correspondence courses. In many countries. I have many degrees. And before you ask, that phrase I just used is German. It means 'my love.'"

"No way."

"You are very difficult to convince, *ma femme.*"

"French, too? All right. Enough playing around. There is no way you could have attended many colleges. You're what? Thirty?"

"Thirty-one. If we are counting mortal years."

He called it skeptical? She'd never been up against such a pathological liar. She was amazed she wasn't projecting absolute disgust.

"Aren't you an island native?" she demanded.

"I was born here, yes."

"So. Pin it down, already. You are a native of this island."

"My mother was an islander. My father was a Spanish sailor."

"Oh. That explains your coloring. Except for your eyes."

Damn it.

She felt the blush as he watched her. He didn't blink. She didn't, either. And, after a span of some time, her eyes didn't burn. How was that possible? But the moment she questioned it, she sent it to her subconscious with the rest of this. What the heck did it matter right now?

"You have noted my eyes? Well. You would not be the first

woman."

That remark sent a flash of something through her. Ire. A hint of anger. Something white-hot and jagged. Was this what jealousy felt like? And why did she waste time questioning it? She had bigger problems. This was getting insane. And he acted like it was nothing.

"My eye color is a throw-back to some previous generation. No one ever found out where that particular gene trait came from."

"The ruins back there?" she asked.

He shrugged. "Perhaps."

"They looked Roman."

"Perhaps."

She sighed heavily again. He matched it again. Kat rolled her eyes. "I really need you to stop doing that. Okay? Just stop."

"Forgive me, love, but I cannot."

"Why not?"

She tried to make her tone acidic. Because he'd called her his love. In words she instantly understood. And that made them more meaningful, or something. She failed with her objective. Her voice sounded breathy. Low. As if this was a singles bar, and she'd just projected her interest. Readiness.

"I told you. I am a vampire. You are my mate. The one. And only. And now that we have mated..."

His eyebrows lifted several times. His gaze flicked over her as if she needed clarification. That look sent fire racing through her veins. She should be all manner of embarrassed. Nope. She was experiencing a mass of sensation that carried thrill and excitement at its base. All kinds of alarm bells started sounding in her ears.

"That means your physiological responses...are now mine."

"Um. Tane?"

"Yes?"

"I don't know what to say. What to do. I feel—."

Her words stopped. She didn't know how to describe it.

"You are feeling the mating urge, darling. It is very powerful between us. Impossible to fight. Even if I desired that. And I do not."

"Yes," she whispered.

Trembling had overtaken her frame as he turned toward her. His eyes sent all kinds of messages, while his nearness created worse. A wave of heat hit her, washed back to him. Re-crossed the five or so inches of space that separated them. Rebounded back to him. It felt like parts of her were already leaping toward him. None of which she had the imagination to conjure up. Her head went back. Each breath came with a sigh of sound.

"You are so...beloved," he told her. "And I am beyond besotted."

"Yes," she replied.

"Mating with you right now....is dangerous."

"Tane."

Some woman spoke his name as a plea. It couldn't possibly be Katherine Clark. *Could it?*

"It will take all my strength...to prevent the change."

"Please?"

"You do not...understand." His voice was a grunt of bass sound. And it shook.

In a moment she was going to be begging. And that was so far outside her realm of experience, understanding, and comprehension, that she couldn't even grasp it mentally. There was no ignoring anything. Her body was too alive. Her senses too attuned. All she could do was experience.

"Kiss me."

She whispered it. And they both pounced.

CHAPTER EIGHT

HER AGGRESSIVENESS WAS SURPRISING. AND highly enjoyable. And then it became torment.

Her kiss was a masterpiece of torture. Tane's fangs had sliced the moment they'd connected with her mouth, and he fought the instantaneous desire for her. Taking her blood was an essential need, but then it grew worse. He reined it back with such force, his entire frame shook. That transferred to the bed, making it shudder beneath them. His mate had her hands about his head, as if to hold him. It wasn't necessary. Tane was locked in place. Her lips were rapture, the feelings she called up with her kiss, completely sublime. And her moans were so sweet! They filled the chamber with sounds of bliss. Delight. She was above him slightly, her breasts pressed to his upper chest, but she kept moving, sliding her tight, little nipples along him. His skin erupted in goose bumps at the contact. While her legs...

Sweet paradise!

She sat atop his lap, her thighs split, her legs enwrapping, but she kept sinuously moving about...teasing. Toying. Grazing his hardness with the slightest touch before shimmying away. Each time she played with connecting them. But then she'd move, keeping just out of reach. Tane was crazed with longing. Desperate with craving. Wild with need.

He lunged backward, bringing her with him. The bed platform squeaked as it bounced, then settled. Her movements grew more sinuous, her moans more intense, her touch even hotter. The combination took his need to take her blood to an almost insurmountable level. He fought against grabbing her. Pivoting. Getting her onto her back. Joining their loins as he stabbed his fangs into her throat. So he could thrust. Dominate. Conquer.

Every moment the incendiary signals between them increased. They lit fuses, sparked fires, sent electrical current that zapped. An uncontainable growl erupted from his throat. Deep. Intense. The sound increased in volume as he grabbed her shoulders and yanked her up and away from further kisses. And she gave a huff that sounded like amusement.

Tane glared. He had his eyes narrowed, his upper lip lifted in a snarl, his fangs on full display. He knew they were blood-tipped already. They weren't just tingling. They were vibrating angrily in his mouth. His every muscle taut with fiery pain. By now he was drawing in such rapid breaths, each one lifted her from his chest.

And she laughed?

At his torment?

"Is that...meant for me?"

He was actually afraid to answer, for fear he'd startle or alarm. This level of restraint scared him. His body jerked, the spasms getting even worse as she slid a hand along his belly. Caressed the length of his rod. Held him erect. Positioned perfectly...

"Poor man," she murmured. And then she slammed down onto him.

Tane lost all control. Rocket-like sensation flared. It shot through his veins. He grabbed her hips and started pumping her. Up. Down. She may have helped. But it didn't feel like it. Her breasts bounced with each move. Her hands gripped to his shoulders. Her legs flexed. Tane heaved into her as she rode him, his body in the grasp of something primal. Almost bestial. She sent all manner of soft sounds into the room. His release drew near. Closer. More intense. His ears were filled with a cacophony of sounds. The thudding of his heart. The heavy rasp of each breath. What sounded like something sizzling on a low fire.

"Tane! Oh, yes! Tane!"

He watched her arch backward. Heard her cry. And then she lowered her mouth to his neck...

And bit him.

Tane roared with pleasure. It erupted everywhere, flashing through him like a thousand little pieces that each carried pleasure. Sublime wonder. Complete and total ecstasy. He didn't note that they rose from the bed, hovered in midair throughout his release. Nor did he care. All he cared about was his mate. The feelings she engendered. Finding her was the best experience of his existence. He didn't bother listing and comparing.

He knew.

~ ~ ~

Time had passed.

Could have been an eternity or a few moments. Tane didn't bother guessing at it. His newly reactivated heart settled to a steady rhythm. The room drifted into a slow spiral that still held the remnants of bliss. They'd almost missed his platform as he'd dropped. The bounce had separated them, but she was still atop him. Stretched out. Giving him needed body warmth.

One of his legs dangled over the edge of the bed. The center of his back had smacked into one of the rock supports. He still leaned against it. He hadn't noted any pain. He'd barely felt it. That was the trouble. The room still spun slightly because he was dangerously weak. Perilously drained. He should have stopped his mate from taking so much of his fluid...but that might have altered something. Taken away from the ecstasy. And that he wouldn't have missed.

Her legs started twitching.

"Um. Tane?"

She sounded excited, animated, and exhilarated. Everything he was not. All at once.

"Yes?"

The word was ragged-edged. Harsh. He'd dragged in a breath to do that much. She matched it automatically. Kat snapped her head in his direction. He hoped he didn't look exactly like he'd sounded. Weak. Pale. He was even shivering.

"I don't understand. What is happening?"

"I am not certain...you are ready...to hear."

She rolled her eyes heavenward before moving her gaze back to him. "Oh, please. Not that again."

"I have...to go out."

"What?"

He put his hands on her shoulders, rolled her from him, and then sat with a slowness that belonged to an old man. Or an invalid. He placed his feet on the floor next, and then he just stopped. His breathing was rapid and shallow.

It matched hers.

"We are...in luck," he told her. "It is a night...without a moon."

"How on earth can you tell? No. Never mind that. What on earth does that have to do with anything?"

"The natives...they have a ritual."

"The guys who tried to kill me?"

He nodded. And then he turned his head to look at her. His heart dropped as he touched her gaze. Her heart had probably done the same. Her eyes widened and then she glanced away.

"Um. Go on. I don't know what it has to do with anything, but I am interested. Which surprises even me."

"One of them is chosen."

"For what?"

"They...stake him out."

"Stake him out? For what?"

"He is a blood sacrifice. To their god."

"B–B–Blood sacrifice?"

She looked exactly like she'd sounded. Stunned. Disgusted. Dismayed. He finally nodded.

"Oh, no. No. Don't say it. Just. Don't. Okay? Please don't tell me you're their god."

"I...didn't say that."

"But that's what your name means. You told me. Remember?"

He turned to look out toward the chamber. Kat slid to the edge of the bed to sit beside him. This was troubling. She was stark naked and incredibly appealing. Even in his weakened state. And then, it got worse. When she stood, it placed her backside to him. She had perfect woman curves on display as she stretched, and then she put her hands on her hips and looked about.

Tane slouched forward, resting his forearms on his thighs.

"Are those...crystal?"

She motioned with a hand toward the smattering of pieces strewn about the floor.

"Yes."

"From...up there?"

She pointed. He had a hard time moving his attention from her to the ceiling. She'd turned around when he brought his gaze back. His mate was exquisitely alluring. Desire was a difficult thing to ignore. He grunted an answer.

"Why do you have a crystal chandelier?"

"I rescued it."

"What? How do you...um...rescue a chandelier? And why am I even asking a question that stupid?"

"My palace was destroyed. That was...one of the only things left."

"You have a palace?"

She looked exactly as skeptical as she sounded. Tane regarded her for long moments before he answered.

"Yes. I have...several. That chandelier came from one...near Vienna."

"You have a palace near Vienna?"

"No." He shook his head.

"You don't have a palace near Vienna? Well. Darn. What a shame. I would *so* much rather be in a palace than a cave."

"You would?"

"I'm being facetious. Okay? I don't happen to believe you have a palace – near Vienna, or anywhere else. And why? Because, if you did, you would *not* be running around the jungle in a loincloth. Swinging from trees. Nor would you live in a cave on some uninhabited island. Oh, wait. It's definitely inhabited. Scratch that part."

He smiled. She was so young! So very innocent! "I live here...because I choose to," he told her.

"You chose something this primitive?"

"It's private...and I do not care for humanity."

"Then why would you have palaces?"

He needed to cease breathing so shallowly. It didn't help the dizziness. "I have lived...many years, *mi amor.* Seen a lot of things. Experienced more. At one point in my long life, I was greedy. I bought all sorts of properties, traded in stocks. I became a very rich man before I realized it was such an empty concept."

"What is?"

"The acquisition of wealth."

"Oh, I don't know. I would still like to see one of these so-called palaces. If you still have them. And if they really existed."

"We can. And we will. If you so wish."

"All right. I'd like to visit the one near Vienna."

"That one does not exist anymore."

"Why not?"

"I told you. It was destroyed."

"Of course it was." She agreed, but her expression and tone said the opposite.

"You are a very...difficult woman to convince."

"No. I'm just very difficult to lie to."

He sighed heavily. She matched it. He wondered if she noticed.

"I don't have that palace anymore because it was torn down. During the collapse of the Austro-Hungarian Empire."

"Oh. Right. And that happened...oh. I don't know. I didn't like history, but I still got stuck learning some things. I'm going to say...World War I?"

"Exactly."

"Why am I having a hard time believing this?"

He shrugged.

"Maybe because it's impossible? Fantastical? And completely fictitious? And I have to tell you something, Tane. I don't believe in paranormal stuff. Never have. Never will. You are just going to have to come up with a better story."

"You are...a very tempting woman, Katherine."

"Really? Well I think you are very crazy."

"You need...to get some clothing on. I...cannot think."

"Oh. Right. Look who's talking."

She gestured toward him. If he wasn't suffering blood loss, he'd have flushed.

"You are so beloved. So very enticing. But we cannot mate. Not until I have fed. Otherwise...I will not be able to prevent changing you."

"Changing me into what?" She arched her brow enticingly then shook her head. "Never mind. Don't answer that. I don't want to know."

He stood slowly. He wavered in place as he looked down at her. "I must go. The natives...will be waiting."

"Oh. That's right. You have to go kill some guy who has

been staked out for you."

"I do not kill. Only a fool destroys his only source of sustenance."

"Do you want me to gag?"

He smiled, then instantly sobered. "Will you...stay here while I am gone?"

She wouldn't meet his eyes. That was troubling.

"I'm not promising that. I can't. I just...can't. My head is spinning. I mean, I can't even comprehend most of the lies you've been spouting, let alone believe them."

"It is no lie, Katherine. None of it. I told you. I am a vampire. And you are *il mio compagno*. That means—"

"Stop! I don't want to...know what that means." She might be trying to sound commanding, but her voice had a breathless tone to it.

"You are my mate. And you are halfway to becoming a vampire yourself."

She jerked backwards, raising her hands. "Oh. No. No way. For such a thing to be possible, vampires would have to be real. End of conversation. This line of thinking is dead. Or should I say undead? No. Dead sounds better."

Tane smiled then shook his head. "Forgive me. I do not have time to explain. I need blood. We cannot delay much longer."

"Talk while we dress."

Tane swiveled his loincloth back into position; tie at one hip, flaps down to cover him. He didn't even break their gaze to do it.

"Oh, fine. Very funny. Explain while I dress, then."

She tiptoed about, avoiding the scattered pieces of crystal as if they were broken glass. That was amusing.

"You possess a lot of energy all-of-a-sudden," he told her.

"True." She shoved her legs into pants. Grimaced. Tane assigned a reason. They were probably damp. Chilled. He could tell she'd chosen her field attire with care. They'd dry, and they weren't even wrinkled.

"Your senses have been elevated. Sight. Sound. Smell. Touch. Taste."

"Also true." Her shirt was in the same condition as her trousers. It looked like it felt as cold, too.

"You have immunity to disease now. If you do get wounded, it will rapidly heal. Very few things will actually kill you."

"What? I'm not immortal? Well. Heck. We were on such a roll here."

"You still do not believe?"

"Nope."

He sighed. "You also have new abilities."

"I'm psychic now?"

"No. Physical abilities."

"I already had some of that." She lifted her knife holder as if that explained her comment. Then she pulled the blades over her head and settled them like an 'X' atop her chest. She patted them before looking at him again. "Crap. This is gonna be a bitch without my mosquito netting. I think we left it in your tree house."

"Insects will no longer bother you. Your blood...is unappetizing to them."

"Really? Well. At least that part sounds nice."

"You still do not believe?"

"Nope. But I've never heard anything quite this original. Really. Well. I'm ready. Where's the door?"

"We are not going through a door."

"My mistake. It'll be called a tunnel."

"We are going through that opening. Up there." He pointed to a shadowy area just beyond the dangling wreckage of his chandelier.

"Okay. And...you have a ladder? Right?"

"We don't need ladders."

"I'm going to just fly up there?"

"I told you, *mi amor*. It's called jumping."

Tane used a vital burst of energy to reach her and then launch upward. They swooped through the darkness, flew out into a moonless sky, and started gliding above the treetops. He aimed for a spot of light that was a bonfire. He didn't stop. He didn't dare.

CHAPTER NINE

T*HE NATIVES WERE RESTLESS TONIGHT.* Kat smirked. She had no one to share it with, but the thought was still funny, in a tongue-in-cheek kind of way. Actually, her entire world had that problem at the moment. How could it not? She was being babysat by a man claiming to be a vampire. *Babysat.* His idea of that was to stick her in a platform about a half-mile above a forest floor, tell her to stay put, and then disappear over the edge.

This tree house didn't have near the amenities of the first one. It was a lot smaller for one thing. Planking enclosed three sides, while the roof was a leaf-covered overhang that kept the elements at bay, and the edge didn't have a railing. There also wasn't a ladder, or stairs, or a rope, or even a vine to swing from. Jungle sounds intruded from every direction. An occasional monkey cry. Bird calls. The soft noise of drizzling rain. The buzzing of insects.

Weird.

None of the cloud of mosquitoes came inside a certain distance. Like the platform had an invisible bio-dome about it, or something. Nice to know there was a definite plus to Tane's explanations...aside from the spectacular increase of power that had happened to her senses.

She'd been out at night before. Chasing nocturnal birds required it. The experience hadn't been quite this vivid, however. The air had a presence. Like a moist blanket wrapped about her. Even the rain carried a smell. Clean. Slightly citrusy.

If she had to be stuck somewhere, this wasn't half bad. At least everything was physically real. The tree house was sturdily built. And it was in an excellent location. Then again, location was everything when it came to real estate.

Kat smiled at that thought, too.

This platform was directly above a clearing where a lot of mostly naked guys danced around a roaring fire. They'd made it large, and kept feeding it against the rain. They had some decent musicians down there. More than three drummers. One fellow played a flute-thing. Another had a large horn. Their rhythm was catchy. She admitted it as her body swayed.

There didn't seem to be any females in the entire bunch. Kat assigned a reason she liked. Their women were smarter. They had enough sense to stay inside on a night like this. Not stripe their bodies with a lot of white, black, and red paint, drink something intoxicating, and dance about with abandon, making a ton of noise in order to attract a monster.

Like Tane.

Kat immediately sent the thought away to join the mass of impossibilities she was already disregarding. She knew she'd have to deal with them at some point. But not yet. And not now. She'd worry about it when she was back to reality. When things got normal again. Maybe, not even then.

Hmm.

She really did possess incredible hearing and eyesight. She had no trouble following the action so far below her. Near impenetrable dark surrounded the tableau being enacted. If this was a ritual, it was a lengthy one. The red orange flames of the bonfire flickered and hissed, tossing sparks and ash. It cast grotesque shadows from the dancers out onto trees and deadfall. Their dancing seemed more erratic. Arm and leg movements much more fervent. The music got louder. They probably thought they were failing. But Tane wasn't playing fair. His sacrificial victim was staked out at the base of an altar that looked like a skull. It was just outside the range of their firelight. Probably so they wouldn't see the poor man get taken.

And feasted on.

Ugh.

She quickly moved her attention again. The natives might not want to see it, but they were definitely interested. While the majority worked at their ritual, she could see quite a few men hidden in the jungle. Unmoving. Silent. They were all focused on the victim. That poor man was on his back, tied at the ankles and wrists, stretched out and indefensible. But it was all for naught. Tane hadn't approached him. He was a shadow of motion, sneaking among the watchers, pulling an occasional man back from the area. Far back. And what he did then, she didn't want to see. Not again. It was just a little too interesting. A bit fascinating. She'd actually found herself salivating. And that was beyond comprehension at the moment.

Crap.

Looked like Tane had just grabbed another native.

Kat lifted her gaze quickly and looked out over the tops of the trees. She could see for miles, as if there was a bright moon illuminating everything and rain wasn't an obscuring presence. The moisture made the outlines of everything hazy. That would be the effect of water droplets as they splashed against an obstruction. It raised a mist that blurred outlines and, courtesy of her new eyesight, she could actually see it.

Oh. That was excellent.

She'd had something to figure out and managed it by extrapolating the physics involved. That was a relief. She wasn't entirely crazy. And then she saw the top of something angular. It was indistinct due to the distance, the elements, and possible overgrowth, but...

Her heart ticked up. There was a strange resonance to the

sensation, but she quickly ignored it. No heart had an echo. It had to be imagined. As such, it was completely inconsequential.

Kat pulled her feet beneath her and stood. Narrowed her eyes. Focused. She wasn't mistaken. She'd just located the ruined wall! The one with the mountain starling nest. The place where all this had started. It was miles in the distance, but a definite fixed point of reference. If she managed to get there, she knew how to get to her camp – after finding her camera and the priceless photos of mountain starlings. And once she did that, she could hide. The pilot was due soon. She'd lost track of time, but it might even be today. Tomorrow at the latest. He'd land on the water of the lagoon. Take her away.

And she'd never see Tane again...

The sensation that stabbed through her breast was quick. Sharp. And debilitating. Kat's legs wavered. There was nothing to grab onto, so she fell to a knee, and her hand thumped as it hit the deck. That didn't hurt nearly as much as it should have, and felt nothing like the pain that lanced thought her chest cavity. It felt like her heart was in a vice, getting screwed tighter with each heartbeat until there wasn't a level accurate enough to describe it. Each breath was a trembled gasp.

This is really stupid, Kat.

What was wrong with her? She'd been locked in some alternate reality, she'd just discovered the figurative door, and bonus! Her babysitter was preoccupied. All of that equaled opportunity. She couldn't care what happened to Tane, the vampiric jungle-man. Why should she? They'd just met. He was just a guy. True... he was beyond gorgeous, had a fantastic body, and some amazing love skills. He stirred her senses beyond anything she'd ever known. She'd reached a heretofore unknown level of ecstasy and rapture and absolute bliss with him. It was also true that he possessed a voice that altered the elements, and a touch that started dreams. What of all that? He was still just a guy. An intriguing, fascinating, and really masculine guy, but still...

Why was she even debating this?

She didn't dare stay. She couldn't. Katherine Clark was a logical, rational person. She didn't deal in emotions or fantasies...or guys who thought they were vampires. And the blur that obscured her vision for a moment couldn't possibly be tears, either.

Kat blinked until she could see clearly again. The vice-like sensation was still there, but it had lessened to a manageable level. She sniffed. Stood back up. Assessed things. Physical things. Her legs held. She didn't feel shaky. Nothing was broken.

Except your heart.

Kat groaned aloud, did her damnedest to not only ignore the instant thought, but absorb the ache it sent through her breast. It didn't work. The longer she stood there, the more it hurt. She sucked in a ragged breath, and made her decision. She was leaving. First thing? She had to figure out how to get down without breaking her neck.

He'd told her more than once that his method was to jump. *Hmm.*

Kat leaned forward and craned her neck to look down, underneath the platform. He'd built this place in a tree with a large trunk. Her arms wouldn't span it. She did a quick visual determination. She didn't bother checking. She was more interested in the branches and this tree had a few of them. Some were wider than others, although she had to decipher the actual wood content. Most were covered with foliage. But one looked especially promising. About ten feet down. Kat went to her belly, shoved until her legs went over the platform edge. Shimmied to her waist, and then pushed off. She hung from the wood for several moments. As if still undecided. Unsure.

She'd been off on the distance involved, too. It was another five feet from where she dangled and the objective. But…if she moved just right…she could land atop it. Kat let go. Dropped. And landed easily, although the force sent her scrambling through branches toward the trunk. She struck it and grabbed on, her arms outstretched, her belly clenched, and her heart hammered, each beat still tipped with pain.

But she'd done it!

She'd been correct on the trunk's width. And sturdiness. And the next branch down looked even farther away. It was on the opposite side of the tree. Kat hugged the trunk as she worked around it, her boots grabbing for any toehold while hard bits of bark bit into her forearms. The maneuver also pressed the knife holder into her chest and belly uncomfortably. She welcomed it. It almost took her mind off the ache behind each heartbeat.

When she was directly above the lower branch, she let go. Dropped again. The branch shuddered with her landing. Some leaves came loose and floated off. Her knees flexed. Her mouth was dry. And her heart was going to launch out of her chest, but she'd done it! Again!

The next three drops were even easier. The branches closer. Her sense of purpose keen. But, overconfidence was a killer. She must have forgotten that. Her foot slipped on the sixth landing, and there wasn't anything to grab. Her fingers clawed at air, her feet scrambled for any footing, but she still slid off.

She'd heard that a person's life flashed before their eyes when they died, especially if it was in a fall. She'd also heard that they would give a long cry. Both were false. All she'd managed was a small terrified squeak, and then physics figures filled her mind. Without any variables, things fell at a rate of 9.8 meters per second. If she'd been a half mile aboveground, that equaled to what in meters? And just why was she thinking in both standard and metric?

Argh.

804.6 meters. That equated to how much time? Air rushed past her ears, sounding like a wind tunnel. The rain wasn't even noticeable. Could that be because she matched the rate of fall of the drops around her?

Numbers, Kat!

804.6 divided by 9.8. She needed that sum!

Crap.

Leaves slapped at her, slowing her descent. That needed to be factored in. She spun and gyrated as if that would help. This level of vision was horrific at the moment. The jungle floor was rushing toward her. She could see it with perfect clarity.

Eight and a half seconds.

That's how long she'd had before her body slammed into the ground. That's when she knew she'd rather not see it. Kat scrunched her eyes shut, started a prayer, and prepared for the worst. And then arms wrapped about her. Her plummeting slowed with a rapidity that made her ears pop. She was cocooned in a sensation of solidity. Comfort. Protection.

"Oh my darling? Did you fall?"

At Tane's query, Kat did something completely uncharacteristic. She wrapped her arms about him, gripped as hard as possible, and then burst into tears.

CHAPTER TEN

IT WAS MID-MORNING WHEN THE call came in.

Tane had forgotten how even weak daylight affected a newly created vampire. Or a half-turned one like Katherine. He had her snuggled into his master bed. Her boots were on the floor at the bedside along with her collection of wicked-looking knives. He hadn't disrobed her further. He couldn't. He was dealing with a level of emotion that scared him.

If he hadn't caught her...?

His heart still stopped at the thought. Hours later. He knew the fall wouldn't have killed her, but it would have caused horrific injuries. Broken bones. Internal bleeding. Incomprehensible pain.

Tane's eyes misted over as he watched her.

She was so beloved! Beyond precious. Infinitely sweet. She looked like she slept. That wasn't entirely accurate. She was in a state of rest. Her eyes had closed despite how she'd fought it. She might have been worried. That's why he'd stopped undressing her. She needn't fret. She was safe. She would always be safe with him.

Tane watched her chest rise and fall with regularity. She looked so small! So perfect! He had her ensconced in a bed he'd also rescued from his palace. The bed was massive. It had been built for royalty. It looked incongruous amidst all the black stone, but it also looked impressive. Especially with the silver-embroidered heirloom coverlet he'd tucked about her.

She'd clung to him the entire way back. Her tears had wet his chest and every resultant breath had chilled. And yet, he'd never felt warmer. His heart had expanded to hold it. He'd never felt such love or devotion. He hadn't any idea it existed. Until he'd found her.

The cry of a Micronesian Megapode interrupted his reverie. That was his ring tone. The bird's call was shrill. Loud. It would increase with each succeeding ring. Tane flew out of the chamber and down the hall to his computer room before that could happen. He grabbed for a phone, smacked the connect button, and answered with the same sense of expediency and lack of finesse.

"What is it?"

"Ah. Greetings, Tane."

Tane swallowed the instant retort. He'd expected Nigel again, but was mistaken. That voice and volume could only belong to Akron Profit, the leader of the Vampire Assassin League. The oldest of them. Most revered. And respected.

"I have Nigel on the line with us. I believe he will find this edifying. I trust that won't be a problem?" Akron continued.

"No, Sir."

"Edifying...? Wait. That means educational," Nigel spoke.

"Exactly. So. To the reason for my call. Tane?"

Tane grunted.

"Let me set your mind to rest on some things. I don't have an assignment. There is nothing on the grid. No alerts of any kind in your hemisphere. Everything looks pretty calm. On the surface."

"Sir?"

"I understand you have found your mate?"

"Now, how the heck do you know that, Sir?" Nigel's asked.

"You really require an explanation?"

"Oh. Never mind. Dumb question. You know everything."

Akron chuckled. "Well. That is not entirely accurate, dear

boy, although I am gratified that you think so, but back to my call. Tane? You still there?"

"Yes."

"Am I right? You found your mate?"

"Yes."

"And she is with you now?"

"Yes."

"Resting, is she?"

"Oh. Come on, Sir. How can you know that, too?"

"It is a matter of simple deductive reasoning. Tane has found his mate. Chances are good she has been exposed to vampire blood. Therefore, she is now nocturnal, whether she wants to be or not. Tane resides on an uncharted island in Micronesia. It's evening here. That means it's the next morning where he lives."

"Oh. Got it. Pretty smart, Sir."

"Thank you, but I have yet to hear if it is correct. Tane? Is your mate resting?"

"Yes," he answered.

"Ah. Good. Well. Here is where I need to...step in. Give you an instruction."

"An instruction?"

Tane pulled the receiver away and stared at it in surprise for a few moments before putting it back to his ear.

"Nigel believes I am interfering without reason. He calls it meddling, but he's a bit off the mark. It's really—"

"It is meddling, Sir."

Nigel had interrupted. That was surprising, but even more so was how Akron allowed it.

"Meddling is for grandmothers, Nigel. I am manipulating events toward a specific outcome. And in a very short time, I believe you will be very happy that I do such a thing."

"Wow. That's cryptic, Sir."

"I know. But we digress. This is not about us. It's about

Tane. And the reason I called. Tane? Your mate? She wouldn't happen to be a woman named Katherine Clark, would she?"

Tane swallowed before answering. *Akron knew that?* "Yes."

"Now, here is where I'm going to use something more than deductive reasoning. Last night. When you caught Miss Clark, she hadn't fallen. She was attempting an escape."

Nigel's exclamation covered over how Tane's heart seized up. He'd already guessed it, but he didn't want it put into words. Especially with her reaction when he'd caught her. She might have thought she wanted to leave, but she'd latched onto him and wouldn't let him go. That was what he was remembering.

"Wow. I can't even comprehend how you know that, Sir," Nigel said.

"We'll work some more on it, Nigel, but in the meantime, this is a satellite link. We have a lot more time than with a cell call, but we don't want to waste it. Technology is always on our heels. Remember that."

"Yes, Sir."

"Besides, I am not stating anything that wasn't already known. Am I, Tane?"

"What do you want?"

Tane tried to keep the confrontational tone from his voice. It didn't work. Akron's tone immediately got firmer.

"I told you. I am about to issue you an instruction. And you will follow it. Understand?"

"Yes."

"You are to return Miss Clark to her camp. And let her go. I have—"

"No!"

Tane's flung the phone at a wall. It shattered on impact, spewing bits and pieces back at him. Some reached him. Dug into flesh. Stung. He was plucking them out when another phone started shrieking. He ignored it through three raucous calls of the Micronesian Megapode. Just before the fourth one, he snatched the phone and clicked connect. Nigel was speaking.

"...be fair! It's his mate. Surely you remember what that feels like!"

"I think you both need to listen to me before you react. I wasn't finished. Tane? Are you back on the line?"

"Yes."

Tane's reply carried bitterness. And anger. He didn't bother to hide it.

"Good. As I was saying, there are two reasons for my instruction. The first one is because no creature likes bondage. Nor do they seem to thrive in captivity. You should know this already. Wasn't that how I found you?"

"Was he a slave or something?" Nigel asked.

"Warrior. Captured and bound by the natives on another island. They'd taken him as a battle prize. I believe he was scheduled for sacrifice. His body had been beaten, every inch of skin bloodied. I found him in a temple complex. Tied with thick rope. But he was still fighting mad and struggling. Weren't you, Tane?"

"She's my mate. This is not the same."

"I think you will find that bindings are still bindings, regardless of whether they are iron bars, thick ropes, silken threads...or soul-melting kisses."

"She is my mate." Tane repeated. Now, he sounded obstinate as well as angered.

"I know that. I believe she is rather fond of you, as well. And if I hadn't called to manipulate events, things would actually progress quite nicely for you both on that front."

Tane's eyes widened. His heart jumped. His body rose several feet without conscious effort before settling back to the floor.

"I don't get it," Nigel inserted.

"That is not my lone reason for calling. There is another

reason she needs to be set free. Tane?"

"Yes."

"Your island is uncharted. Believed to be uninhabited. Never visited. That's the reason you live there."

"Yes."

"The reason for your privacy is because there's a curse about the place. For centuries now, people who go there don't seem to return. It's a verbal thing. Nothing on record, really. Just rumor. Isn't that true, Tane?"

"Yes."

"That was because those disappearances happened before technology. Cell phones. Internet links. Global satellite positioning. Spy drones. Is any of this sinking in, yet?"

"No."

Nigel and Tane answered at the same time. Akron sighed heavily.

"Katherine Clark is a renowned photographer. Her work has been featured in major magazines and exhibits. Major ones. What are you doing, Nigel?"

"Internet search...and yep. She's got a website. Lots of photos...and look. A bio photo. Hmm. She's cute."

Cute?

Tane straightened as if insulted. His mate was wondrously fair. She possessed breathtaking beauty. A vision of feminine perfection brought to life. Nigel needed better descriptive words.

"A little on the butch side...but cute."

Tane growled.

"I believe Nigel means she looks confident. Assertive. The type of woman who can take care of herself. Apologize, Nigel."

"Oh. Yeah. That's what I meant. Sorry."

"I also believe that Nigel has just proved my point."

"I have?"

"Tane's mate is too well known to just disappear. There

will be a search conducted. A large one. They will find a heretofore unknown tribe on that island. And then find the ancient ruins. You will be overrun with anthropologists and archeologists, and that's before I factor in the miles of pristine sandy beaches."

"So?"

"You see perfect beaches. I see a developer's dream. A resort would probably come first. Followed by condo units. An airport. You can't have a newly discovered island retreat without an airstrip. They'll build roads. Housing. Maybe a mall or two. Some piers to dock sailboats. And then a big dock for a luxury cruise liner or two."

"Stop!"

Tane's exclamation wasn't loud. It created a well of silence. And then, Nigel spoke into the breach.

"Wow. That sounds like my idea of paradise."

"It would," Akron answered.

"We can leave." Tane spoke up. "She wanted to visit...my palaces."

"You have palaces?" Nigel asked. "Dang. All you older guys have so much cool stuff. I was born in the wrong century. Everything was already staked out, grabbed, and sucked up."

Akron answered. "Not entirely, Nigel. I know of a beautiful island you could buy. If it is discovered, listed, and placed on the market. Which is a likely event at the moment."

"Really? Where?"

"Micronesia, of course."

"Really? Doing a search of the area..."

"Nigel. Stop. I meant the island that Tane lives on. And what will happen if he fails to follow my instruction."

"Oh. Well, crap. That's completely unfair. I'd have to bid against him for it. And I don't have his bank accounts."

Akron sighed heavily. "I really do enjoy your company, Nigel. It's so...refreshing. And entertaining. But, you are both wrong. We don't have to alter the current situation."

"We don't?" Nigel asked. Tane remained silent.

"Katherine will have to be returned to her camp. And let go. Few men have the strength of will for this. I believe you do, Tane. It will feel like cutting your own heart out. Trust me. I know."

"I think he should just take her to a palace. Let the island get discovered. And let me buy it."

"Tane?"

He grunted something they could take for agreement. Or rebuttal.

"Buck up. Both of you. I wouldn't have called to medd—ahem. I mean manipulate events if I didn't have a solution."

"You have a solution? And he can be with his mate?"

"Katherine Clark has a very large exhibit planned next Saturday. In New York. Yes. Check it, Nigel. Am I right?"

"Um. Yeah. I am doing an internet search...but how the heck did you know that, too?"

"Later, Nigel. For the moment, we need to schedule a flight for Tane. And he'll need to...adjust his wardrobe slightly."

"Where's he going?"

Akron sighed again. "I try to be so obvious. I don't know where I fail. I really don't."

"What?"

"Disappearing in New York can be a life choice, Nigel. With the appropriate notice to the post office and some other minor correspondence, it might not be considered a missing persons case at all."

"Oh! Yes! I knew you had it in you, Sir! You need to get to Pohnpei, Tane. I'll have a private plane there in...two days? What the heck? It can't take that long. What is wrong with the air service over there?"

"He has time, Nigel. You have this handled, then? I can leave it in your hands?"

"On it!"

There was a click. Tane assumed Akron had disconnected. The assumption was borne out as Nigel started speaking in a rapid-fire manner.

"You'll need a tux, Tane. And everything that goes with it. Scheduling a tailor now! I'll put you up at...oh. Let's see. You'll need a suite booked at the...never mind! I'll handle all of this. You just get your mate back to her camp. I'll be in touch."

And with that, the line went dead.

CHAPTER ELEVEN

"**M**ISS CLARK! MISS CLARK! ARE you there?" Noise blared through her head. Loud. Boisterous. It was followed by a blinding amount of light that sent spears of fire through each eye.

"Miss Clark!"

"What?"

Kat yelled it and lifted the front of her sleeping bag over her head. Her ears throbbed with the volume she'd used. Or something equally impossible.

Like her presence here.

The last thing she remembered was being with Tane. His blue eyes had been so warm. So loving! He'd held her close as he'd entered a different cave room than before. Smaller. Much more cozy. He'd placed her in a bed – a real one, and then covered her with a comforter. He'd whispered of love and devotion and forever companionship...

"Oh, good! You are alive! I was a mite worried."

"Who are you? And what do you want?"

Kat tilted her head toward the top of her bag to yell it. She didn't feel her knife holder on her chest, or she'd have slipped a blade out. Maybe two of them. Without them, she'd have to use an elbow to the interloper's windpipe. Thumbs into his eye sockets. A perfectly aimed knee to his groin. Or something as equally devastating. Because you didn't accost a lone female in her camp with a bazillion-watt searchlight beam and expect to come out unscathed.

"Whoa! No need to take my head off! I'm Frank. From the mainland."

"Who?"

"Your pilot!"

"Aren't you supposed to come tomorrow? At least...wait for morning!"

"It's midday. And we've got a bright sunny day for a change! Excellent flying weather."

"No way. That's...the sun?"

"Yep. Hard to remember what it looks like with the rainfall we've been experiencing, but it's out today! In full splendor! You...awake, then?"

Of course not, Frank. I'm talking in my sleep.

Kat almost giggled at the withheld retort. The urge instantly died. A wash of emotion surged up her throat. Her eyes filled with tears. It wasn't possible. Not unless he'd guessed the reason for her fall. Knew she'd tried to escape. And this was a demonstration of the depth of his regard. He'd given her freedom.

Tane!

She should have told him. Last night when he'd cradled her close, held her to his heart. Whispered words just for her. She should have said it then! It didn't matter how insane his world was, she wanted to stay in it! Because she loved him!

Kat pressed her hands to her eyes and shuddered through a wave of sobs. Swallowed over and over to kill any sound. This was ridiculous. Embarrassing. Feeling anything was beyond stupid. It was obscene. She mentally castigated herself but it didn't help. She felt like she'd lost something infinitely special.

Because she had.

"Do you need some help? Maybe a hand with packing up? I mean, I'm available, but it'll cost extra."

Kat pulled in a breath. Held it. Trembled the entire time. Eased the air back out. "Um. N-no."

"Fine. Suit yourself. I'll just take a nap while you pack up then."

"I'm not going."

Despite the physical impossibility, at the words a spark of hope lit deep within her heart. It flickered. She could actually feel it.

"You're staying?" Frank asked.

Oh, yes.

She was going to get back to the ancient wall, climb it, and locate one of Tane's tree houses, despite how well-camouflaged they were. It shouldn't be a problem with her enhanced vision. And then she was going to reach that tree house, no matter what. There had to be some way to get Tane's attention from there. She might even try giving a mating call.

Kat swabbed at her eyes with the sleeping bag. It was manufactured of rugged material. Great for absorbing moisture. It worked.

"Well. Well. Listen to this. You're already gonna be a legend. Might as well add to it."

"Excuse me?"

"You survived almost a week out here. By yourself. You didn't disappear. I haven't seen you, but you sound fine. And now, you don't want to leave? Well, heck. I might be able to make this a full-time gig."

"A full-time gig? At what?"

"Transportation can be big business...if there's a market. Starting with you. You'll need more supplies. And more cash. For my fee. Let me think about this."

Oh. Snap.

There were over seven billion people on the planet, most congregated in cities. Kat rented a flat in New York. Not by herself. The rent was astronomical. She had two roommates. She only needed it for a home base. She wasn't fond of cities. She wasn't fond of crowds. Sending even a fraction of the world's population to this island paradise sounded like complete desecration.

And it would be her fault.

She sat with alacrity. The sleeping bag gapped open and slid off her shoulders. And sunlight hurt like hell. Kat groped for her personal bag. She always carried necessities in a worn leather satchel. Toiletries. Feminine hygiene. Change of clothing. Sunglasses. Floppy hat. She found the glasses by feel. The dark lenses eased the sun's effect, but didn't entirely cancel it. The light was still beyond bright, and burned her eyes if she didn't keep them narrowed. A quick check showed she was dressed in her field attire. Nothing was wrinkled. She even had on her boots on her feet. She could feel them.

"No. No, Frank. It's nothing like that. I just...haven't finished my work. I'll need more time."

"You didn't get any photos, then?"

Kat glanced about the interior of her dome tent, wincing as the light pained. There wasn't any space that wasn't in use. Her field camera was missing. She knew just where it was – at the base of the ruined wall. She wondered if Frank would wait while she got it. The photos it contained would be the crowning achievement at her exhibit.

But they'd also bring notice to the island.

And even more crowds than Frank imagined.

Kat closed her eyes for a moment. Made her decision. "Um. No. I didn't find the bird I searched for...if that's what you're asking," Kat lied.

"What a shame."

Kat finger-combed her hair into a ponytail and secured it with a band from the bag. "Hey, Frank. I've got a function in New York to attend, but I'll return. Will you be available to bring me back out here?"

"Next week? Next month? What are we talking? I mean...I might be busy. The price would reflect that."

Kat rolled her eyes. Frank was probably adding to his fee as they spoke. But what did she care? The tiny flame of hope was still there. She could feel it. Entrenched in her heart, pumping out warmth.

"Two weeks, max. I think my camp will be fine."

"Want me to check on it for you? I mean I can do it, but it'll cost."

"Oh. I think it'll be fine. This island is...uninhabited, you know. What could possibly happen?"

Kat pulled a pair of panties from the line where they'd been hanging to dry, placed them in the bag, and then shoved the hat onto her head.

And she was ready.

Frank and his plane were just as un-groomed, uncouth and uncivilized as before. Except for being in a week of rain showers, Kat hadn't bathed. She thought she might smell, but there wasn't any competition with Frank. Her enhanced sense of smell added to her vision problem, giving her a massive headache before they reached Kolonia, the capital of Pohnpei. She was going to have to find another pilot before her return plane trip out to Tane's island. She'd put out notice while she was gone. She got a ride to the Village Hotel. Enjoyed a long shower, and hid under the covers until sunset.

The flight to Guam was a long one. Felt like eternity had passed before they finally touched down in Hawaii. She'd booked her tickets in advance. Checked in online. Didn't have any luggage. She was still offered a cash incentive and a later flight in Guam if she'd give up her seat to Hawaii.

Not a chance.

She had a lot to do. She had to get to New York. Reach her flat. Make sure her cocktail dress was back from the dry cleaners. File a change of address.

To where, Kat?

She could rent a PO Box somewhere. Send her mail there.

But that would require time waiting in a line or online. She could just file a temporary hold. Worry about her final address later. Then she'd give her roommate the required 60-day notice for vacating. Make sure there was enough in her account to cover rent deductions. Pay off any balances on her cards. Give any excess clothing to charity. She wouldn't need much. The island had a very temperate climate.

It wasn't until the lights of Honolulu came into sight that she realized she might be preparing to change her entire life over an emotion, but she hadn't completely changed. She was still Katherine Clark, the woman who'd been called a cyborg. She still listed things, but now it was a mental exercise. That would come in handy. Paper wouldn't hold up in a humid climate.

She didn't look at anything from her prior, reality-based perspective. It was like she'd been reborn. It didn't matter if what she planned was beyond insane. She didn't even consider it. Because she was in love!

With a vampire.

CHAPTER TWELVE

SHE WASN'T THERE.
Tane stood in an alcove, shadowed. Intent. Silent. By his watch, he'd only been here six minutes. It had been enough time to check every bit of the gallery. But he was early. He needed to practice patience.

Patience?

When every bit of him was tense with excitement? Alive with emotion? On edge with thrill? The last thing he felt was patient! Tane wondered what would happen if he ripped the tuxedo off, gave a huge howl, and started prowling for her like he wanted.

The thought was almost amusing.

The gallery was a multi-level establishment. Mostly white. Extremely spacious. Partitions intersected the space, making it impossible to find a good vantage regardless of which level he gained. The ceiling was as high as his cave, making the attendees look small. The area was filled with people, each seeming to out-vie the next in appearance. There was a lot of jewel-covered skin being displayed. And every gentleman wore a tux. Waiters in white suits walked about proffering trays that held champagne flutes or *hors d'oeuvre*. An orchestra played softly in the background.

Tane was doing his best to go unnoticed. It wasn't working. In his quest to find Katherine, he intersected all sorts of glances. Some of them caused him to flush. Again. He felt like a foreigner in a strange land. And all of that was Nigel's fault.

It had started the moment he'd exited the limo this morning. The staff at his hotel appeared to be well-versed in eccentric guests. Nobody at the front desk had lifted an eyebrow when he'd arrived and checked in at three a.m. Without luggage. They didn't look askance at his baggy denim pants and ill-fitting pullover when they gave him his room card. He didn't have another clothing option. It had been a long flight. He'd rested when he could. Showered. Found something to wear that belonged to one of the twins, whoever they were. Tane didn't know. He didn't care. Apparently the Icelandic twins were large vampires. They had him by a good two inches on height, and several inches in muscle. Didn't matter. He was clothed. He should have taken time to pack before he'd left, but hindsight was always 20/20.

He'd done what had to be done. Kat had been delivered to her camp. She hadn't felt the kiss he'd placed to her forehead. She hadn't noted that he left. Akron was right. It was akin to ripping out his heart. Tane's chest had turned into a huge pit of pain. The world had looked especially bleak. He'd actually gone back. Three times.

And somehow he'd existed through four days to get back to her. And she still wasn't here.

Where the heck could she be?

This was her show. She had to attend! New York was a labyrinth of steel, glass, concrete...and it teemed with humanity. If she didn't attend, how was he to find her? And...if he needed to do so, he wanted to start now! Not stand around, wasting time watching people as they socialized. Occasionally discussed a photograph. Sipped at their champagne. Nibbled on appetizers. Lifted their heads occasionally to laugh, showing off long, blood-filled throats.

Hmm.

Tane's fangs tingled at the thought. He sucked on them absently. Forced them back. Could something have happened to her? An accident? Humans were so fragile, even half-turned ones. His heart stopped. He took a deep breath to restart it. The back of his shirt pulled tight at the motion, demonstrating how closely the tailors had fit it, which was exactly what they'd wanted.

Nigel had booked their most expensive suite for Tane. Called an Inferno Suite. It took up the entire top floor of the hotel. That hadn't even created comment with the front desk, not until he walked around the corner, anyway. He heard the whispers. One of the night clerks had remarked how she sure wished she was "room service right about now because this guest needed his bed turned down," and the others had giggled.

Well. If his arrival created comment, the desk clerks had probably been agog over the appearance of four tailors from the Carlotti menswear firm being accompanied by one of the Carlotti owners, himself. They'd arrived at four a.m. On the dot. That was followed by hours of measurement taking, fabric swatch selection, evaluating and adjusting the length of creasing atop his shoe called break, and something he'd never heard of or considered. Balance. That was the term for the adjustment of front and back length on a jacket due to – in Tane's case – a supremely muscular physique. The tailors reminded him of bees in a hive. Busy. Constantly moving. While their boss watched and occasionally commented. Tane hadn't said anything. He'd been too busy controlling a flush... and his fangs. There had been a lot of sustenance before him. They had no idea how temping it was.

But that was before the salon firm arrived for him this evening. Just after the sun had gone down. Again. Courtesy of Nigel.

Men's grooming had certainly changed, as had the practitioners of the craft. Two women had been sent to his suite, along with two men. Neither man had acted in what

Tane considered a masculine manner. They'd be in trouble on his island, captured the moment they were seen, slated for sacrifice. Their expertise was evident, however. So, Tane had endured a pedicure, manicure, haircut, and styling, none of which would be in evidence when he next woke. He'd given silent thanks that due to his mother's heritage he didn't grow much body hair. Otherwise, he'd have been waxed with the heated preparation they'd set up. Somebody would have paid for that. With blood.

Hmm.

Katherine still hadn't arrived.

Tane absently lifted his arm to view his watch. The fabric about his bicep pinched at the movement. Formal menswear was tight and restrictive nowadays. This suit had been crafted to his exact frame. It was snug if he just stood in it. Extreme movement was going to rip something. And only four minutes had passed.

Patience, Tane…

Patience. Didn't that mean endurance? Tolerance? Lack of complaint while one waited for something? Well. Patience needed a new description! This wasn't serenity. It was gut-ripping frustration. Tane took a deep breath that held anger. The shirt gripped about him like bondage. And then something happened over at the entrance. The crowd had stirred, started moving that direction. Phones got lifted as people took pictures, got video. He saw a cadre of dark-clothed men. Large men. With a smaller person between them.

And his heart leapt.

Tane jumped down to the first floor. It was a drop of thirty feet or so. He didn't note if anyone saw it. He didn't care. He maneuvered his way through people. Tried not to react. Snarl. And worked especially hard to hold back an urge to shove.

But he couldn't get to her in time!

The group of bodyguards about her rushed through the

assemblage and into an elevator. Tane watched with red-colored vision as the door shut behind them. He didn't know how he reached the area, or who he moved out of his way. But he stood there, snarling at the chrome doors right as they closed. The crowd's reflection was visible all about him. And behind him. He didn't have an image. That was probably going to get noticed. But he didn't care about that, either. He was fighting a wave of emotion that demanded action. He yearned to smash his way through the elevator doors. He shook. His canines elongated. Something in his suit ripped as he lifted both fists.

"Yo. Buddy. You don't want to do that."

Tane regarded the elevator door. A young man in a black suit stood beside him. He had an earpiece in his ear. Carried weaponry beneath his coat. His reflection was clearly visible. A security guard. His presence meant attention. And Tane had been trying to avoid that very thing.

"I need to speak with the photographer."

"So does everybody else."

"No. I need to speak with her now."

"You need to calm down. Okay? We really don't want a situation tonight."

Tane looked up and glared at the ceiling far above him. Took deep breaths. Felt the back of his shirt tear further with each one. By the third one, the red haze had faded to pink. And his canines started retracting.

He lowered his head, turned, and locked gazes with the man. Waited until the guy's pupil's enlarged.

"Can you get me to her?"

"Well, I—"

"No, he can't."

Tane turned his head further. That had been quick. Now, he had three similarly-clothed gentlemen facing him. The crowd behind him was enlarging, too. He could enthrall all of them, but it would take time. And effort. And he just wanted to be with Katherine! It would be so easy to leap upward. Smash his way through the ceiling. He could find her. He knew he could. He'd just follow the echo of his heartbeat. But, that would be a mistake.

Katherine deserved a gentleman, not a savage.

Tane regarded the man who'd spoken in silence. Then he sighed. Tried to look non-threatening. Started acting like one of the male beauticians. Slightly effeminate. That felt even more foreign, akin to being an alien on a strange planet.

"I just want to see her for a moment. Surely, that's doable?"

"Maybe."

"Why don't you tell me? What would it take to get me in to see her?"

Somebody snickered. Tane ignored him.

"She'll be down eventually."

"I'm asking what it would take...now."

"You might try buying the entire exhibit," one of them said.

"How much?"

"One-point-eight million."

Tane reached for his wallet. Pulled out his card. Nigel said he had no limit. Guess Tane was about to find out.

"Who do I see?" he asked.

CHAPTER THIRTEEN

"THAT'S NOT ACCEPTABLE. IT CAN'T be booked. How many people can possibly be going to Guam next week? Check another flight! No. I will not hold again! Wait! Ah!"

Kat almost slammed the phone onto the table to vent the frustration. She was in the sitting area of the director's private apartment. He had a fortune in artwork on the walls. Some potted plants. Two over-stuffed leather sofas. Mirrors that didn't reflect her image with any clarity. Long drapes that covered a wall of windows. She gritted her teeth and walked about the room while horrid music wafted through her ear.

Why do companies use the most horrible music on the planet when they put you on hold?

So, you'll hang up, she answered herself.

She'd been trying all day to get a seat on the flight back to Pohnpei. And Tane. Because love was that special. It even transcended reality. She'd always thought physics ruled the universe. Well. Now she knew the truth. Love was the real power. And she'd found it. With Tane. She loved him. She needed to be with him. And she was not accepting that every seat was taken until Tuesday! She didn't care if it was a prime holiday week. That was three days from now! She wasn't waiting three days! She didn't want to wait three minutes! *Oh!* If she only had unlimited funds! She'd book a private flight. But she might get irritated enough to max her cards out and do it anyway.

'Thank you so much for holding. Your call is important to us. Please stay on the line—'

"Uh. Miss Clark?"

Kat welcomed the interruption from the recorded message, but not the interference. She looked over her shoulder at one of the guards they'd sent for her.

Her.

Katherine Clark.

She had bodyguards attending her. That was unreal, but it didn't really compete with the level of strangeness she embraced anymore. She knew she was acting erratic. Strange. Completely unlike herself. But there wasn't anybody she could confide in. Nobody who'd understand. They'd probably lock her up and toss the key if she tried to tell someone what had happened and how she felt. How do you explain that the love of your life is a vampire? Was there a level of insanity in the asylum for that?

She doubted it. So, she stayed silent about what had happened on the island. She didn't search out anybody, and nobody approached her. That would be tough tonight. She had eight bodyguards, all big, beefy guys. She'd been surprised when they'd arrived at her flat. She didn't think anybody needed this much security. Once they arrived at the gallery and she saw the crowds, however, she was grateful for them.

Until now.

"What is it?"

She tried to speak tactfully. Keep the acidity from her tone. She already told the sponsors she'd attend the show. And she would. Eventually. She just wanted her plane ticket booked first! Or she'd settle with being able to speak with someone who spoke English. She'd been on hold for so long already, she didn't dare disconnect. That's why she'd given instructions not to be disturbed. And what happened?

She got disturbed.

"There is a gentleman out here who wishes to speak with you."

"And you let him up here?"

"Well...he did just buy your entire exhibit."

Kat's mouth fell open.

"One-point-eight million. He just pulls out a credit card. Cool as you please. You wouldn't have believed it."

Oh, sweet heaven!

Her first thought was she didn't need the stupid commercial flight! Her finger clicked the disconnect button without looking. Her second thought was she didn't have to go meet anyone, either. The sponsors had their cut. She didn't have to schmooze with anyone. Ever.

"Is he...here now?"

"In the hall outside."

"Oh."

"Don't worry. We'll be at your side if you need us."

"Why would I need you?"

"This gent. We were told he was a bit...aggressive downstairs."

The bodyguard patted the revolver beneath his coat jacket to reassure her. She was very grateful to have him. And the rest of them. The emotion toward her unknown benefactor had started as a rush of gratefulness. It turned to wariness before she could prevent it.

"Um. Thank you."

Kat turned to the large mirror to check her appearance, before remembering it would just be a big blob. Earlier, she'd arranged her hair into a bun by feel. Now, she patted any stray hairs back as if she could see them. Retouched her lipstick. She used the time to brace herself. She didn't need more lipstick. It wouldn't even show. She'd chosen a nude shade tonight because of that. She couldn't tell where she painted it on...not exactly. She wore a black figure-skimming sheath. Flats. A string of real pearls. She just needed to get through the next few moments. Accept whatever praise he might utter. Say some words of thanks. And then she'd be off.

She started listing things.

First, she needed to find a private plane. Book her itinerary. She had enough credit on two cards to charge it. She could pay them both off when the transfer for the exhibit reached her bank. By then, she'd be well on her way back to Tane. In his arms. Close. Her eyes stung with tears at the beauty of the thought. She blinked rapidly. Everything felt like it was awakening within her as if water had just reached a parched flower. Her heart started pounding. Her breath shook.

Wait a minute.

Both her heartbeat and her breathing had an echo, while a sensation of warmth surrounded her like a soft blanket. He felt so near. And, oh! How she'd missed these sensations!

She heard words said in a conversationalist tone, as if the door was already open. She wasn't really listening, though.

"We didn't catch your name, sir."

"That's all right, gentlemen. She won't need it."

She recognized the voice! In seeming slow motion, they opened the door. Her bodyguards were all standing in the hall but her eyes went to the man leaning against the wall opposite her. Shock held her rooted. And everything stopped.

It was Tane, all right, but he looked unlike anything she'd seen or imagined. There wasn't a description for his range of handsomeness. His hair was cut and combed back. A tux had been fitted perfectly to him, highlighting a form that haunted her. And she must have forgotten the impact of looking at his neon blue eyes.

She was stunned. Close to swooning. Her legs wobbled warningly.

"Well?" he asked. And then he opened his arms.

"Tane!"

Kat launched at him and he caught her. Hard arms enfolded

her. Lifted and then held her to his chest. His lips met hers. All kinds of light filled the hall, coming from somewhere to envelop. Fireworks erupted all around them. Her heart swelled to bursting. Some of the bodyguards cleared throats.

"You...know this gentleman?"

One of her bodyguards asked it from behind her somewhere, bringing her back to reality. Tane had lifted from the kiss instantly. He moved his lips close to her ear.

"You will marry me. Yes?"

"Oh, yes!" she whispered back.

Tane lifted his head to look out at others. "The lady and I are affianced," he announced.

"Oh. Well. No wonder you were pissed."

Several men chuckled. Kat didn't care. She was in a whorl of wonder. A plateau of joy. She closed her eyes and leaned into Tane's chest, and listened to their hearts beating in tandem. His every breath matched hers as well.

She knew none of it was physically possible.

But it still happened.

"Uh...we were hired to protect the lady this evening."

"I have a limousine downstairs," Tane replied. "If you can get us there, I think you can consider it a job well done. We shall just...disappear."

Tane looked down at her. Winked. And that's exactly what happened.

~ ~ ~

"Well. Well. She disconnected from her call, Sir. She'd been holding forever to get a flight. I was monitoring it. You think that means...?" Nigel left the sentence open-ended.

"I believe that means Tane won't be available for assignments for a span. And we have a new associate. Before you shut down for the night, Nigel, we need to discuss something. Do you have a moment?"

Nigel turned from the monitor and looked over at Akron's

desk. The man wasn't sitting at it. He was standing in the shadows behind the desk. But that was normal.

"Sure. What have you got?"

"Remember when I said I'd have to do some manipulating of events in the near future...and I mentioned how you'd be grateful?"

"Yeah."

"Well. It concerns Paul Henry."

Nigel shot from the chair into the center of the room, smacking his head on a ceiling beam before he landed. "My grandson?"

"Do we know another Paul Henry?"

"What about him? Quick! Tell me! Now, you have me scared."

"Well...I don't know if I should interfere. It could be termed meddling."

"Akron! Please. What is it?"

"I need a decision. I can't get it from him. And we have about...oh. Thirty seconds."

"Yes! The answer is yes!"

"I haven't even posed the question yet, Nigel."

"Speak faster, then!"

"Would you rather have him dead? Or a vampire?"

"Dead?"

"Really? I would have guessed you'd want—"

"No! I don't want him dead. That was a question—never mind! We don't have time for this! Is he...?"

"His private plane has experienced a carbon monoxide leak. The pilots expired some time ago. The plane is on auto-pilot, so that hadn't been an issue...but now the gas has seeped into the cabin. Paul Henry has just lost consciousness. They will go down somewhere in the Indian Ocean. Unless I intercede, of course."

"Intercede, already!"

"He's not fond of us."

"I don't care! Make him a vampire!"

"He might blame you."

"I don't care! Vampire!"

"He could hate you for it, Nigel."

"I don't care! Vampire!"

"Are you certain?"

"Please? I'm begging you!"

"As long as you're certain."

"Akron!"

Akron Profit disappeared. Some words followed his departure as if he was still in the room. Nigel didn't know how the man communicated psychically, nor how he teleported. And right at the moment, it didn't matter. His throat had closed off with worry, and his eyes stung.

"You are such a Mother Hen, Nigel. We still have five seconds."

Nigel sagged to the floor, put his head in his hands, and barely kept from weeping. And that's where his mate, Mandy, found him.

ALLEVIATE

THE PORTALS OF TIME

JACKIE IVIE

CHAPTER ONE

"WELL. THAT'S ENOUGH SLACK TIME, intrepid explorers! Everyone ready? Gear stowed? Life jackets tight? Everyone have their game on?"

Elena smiled slightly at being called an intrepid explorer, just as she'd done the first time it happened. That had been days ago...at the lodge, where they'd been wined and dined and given all kinds of information. Along with a heavy dose of safety rules. That was the last time she'd had a drink. And she could sure use one. Her body was in revolt, but they didn't allow booze on this trip.

Or wine.

Or even beer.

Elena sighed in resignation and checked her life jacket again. Re-cinched all the straps. Waited her turn to load. The evening at the lodge felt like a dream. She hadn't paid much attention to all the rules and regulations at the time. No need. She'd pored over all the information for months now. She'd prepared. She'd even bought a special wardrobe from an outdoorsy outlet mall. She was going natural. She hadn't even packed her special mastectomy bra or the inserts. Besides, she'd known this trip was a dry one. That's why she'd booked it. That's also why she'd gotten a few doubles under her belt before retiring for the night.

She was going sober. Cold-turkey.

Nobody had noticed her inebriation level. Nobody seemed to pay much attention to her. And nobody had complained when she'd gone into the gift shop and dropped a large chunk of change on the counter for a little golden ring. The lady in the shop had been a Native American. Something about her had given Elena pause. The woman had some kind of mystical aura. Or the vodka in that lodge had something weird in it. The shop lady told Elena she was going into one of earth's most powerful places. She'd need this ring. It was her destiny to own it.

Elena regarded the spiral-shaped ring sitting on her middle finger right now. What a stupid purchase. She shouldn't have imbibed so much. But she used to say that every morning.

"Listen up, my intrepid explorers!"

There it was again. Intrepid explorers...

It was cute wording, but Rob, the lead boatman, was that. Then again, all of them were cute. Very cute. Every raft had five boatmen. All fit. Late twenties to maybe...forty. Nicely muscled. Like a small army of beefcake, displayed in identical khaki-colored uniforms. Looking sharp. The first day, she'd picked out her favorite - Mike. He had the longest hair, although he kept it pulled back and tucked beneath his collar. He also had the most tattoos. She'd joined his boat with alacrity. Days into this excursion and her choice hadn't changed. He was very cute. But he was married. Told everyone he had a really cute wife and two cuter kids back in Glen Canyon. Elena hadn't even asked.

Rob started speaking again. He had a voice like a bullhorn. He used it efficiently. The words had a distinct echo as they bounced off the canyon walls.

"Today is the day! We're going through Cataract Canyon! That means we've got some major rapids on the menu! This is the section with the big, dangerous drops. We spoke of them. Everybody remember?"

Mister Smyth opened the map card he'd zipped into a plastic bag and pointed it out to his wife without saying anything.

That was a blessing. The Smyths had told everyone they were on their anniversary trip. The first night out here the groups had gathered around the campfires. Shared stories. Elena hadn't offered much, but they all knew she was a paralegal. And they knew she was single. Which got her an interested look from Marv, the chubby accountant from New Mexico somewhere, and a couple of stupid come-on lines from the Utahan Ronald, who might be in excellent shape but looked old enough to be her father, if not her grandfather.

Well.

It looked like her ex-husband, Don, was wrong about one thing. There were other men who would want her. Even without breasts. Elena had been married to her college sweetheart, a football receiver with looks to match his physique. He'd been gorgeous. Ripped. The first two years of marriage had been absolute fun. They'd had a great sex life.

Too bad that hadn't been enough...

Wow.

Elena swiped at what could be a tear if she allowed it existence. She could sure use a drink. Of something besides the constant stream of water the boatmen kept on hand. They didn't use bottled water. They had a supply of special filters that supposedly made any water drinkable. She'd been given one at the lodge meeting - it was in the welcome packet - but she'd already bought one. It might make the water drinkable, but it sure didn't make it vodka.

What was she mooning over the divorce for, anyway? She didn't even know any happily married couples. Her boss avoided his spouse, and required her help with it. The senior lawyer in the firm had a collection of 'girlfriends' his wife didn't know about. The Smyths were just another example. They might smile happily if anyone was looking, but it was a farce. She'd rarely heard more scathing tones and words than when they spoke to each other if they didn't think anyone was listening.

"Today we're going to go through a hydraulic called Satan's Gut! That section is aptly named! It will get your heart pumping! That's a guarantee, ladies and gentlemen!"

The boat rocked side-to-side as Elena reached her assigned seat. She swiveled and wedged her butt into the spot, trying to look smaller. She might have lost some weight on this trip, but not much. They'd put in the brochure that physical fitness was of prime importance. Well. She hadn't considered herself unfit. She always hiked the stairs at her office building. Walked everywhere. Everyone in New York did. But she still carried a few extra pounds left over from the rounds of chemo. And they really counted negatively on this trip.

Rob wasn't finished. He kept up the diatribe as the boats loaded. It was part of the package. The boatmen got the camp site cleaned up and everything stowed quickly while breakfast was cooked. They got everyone fed. Prepared for the day's ride. Geared-up with safety equipment. Loaded into boats. And it was all accompanied by a lot of words to pump up the enthusiasm.

Rob would have made a great football coach.

"But this is why you booked this trip, isn't it? The excitement and danger lurking around every corner! Isn't that right?"

Most of the boaters agreed. Elena snickered. She hadn't booked this trip for the excitement or the danger. She hated the holiday season. It meant loss. Depression. First she'd lost her still-birthed daughter, then her boobs with the double mastectomy. And then she'd lost her hubby. She'd come on this trip because she was escaping Christmas...just like she did every year. Only this time she wasn't using a bottle.

She needed a break from snow and cheer and merriment and twinkling lights and decorated trees and gingerbread smells and office parties and...

Crap.

There was too much to list. Every moment of each day was filled with somebody trying to make sure nobody forgot it was the holiday season. Time to celebrate! Be of good cheer! Gather with your loved ones! Exchange presents!

A river rafting trip down the Grand Canyon in Arizona was the farthest thing she could come up with. And so far, it just might be working.

The boats shoved off. She was in the last one. On purpose. Elena wasn't adventurous. She didn't want to be the first. Then again, nothing about the morning looked dangerous. Or exciting. There seemed to be a slight current in the center of the river. It bobbed them about placidly for nearly an hour. And then things started changing. Mike and the other boatmen put their paddles in the water and fought progress, as they slowed up. It was to get distance between the boats. They needed room in the event of a problem, so one boat in trouble wouldn't become two of them. Elena remembered that from the talk.

She could hear the upcoming rapids before they came into sight. Sounded like a big waterfall. Then a huge one. And then it sounded like they had dozens of them. The canyon narrowed next, the tops of cliffs reaching toward each other overhead, darkening the area. Elena started subconsciously tensing muscles as the roaring sound got louder. And louder. The boat started bobbing, as if in concert. Her heartbeat quickened. Her throat tightened when she swallowed. But then she didn't need that. Her mouth went dry.

Well ahead of them, the canyon curved. Elena squinted to see the lead boat go around it. And then they all heard a lot of yelling. The second boat disappeared around the bend, with another burst of sound. Elena's eyes widened and her hands gripped to the ropes along the side as she got her first look at Rob's version of excitement and danger.

Holy shit!

The water had turned into a live thing as if giant turbines had been slammed into the river. The front of the boat dipped nastily, sending her skyward. Then the front launched upward, soared several moments above the water before slamming back into the river with a stomach-dropping thud. Water shot up and over everyone, drenching. Frightening. The front dipped again. Elena's tightened her knees in a crouch, as if that would keep her secured in place.

"Isn't this cool?!"

Cool?

Someone yelled it. Elena guessed it was Marv. She'd smack him later. Right now she had to hang on tightly as the boat jerked to one side and then the front rocketed into the air again. The ridges in the seat weren't too tight after all. Elena's butt slid right out. She slammed against something in the bottom. Took a moment to realize it was a cooler that was also lunging against its restraints. The ropes burned her palms as she slipped. Her arms strained. She tried not to panic. According to the report of one fatality on the river, there is a tendency to panic if you fell overboard, to hyperventilate, and all that only made the likelihood of hypothermia greater. A person could slip into unconsciousness within moments.

The boat rocked and gyrated about her. Over and over again. Elena squatted in place beside the cooler. Getting drenched. Feeling seasick. And watching the world go crazy. Soaring rock face cliffs meshed with sky. White foam filled the view before it splashed over them. And even if they hadn't wanted to proceed, the water forced it. There was no way out.

And then everything went calmer. Mike gave a huge whoop. It was followed by his men.

"We made the first Big Drop!"

A chorus of cheers came from the others in the boat. Not Elena. Even if she'd wanted to celebrate, her throat was too tight.

"And we've got Satan's Gut just ahead! Everybody ready?"

Oh.

Hell no.

Nothing changed for long moments. The boat rocked side to side, each one getting wilder, as it slid along the water. Elena turned forward. Peeked ahead. Watched with shock as the back of the second boat lifted well above the waterline. And then it disappeared! She didn't realize what had happened until the boat she was in started moving quicker. Pulled forward by the current. Toward a ledge. It looked like the water just ended as they approached what couldn't be...

Oh! My God!

It was a waterfall, the drop beyond comprehension. Elena was hyperventilating as the front of their boat went out into space, and then dropped forward as if in slow motion. The rear went perpendicular next. Elena screamed as her body jettisoned out from the boat, leaving her hanging by her handhold. The boat slid into a precipice of doom, taking everyone in it.

Elena screamed. She was actually watching as the cooler swung outward from its mooring, and then came right back at her. The boat slammed into the vortex of water called Satan's Gut. The cooler barely missed her head. And she lost hold.

It wouldn't have mattered.

The boat was upside down. Everyone had been ejected. The stupid warnings in the paperwork hadn't been succinct enough. They were right about an involuntary gasp. Elena did that as she entered the water. That added a lungful of water. That sensation combined with an instant dunking in freezing water caused an instant need to hyperventilate some more. All of that had been covered. But nothing had been mentioned about a rainbow of color that seemed to swell up from the bottom of the river and start swirling around her. Nor was anything said about weird shards of crystal. They permeated the rainbow, glinting with all manner and variation of light.

She should be flailing, her arms pushing at the water, her legs churning her toward the surface. None of that happened. Because nobody had said a word about how warm and comforting losing consciousness would feel.

CHAPTER TWO

1790

"**WE'VE BEEN OUT HERE FOR** hours! Listen to reason! There's nothing to find. No treasure! And no one you need to save!"

"Not! Yet!"

Morrigan yelled the response, breaking it into two words due to the storm's intensity. The speaker had been Cedric. The man had a wealth of breath available to him, mainly because he stood atop the oaken keel, running the center of the boat. The man didn't work an oar. He spent his energy directing. Yelling. That's what came of being born to the village leader.

Cedric's words were wasted. Everyone knew it was a bad night to be out. Nobody needed the reminder. Bone-chilling waves washed over the boat edge with unfailing frequency, drenching every rower. Especially those in the front row. Where Morrigan sat.

Cedric had a booming voice. They could hear his next taunt even over the maelstrom. "Then mayhap you should not sit about like newly-birthed babes! Put your backs into it this time! Heave!"

Christ.

Cedric was an ass. Ill-equipped as a leader. Morrigan itched to challenge him despite it being a mistake. He'd joined this village three months past because it was isolated. Primitive. Easy to disappear in, while his brother's men searched. He didn't plan on staying.

"Heave again, you wastrels!"

The taunt added impetus to Morrigan's motions. Warmth to his exposed hands. Power to his movements. He pulled at his oar with a gesture that bumped his shoulders into the man beside him before lifting the wood, swinging it backward. Dropping the end back into the water and pulling again. Morrigan was one of the largest men in the boat, probably the strongest. Cedric's words added unnecessary impetus. Morrigan's side of the skiff reacted with his strokes, shuddering slightly as it sent the bow against a riot of seawater.

"This is your doing, Morrigan!"

Morrigan shoved the oar into the water again. Ground his teeth. Yes. It was his doing. They were out here because of him. He still wasn't giving up and going in. Not yet. He knew the odds of finding anything diminished with every second that passed. But something kept nagging at him. Despite the temperature, how difficult it was to see, and the chunks of debris that filled the ocean waves, making progress even more hazardous.

Gut instinct drove him.

He was following it.

There had been a big ship out here. He'd been the lone one to spot it from shore before the sun gave up trying to break through clouds and had disappeared altogether. The ship had hit Satan's Reef. That's how Morrigan had gotten all these men out here. Looking. Pointing. Arguing. There shouldn't have even been a discussion. The ship had been a Spanish Galleon. Unaccompanied. And vulnerable. It was a supreme stroke of luck. Those ships rarely came this far north and never this late in the season.

Then again, it had been a season wracked by storms...

The villagers hadn't been difficult to convince. This was a Spanish Galleon on the brink of sinking. The salvage could be astronomical. Those ships came from the New World. They were filled with treasure. This could make everyone rich. But that had been before a series of explosions had lit up the sky, blasting the ship apart. If anyone had survived that, it would be a miracle. Still, Morrigan wasn't going back in until he was certain. Some cargo might have survived the blast and could still be awash. He'd already argued with Cedric over it. That exchange felt like it had happened hours ago.

"This is foolish? We are all going to die!"

Cedric's complaint was actually heard over the storm. Morrigan considered them as he worked his oar. Sounded like he might need to speak again. Perhaps threaten. But just then something smacked into the wood beside him with a jolt that nearly unseated him. Morrigan released his oar, leapt it, and grabbed a long grappling hook to send it over the side. He barely missed hitting other rowers' fur-covered heads. They all wore furs. Dark with moisture now. He fished about vainly until somebody assisted by lifting a lantern. The flame struggled for life behind glass panels. It wasn't much help. The light barely illuminated. The seas were rougher than he'd imagined. The waves flecked with foam. Filled with boat-damaging debris, and...

Wait!

There was a mass of netting in the water beside the skiff. Amidst it, Morrigan could plainly see the rounded top of an ornate trunk. Metal embossing glimmered as flickers of light reached it. Morrigan's next lunge with the hook speared the net. He yanked, bringing the trunk close and another trunk became into view. A third one trailed it. A fourth. The edges of even more containers were visible as far as he could see. They were all entangled in the netting. Morrigan would have grinned if the temperature of air wouldn't have iced his teeth painfully.

"What is it? What have we got?"

Someone yelled the question. Someone else answered it. "Treasure!"

A cheer went up. The burst of excitement gave Morrigan strength. It took mere moments to get the first container close, snag a side handle with one hand, and yank it up and onto the deck. He hadn't even needed help. He flung the grappling hook down onto the deck and started hauling at the net. The next trunk came near. Knocked against the side of their skiff. Morrigan dropped the net and reached for it, but the entire boat dipped that direction, plunging his arms and chest into freezing water, while swamping his lower legs as seawater gushed over the side.

"Everyone! Get back! You fools! You want to sink us, too?"

Cedric yelled it. Good thing he possessed such a large voice. The skiff re-righted with a shudder as his orders were obeyed.

"Shove that trunk to the middle! You! And you! Start bailing!"

Morrigan heard the sound of the first trunk sliding across wood as he grabbed for the second one. This one was larger. Heavier. He had to use both arms. He grunted loudly as he heaved. The trunk made a thudding sound as it landed behind him. He heard them sliding it away, too.

"How many are there?" someone asked.

"Six!"

Someone answered. Morrigan pulled on the net again. One of the oarsmen from this side of the boat was at his shoulder, assisting. That fellow pulled the third trunk aboard. Morrigan snagged the fourth.

"Nae! Seven!"

"More!"

"Oh. Holy Mary, Mother of God."

Morrigan didn't know who said it, their voice reflecting shock and reverence. It sounded like a prayer. Or homage.

"Balance the weight! Shove them in the center. Move your

arses!"

Cedric was still spouting directions. Someone spoke up.

"We cannot take many more aboard!"

"Well! We are not leaving any!"

Cedric yelled it. Morrigan's shoulders ached. The muscles in his belly burned with effort. His teeth were gritted tightly together. The trunks kept getting heavier and larger. A third man was assisting now, his weight at the side counter-balanced by the trunks already aboard.

"We may...need to head...for shore!" Morrigan's announcement was broken into thirds due to lack of breath. It was a chore to yell, but he had to shout to be heard above the elements.

"And leave a bounty? Are you crazed?" Cedric yelled back at him.

"We can...tow them!"

"Oh! Right! Hook the net, lads! We'll start for home!"

Morrigan watched the length of sodden rope slide away. Several men wrapped it about the mast, securing it. The net settled atop a mass of trunks in the center of their boat, molding and defining them. He wasn't the lone man looking. Morrigan nearly whistled in disbelief. The trunks hadn't been heavy enough to contain silver, but they might contain all sorts of marketable goods. Merchandise.

But his gut was still giving him trouble. That was odd. They had a good haul. And that's why he was out here.

Wasn't it?

Exhaustion hit without a shred of warning. With it, the elements. He was wet. Cold. And shaky. Morrigan sagged onto his knees before his legs dropped him.

"Come on, boys! Row for home! Everyone! Back in your places! Morrigan? What are you doing? Get to your oar!"

A muddled cry stopped any answer.

"*Madre de Dios! Ayuda! Ayuda!*"

"Wait! There's somebody out there!"

One of the men pointed. Morrigan looked. There truly was someone out there. Hooked in the net. Waving an arm.

They had a survivor?

Strength instantly returned. He didn't even wonder at it. Morrigan stood and started hauling at the cargo netting again.

"Ayuda!"

"Who speaks Spanish? Anyone? What does he say?" Cedric demanded.

"I think he says 'Help'! That's Spanish for help!"

Morrigan didn't need the translation. He recognized the plea by the man's tone. It was definitely a man. Thin. Dark-skinned. He clung to a trunk edge. Morrigan grabbed for his collar and pulled.

"No! No!" The fellow shimmied out of his grasp, fighting removal.

"Come...aboard!"

"No! Es mi amante! Es me amante! Por favor!"

The fellow was spouting gibberish. Morrigan reached for him again. The man pulled farther away.

"Will someone translate...while I can still feel my arms?" Morrigan shouted.

"He says he can't leave without his mistress. Says she is attached to him. With a rope!"

The poor man had a corpse attached to him?

"I'll get him free. Tell him."

And if he could feel his fingers, he'd have done it already. Morrigan pulled out his dagger. The fellow moved back again, screaming more words.

"Now, what is the problem?" Cedric yelled.

"He says his mistress needs help! These are her belongings."

"Not anymore, they're not! They're ours!"

Cedric's announcement was met with a disjointed shout of approval. Then some cheering. The interpreter spoke again.

The survivor was spouting more words, in an even quicker fashion.

"No! Wait! He says she spoke just moments ago. She is not dead. He begs us."

"Cut the bastard loose!" Cedric ordered.

Morrigan didn't waste another moment. He dove outward, grabbed the fellow's shoulders and twisted them, breaking the fellow's grasp on the trunk. Someone had snagged Morrigan's legs as he lunged. He was hauled back into the boat, dragging the man, a lot of water, and even more netting. He groaned as he hit the deck. The surface was hard. Unforgiving. Hitting it hurt worse because cold was seeping into every experience. The man definitely had something about him. It started dragging him back toward the sea. Morrigan struggled to his feet, grabbed the rope about the fellow's waist, and started pulling.

Whatever was attached to the man was heavy.

Morrigan slid. His body smacked against the side of the boat. It took every ounce of strength to continue. Not one man came to his aid. The rope slid more than once, burning his palms as if it fought him. A mass of hair came into view finally, resembling seaweed. The body was face-down. Morrigan flung the rope down and jumped atop it, preventing it from moving. All so he could reach out. Grab a shoulder. Roll her over. Even in the feeble light of their lantern he could tell it was a woman. She was a beauty. And she wasn't breathing.

He looked back over his shoulder at the others. "Tell the poor man, it's useless. She's dead."

And that's when the bolt of lightning hit them.

CHAPTER THREE

BRILLIANT LIGHT FILLED HER VISION. Elena watched it in wonder. It was imbued with color as if a watercolorist was at work, using every shade in the paint box. A thunderous boom filled her ears on the heels of the light, sounding as if the drummer was right behind her with a megaphone. Her body should have jerked involuntarily.

It didn't.

Shock held her spellbound. Awe kept her entranced. The world still spun uncontrollably, but it had turned into a kaleidoscope of color and light and sound. But then it changed. Something about her waist started tightening, cinching her nearly in half. The spiral about her slowed, the colors turned into strips of light. Elena started sliding downward, going ever quicker, as if caught in an immense water slide without a hint of definition. It got darker. The colors faded to a charcoal shade. And it was filled with what sounded like a squeal of rusted equipment. Her heart turned into a pounding entity in her chest. A huge knot lodged in her throat. Each breath was a chore, and her pulse moved as rapidly as an operatic aria.

And then the thing that had held her evaporated, dumping her body into ice-water.

If she had breath, Elena would have screamed. Freezing water encased her, sending liquid pain. Water filled her mouth. She inhaled and choked. Tried to breathe, but coughed. A sodden mass encased her limbs. Struggling only made it tighter. Everything hurt. But the restriction about her waist was the worst. It felt like she'd been grabbed by a vise and it kept ratcheting tighter.

And tighter...

"Listen! She breathes!"

The speaker sounded like he'd spent too many hours screaming at a rock concert. He also spoke with an odd accent. That was weird. To her knowledge, nobody on the river rafting tour was a foreigner.

"Someone help me!"

The hoarse voice yelled words again. She was gripped about the shoulders, relieving some of the pressure about her waist. The relief was instantaneous. She really needed to open her eyes. Get her brain in gear. Figure this out.

"Wait!"

Another foreign-sounding voice shouted the word. The reason for his volume was obvious. She could barely hear him above a huge whining sound. That was odd. It didn't sound remotely like the waterfalls in Cataract Canyon somewhere in the Grand Canyon of Arizona.

Wow.

This was worse than waking up to bright sunlight.

Without a drink.

Her eyelids were leaden. Her joints locked. Her muscles were active, but they weren't under her control. Every limb was experiencing uncontrollable spasms. She might as well have fallen through a skating pond in Upstate New York. Cold permeated everything. Elena had her teeth clenched tightly to keep them from chattering. While all around her a storm raged. And men argued.

No.

She was losing her mind.

That had to be the sound of the boatmen calling out. They yelled because they needed to be heard over the Colorado River as it turned into waterfalls. Smashed against obstacles.

It could be the sound of their boat as it got ripped apart by churning water. Might even be noise from the area of river she'd fallen into – appropriately called Satan's Gut. Perhaps, if she were supremely lucky, that was what river water sounded like as it smashed against the sides of a canyon. If she could just reach it, she'd be safe. Able to get out of the wet. Dry off in the sun. Get warm. Somewhere there had to be warmth.

"No! You wait!"

The hoarse man yelled it. He sounded closer. So did the other guy when he answered. And if the freezing sensation that was sucking at her life force would just back off a little, she could figure this out. Decipher things. Ready a strategy.

"Let her go! Now!"

The other voice was difficult to understand, as if English wasn't his first language...or even his second. He sounded commanding, though. She recognized that even as his words filtered through. Surely, he didn't mean her?

"No!"

"This is not her treasure! It's ours!"

She heard a yell. Followed by a shriek. A huge swell of water washed over her again. Elena choked. Sputtered. Something smacked into her. And then it was gone.

"What have...you done?"

"It is not his treasure, either!"

Elena got yanked upward, despite how the water sucked at her, unwilling to release its hold. The instant sensation of air was actually worse. It wrapped her in a blanket of frost. Freezing cold infiltrated her frame. Found every inch of skin. Elena moaned as she slammed into a solid mass. That hurt, too.

"Cedric!"

"What is one less Spaniard to the world?"

The pressure about her waist was back worse than before. She needed to get her eyes open. Guzzle down a really stiff drink. *No.* Two of them. She wished she'd never come on this trip! She'd rather deal with holiday crap. So, she had to deal with depression. Loss. Apathy for Donald, the ex-husband... and by extension, men in general. So what? At least all of that was normal.

On that thought, her eyelids finally worked. Elena forced her eyes open. Glanced upward. And if she hadn't had her teeth clenched, her jaw would have dropped.

Oh.

No way.

It was a movie version of the Norse god, Thor. The guy was large. Long-haired. Blonde. Had a scruff of beard. And he was absolutely gorgeous. His left arm had her pinned to his side. And everything felt a lot warmer all of a sudden.

"Put down your blade, Cedric."

Elena turned her head to see who Thor addressed.

Wow.

This was like watching a play. Her man had a long knife in his other hand. Light glinted off steel as he brought it upward, slicing through what looked like a thick rope. It took a second to recognize that one end was tied about her waist, while the other end slithered out of sight over what looked like a balcony edge. The instant easing of the vice-like pressure was pure heaven. She'd have thanked Thor, but he wasn't paying any attention to her. He was facing an adversary, the knife now out between them.

Hmm.

If Cedric was the man facing them, the poor guy was seriously outgunned. Even dressed in a fur hat, with another animal hide over his shoulders, he looked diminutive. But it was hard to be certain. The scene was chaotic, poorly illuminated, and constantly moving. The floor rocked upward with huge surges, before dropping with a sickening motion. Thor must be as strong as he looked and felt. They swayed back and forth with the movement, but otherwise, didn't shift much. She didn't know for certain, but it really looked like...

Now, wait just a minute here.

She was aboard a ship?

Out in the ocean?

In a storm?

As incomprehensible as it seemed, listing things didn't change anything. The world outside the immediate vicinity was a boiling mass of water. Heaving waves. A lot of darkness...

It was night, too?

This wasn't possible. None of it.

"You challenge me, Morrigan, and you're no longer welcome in my village."

Ah. Her man had a name. Morrigan. *Hmm. Nice.*

"If I challenge you...you're a dead man," Morrigan replied.

Wow. That was a great line. It gave her goose bumps. This was quite the dream. She was locked into something resembling a historical movie. She couldn't tell the era. Clothing wasn't helpful. Everyone wore fur. There were a lot of actors on the set, most sitting on long benches in rows. One guy stood atop a ledge, holding a lantern aloft. Another stood in the back holding what appeared to be a big drum. The rest of the men rested muscled arms onto long oars as if re-enacting a Viking scene.

Was she dreaming of Vikings?

Could be.

The men all watched the *tableau* without interfering... except for one guy. He was beside Cedric. He looked even smaller than Cedric. And then both men started dancing back and forth, as though compensating for the waves.

No. That's wrong, Elena.

They weren't dancing. They were grappling. And yelling in that hard-to-understand English. Both had long knives out. This was insane.

"Cease this, Cedric!"

"I will kill you, too!"

"Who will translate...then?"

"It's a woman. Who cares what she says?"

Oh. She had historically-accurate misogynists to deal with, too?

Elena narrowed her eyes. Watched the battle. Silently rooted for the translator fellow. Hated it when Cedric flung the other man off. The fellow crumpled to the deck. Dark water in the bottom sloshed against him. Cedric stepped over the body.

This was an incredibly realistic movie set. Fraught with intensity. Imminent danger. The set designers were fantastic. She could swear she was aboard a boat, a large boat. Seventy foot yacht-size. It was the dark of night. A hurricane-strength storm swirled about them.

And these two males were about to have a knife fight?

She hadn't seen this much overacting since she'd watched her grandmother's soap operas. The translator fellow was even starting to stir. Get to his knees. He didn't know enough to stay dead until the scene was over?

Elena snorted. Cedric couldn't have heard it. Morrigan looked down at her. A surge of fire rocketed through her as their glances touched. He turned back to the smaller man while she tried to absorb all kinds of sensory signals.

Holy crap.

That was amazing. Morrigan was the sexiest thing she'd ever envisioned. He sent vibes that scorched. His look sent a solid sensation of warmth, heating her through sodden layers of...

Stop the action for a second here. She needed to check wardrobe. What on earth was she wearing?

Elena lifted an arm. It was covered in some strange shiny fabric, impossible to tell color in this light and with the amount of saturation. Whatever it was, the material molded to her like a clammy outer shell. Water sluiced off of it in rivulets. And there was something more. Tendrils of dark hair clung to her arm. Long hair. She could feel it pulling at her scalp as she moved. She had hair again, too?

Wait.

Did that mean she also had...?

Elena looked down. She definitely had breasts! Large ones! They rose and fell with each breath.

Oh! This was an awesome dream!

"Well, Cedric? What's it to be?"

Morrigan slashed the air with his blade, grabbing her attention as he restarted the scene. The ship rocked up and down. Cedric skidded and pranced to one side. Returned. She and Morrigan had barely moved. It occurred to her then that Morrigan's words were easy to understand. Even with his accent. It was a really cute accent. She'd heard it before. In other movies, maybe. It could be Scottish.

Cedric pranced sideways again. Returned to face Morrigan. Went the other direction. That was really funny. Elena caught the smile, but didn't quite stifle the chortle. Morrigan's arm hardened about her, sending more heat. A lot more sparks. And all kinds of sensation that stopped every hint of amusement.

"What...should it be?"

Cedric managed to stay in one place long enough to spit the words at Morrigan. The light hit his face. The casting director had done a great job with the villain. He looked about twenty-five. He was a ginger, his hair as red as his beard. A snarl contorted his face. And he was missing two front teeth. Elena only got a moment's look before he was on the move again, stumbling sideways as the ship continued rocking.

Morrigan waited for the man to return before he answered. And that's when she nailed his accent. He had a really thick Irish accent. And it was very cute.

"You're their leader. Cease this."

Cedric was the leader? Oh. No. No. What group of men would follow him? Somebody needed to rewrite this entire scene.

"Aye! That I am!"

Cedric slashed at the air with his long knife. It looked pitifully weak against Morrigan. Elena watched in surprise as Morrigan lowered his weapon.

"Start the drummer. Head for shore."

'No! Take his head off!' Elena inserted silently.

Cedric went dancing off again. Swooped right past them with his return. It took two or three motions before he stood before Morrigan again. Most audiences would have burst into laughter. Elena glanced up at Morrigan. Back to Cedric. Chewed on her lower lip.

"The woman...comes with me!" Cedric shouted.

'Oh. Hell, no.' Elena replied in her head.

"No." Morrigan stated it without inflection and then he added words that sent another dose of warmth through her entire side. "The woman stays here. Beside me."

"She'll freeze."

'I already am, Cedric. Duh.' Elena continued adding silently to the script.

"I will handle the woman. You go handle the beat."

"This is not finished!"

"Go. Get us to shore."

'Yeah. Go do that, Cedric. Make yourself useful.'

Cedric glared at Morrigan for a second before the ship motion sent him stumbling away. He didn't return this time. Elena watched him make his way to the back of the ship until he reached the drummer-guy.

"Here, lass."

Morrigan released his arm from about her. Her attire gave an audible thump as it hit the stage.

Crap. Her outfit weighed a ton.

Elena instantly grabbed onto his fur covering, receiving a

handful of water from it. Morrigan sheathed his knife. Gave a heavy sigh. It lifted the fur she held. And then he slid the robe off his shoulders, turned to her, and wrapped it about her. It took time for the folds of frozen material about her to thaw. But it happened. Elena's eyes actually filled with tears at the sensation of warmth. Comfort. Security.

But, she couldn't take his covering.

Before she voiced it, Morrigan lifted her, took two rocking steps, and then dropped to a knee. He set her down and pushed. Elena scooted back, stopped as her back met the indentation of the ship's bow. She bent her knees, pulling her lower legs into the warmth with her. Something solid smacked her ankle. She winced and rubbed at it. She knew they used to weigh skirts to keep hems from flying up, but this was ridiculous.

Elena snuggled further into the fur. His cloak almost completely covered her. She was fine. She even had a ridge above her head, protecting her from spray that jetted over the bow. She could see it.

But she could also see he was getting saturated. She started pulling the fur off. He stopped her motion with a hand atop hers. Elena's heart dropped. She stilled as all kinds of sensations suffused her entire body.

Oh. This was bad.

She didn't dare feel anything. Not for a fictional character.

"You cannot understand me, but you need to be quiet." He made the universal sign for silence, a forefinger atop his lips. Elena nodded. "Do not fear. I will protect you. You have my word."

A drumbeat started up. She watched with wide eyes as he stood. He wasn't dressed for the elements. He wore a white shirt. Dark trousers. A heavy-looking jacket. None of it disguised him. She'd been dead-on about his physique. He was really well-built. Strong. And handsome enough to send any female's heart racing. She shouldn't feel annoyed that it happened to hers.

She watched him take a step, swivel, and sink onto a bench. He reached for an oar. He had a partner. The man was smaller. *Hmm.*

He had his back to her, and that showcased some really wide shoulders. Nice arms and back. Muscles got delineated as he pulled at the oar. Lifted it. Pushed forward. Pulled back again. She could feel the boat's movement beneath her. Hear the drum cadence. Smell the fresh ocean water. But the view was really incredible.

She'd been so wrong.

Whoever had written this script needed a raise.

CHAPTER FOUR

GUT INSTINCT HAD RARELY FAILED him to this extent. Nor this quickly.

Morrigan worked the oar, feeling the wood shift rhythmically in its oarlock beside him, while everything else diminished in importance. Even the elements. The storm was still raging, sleet hitting his back. Shoulders. Arms. Moisture plastered his hair to his head and neck. He disregarded it. All of it. His vision never wandered from Cedric, but his mind was a whorl of thought. This foray into the ocean changed things. It was time to leave. He had to. Cedric wouldn't survive another confrontation.

Morrigan had hoped to stay hidden until spring. Approach his maternal uncle then for help. He'd already sent two missives, one when he'd fled his ancestral home. The other he'd snuck out with a visiting priest. Neither had been answered. That didn't mean his uncle wouldn't assist him. Grant him enough men he could return to KilCreig Castle. Clear his name. Claim his inheritance.

First though, he had to get through the next few hours.

Morrigan's face was set in a frown. His gut churned. That emotion transferred to strength. His oar shove lifted his partner more than once. The man had glanced toward him each time. Morrigan ignored him, keeping his gaze on Cedric. His oar-partner hadn't looked at him for long.

The man didn't know Morrigan. Nobody in the village did. He had his reasons for not accepting Cedric's challenges.

None of them were any more palatable than the last time he'd considered them.

Anyone removing Cedric from this earth needed to take over as village chieftain or select a replacement. No other man seemed capable, and none appeared willing. The situation with the woman was further proof. The only man who'd tried to help had been the translator, and he'd proven too weak. The man was rowing now near the mast, his head bowed, his face averted, but at least he'd tried. The rest of them had been silent. Inactive. Passive.

Cedric might be arrogant and cocky, but he was the son of the prior chieftain. He had right of blood on his side. He possessed some leadership ability. He must. The entire village had enough wood cut for their fires. Meat had been butchered and salted. Grains and vegetables gathered and stored. Nobody went without.

Cedric was also a family man. He claimed more than one wife, multiple daughters, and three young sons. Another babe was due any day. Taking his life made widows out of his women, and orphaned his children.

Morrigan didn't have much choice. But it still irked.

Sneaking away was a poor option, but the best one. He'd need a diversion but some things were already on his side. It was night. They were all tired. No one would expect it. Everyone in the village, even those waiting onshore, should be occupied with offloading the bounty they'd brought from the shipwreck. He wouldn't participate. He'd slip away. Get to his croft. Gather foodstuffs. Pack enough to survive. Only the desperate traveled during the winter months, but snows hadn't come yet. He had a strong horse. He could be on his way toward KilCreig Castle before anyone noticed his absence. With luck, he'd reach it within a sennight. Mayhap sooner.

Except that now he had to do it with a woman. Worse

still, she was a foreign woman. He already knew she couldn't understand him. Chances she'd obey quietly were dismal.

Maybe he should stay. Help transfer the trunks to shore. At least see what they contained. Take his share. He needed funds to pay for an army. That alone was worth stifling any urge to respond if Cedric challenged him again. For that to happen, he needed to get the woman to his croft first. Stoke the fire. Find her something to wear while her attire dried...

At the thought, Morrigan pulled the oar with a hard yank that unseated his bench-mate again. The fellow grunted something that sounded like irritation. He didn't voice it, despite the time Morrigan gave him. The man turned away finally, continued rowing. Morrigan went back to considering things.

Keeping the woman was fraught with complication. Something had happened out there when he'd pulled her from the sea. Something...unreal. Her nearness affected him. Direct contact went beyond his experience. It sent a strange sensation – like little sparks shooting through every limb. He'd experienced them as he'd held her, dripping wet and shaking. Nothing had abated, either. He could swear he felt the same thing now...and she wasn't even in sight.

All women were trouble.

This one was worse.

It started with her comeliness. He'd been around many lovely women, all self-absorbed and vain. Few compared with this woman, however. Even bedraggled from a near-drowning, her beauty was obvious. She had a mass of dark hair. Riveting dark eyes surrounded by lush lashes. Unblemished, pristine skin. She also possessed womanly curves. Impressive ones. Morrigan hadn't given her his fur simply to protect her from the elements. He had to cover up a large bosom, a tiny waist, and all kinds of other allures that kept snagging his attention.

He shook his head at the madness of this. Concentrated for

a moment on pulling the oar. Lifting it. Pushing it forward. Dropping it into the water. It didn't help.

Readying this woman for travel would test a saint. Even if she understood, she'd probably argue. Loudly. Noblewomen usually did. He didn't know her exact status, but he knew clothing. She was richly dressed. That woman wore heavy satin. It had been trimmed with something that had sparkled. Drawing the eye to the tops of her bosom...

Argh.

Morrigan nearly voiced it. The emotion transferred wordlessly to his stroke again. His oar-partner's buttocks left his seat again. The drumbeat slowed. The rowers matched it. And then Cedric shouted above the other sounds.

"Steady up, men! We're home!"

Home?

Morrigan didn't even know where that was anymore.

He lifted the oar automatically, feeling it skim along the water, following his partner's lead. Waves returned from shore, washing against the boat, rocking it. Morrigan glanced up. Back down toward Cedric. The cliffs of the cove loomed directly above them. Cedric's orders had nearly beached them. And a moment later the bow smacked into sand. Wood groaned at the collision. Morrigan slid onto his backside. His boot slammed into a bench support, stopping any further skid, although his shoulder smacked into something. That hurt. His oar-partner hadn't been as lucky. That fellow had joined the jumble of bodies amidst the trunks. Morrigan couldn't even tell where Cedric had gone. And then, over everything else, he heard the woman speak. English words. Easily understood although she said them strangely.

"All right. That's it! Whoever put him in charge should be shot. Drawn. Quartered. Or whatever you do in this movie. I'm leaving!"

And then she said a very unladylike word that shocked.

Morrigan's mouth dropped open as he looked over his shoulder.

"This dress weighs a ton! And don't just sit there. Do something!"

She looked like a little bear, crouched down. Every time she tried to stand, she sank to her knees. She had both hands on her skirt material. She glared across at him like it was his fault. And that's when it dawned on him. Her fortune had been sewn into her clothing!

Of course! It made perfect sense. He was such a dunce. Gut instinct was well and thriving. He didn't need the trunks. He just needed the woman.

Well.

Actually, he only needed her clothing.

Morrigan jumped to his feet with new-found alacrity. Wrapped his arms about her legs and heaved her onto a shoulder. He expected the weight, but it still made his knees waver momentarily. She gave a choked sound.

No one answered. Morrigan regarded the mass of men and trunks, some groaning but most moving. He didn't need to wait for a ramp. The ship's bow was beached. The rest of the ship swayed slightly but where he stood was solid. And about four feet above ground. Diving over the side with his burden took a feat of strength he wasn't certain he possessed. He almost failed. He managed a squatted landing, his feet sinking into wet sand, while his buttocks met the same. But then he was up. And jogging.

He was almost singing.

CHAPTER FIVE

ALL RIGHT. THIS WAS GETTING out of hand. Not the fact that she was being kidnapped.

That would have made sense.

If this was a movie, it would be a box office bomb. Nobody would pay to watch an hour or so of men rowing. She hadn't brought her watch on this trip, so she couldn't tell time. It felt like at least an hour. The director should be fired. He was slow-witted and slower acting. No one needed this much time for the perfect shot. And it had started out with such promise!

Elena had been sodden, but nicely warm within the fur. Scrunched beneath the bow edge hadn't been uncomfortable, and it was sheltered. And she mustn't discount the obvious – that incredible view.

Morrigan was quite the male. His acting needed work, but his physical attributes more than made up for it. He had a fantastic upper body, and she was only watching his back and shoulders. The guy probably had washboard abs. This was obviously the gratuitous shot of a gorgeous male, to tempt women into a theater. And it would have worked if it hadn't gone on for so long.

She knew it worked because she'd experienced it.

Sweet heaven.

She had breasts again!

They'd tingled and swelled, and her nipples had even tightened against her bodice! It was such a wondrous feeling.

She thought she'd never have it again. That alone was reason to stay locked in this weird realm. Watching Morrigan. Experiencing waves of shivers. Thoroughly enjoying each one. But...it had gone on too long. The sound of storm and oarlocks and drumbeat had mixed together and faded to a dull hum. Her eyelids had drooped. Why...she might even have dozed off before Cedric woke her with his shouting.

She didn't know where she'd had the presence of mind to grab onto the wooden rail above her. She was just grateful. That saved her from joining the heap of bodies in the center of the boat. If this was a movie, it was a disaster in the making. If it was a dream, she really needed to wake up.

While it was nice that she had hair and breasts again, it was still fake. Totally imaginary. She had to face reality, just like she'd had to three years ago in the oncologist's office...

Morrigan slowed his paces, swiveled, and then smacked his unburdened shoulder against something solid. Elena swayed with the move. He dipped them forward and entered someplace warm. Dimly-lit. And protected. He was heaving for each breath. He bent forward and set her on her feet. Elena's legs immediately wavered. She would have fallen if she hadn't grabbed at the post beside her and wrapped her hand about it. The clumsiness wasn't her fault. It was the combination of huge fur cape thing he'd given her as well as the damn dress.

"Quick, woman! Divest yourself of your clothing!"

Morrigan said it over his shoulder. Elena's mouth dropped open but he didn't see it. He moved toward the back of the space and a fire. It was in stone-built hearth. The walls behind it were lined with something that gave off a dull silver finish. Flames reflected in it as they crackled to life, sending flickers of light, and a lot of blessed heat. Morrigan turned, opened a bin beside his fire pit and started tossing things onto a long bench set against the wall on her left.

If that was a wall.

Elena narrowed her eyes. The wall looked like chunks of grass and mud had been shoved into place between wooden slats. The mud had dried into a light-colored uneven surface, but strands of old grass could be seen. They flaked off occasionally in visible bits as he kept chucking things onto the bench. It was covered with burlap. Barely padded. A quick scan showed she stood in a small room, maybe ten by twelve feet. There weren't many furnishings. A three-legged stool sat beneath a small table against the wall on the right. The fire-pit was in the far corner. The door was obviously behind her. She couldn't tell the floor surface. It was covered with a lot of overlapping woven rugs, all in dull shades. She held onto the only post. There was a depression around the base of it. Shining with a puddle of...*was that water?* A glance upward showed a cross-hatching of beams above their heads, some dark objects at the sides that could be anything, and above that a vaulted ceiling made of straw with a hole in the center. Elena lifted her hand just as water slid over her hand. And then she had to lock her knees to keep from falling with the weight of her attire.

Good Lord.

This was beyond primitive. And he expected her to undress?

Morrigan was ignoring her, despite his words. He kept gathering things and tossing them. Most were basically identifiable. It might be chunks of stale bread. There were a lot of those. A couple of large hunks of jerky. She recognized potatoes, and what looked like squash. He added a couple of blankets. A pair of socks. He reached over his head and brought down two shadowy objects that turned out to be folded woven blankets. He reached up again to pull down a large leather bag that had been hanging from a hook. He really had some well-developed shoulders and arms. She barely stopped a sigh.

Elena dropped her gaze and watched him start shoving most of the items from his pallet into the bag. He left the blankets in place, and then he turned his head to look at her. A frown sculpted little lines across his forehead. He stood next, lowered his chin, put his hands on his hips, and just regarded her.

Holy shit.

Her heart sped into instant palpitations. She must not have seen him in good light before. He was beyond gorgeous. His looks alone would stop traffic. He looked to be late twenties… maybe early thirties. The firelight burnished the sparse beard on his face and his hair into a reddish shade. And then she had to factor in the rest of him.

Oh, Elena. Elena.

Praise heaven.

If this was a dream, why on earth did she want to wake up?

His jacket hung open. It was saturated. Two streams of water dripped from the open edges. His shirt was just as wet, but that just made it nearly see-through. It was glued to all kinds of muscle, too. Large pecs. Defined abs. The perfect 'V' of his obliques. Below that was just more magnificent male. He wore tight leather pants that didn't disguise anything. The man was well-built – everywhere.

And he didn't look remotely disinterested in her.

Good heavens!

She thought she'd turned into a passionless, frigid woman after her surgery and the rounds of chemo. Wrong! She was close to panting. She needed to get her mind involved before she did something totally against-type, like lunge across the space for him.

She moved her focus upward. He took a deep breath that enlarged his chest. All kinds of havoc went through her. Alarm bells were sounding somewhere in her head.

"I know you can understand me," he finally said.

"Um. Per...fectly."

"Then why haven't you disrobed?"

She lifted her chin to meet his gaze. He had especially vivid light blues eyes. They were a riveting shade.

Oh, crap.

The alarm bells got louder. She needed to stand on the stool to face him. This was completely unequal. Either he was more immense than a professional basketball player, or she'd lost several inches in height. She wasn't used to being this small.

"Well?" he prompted.

She cleared her throat. "Maybe it's because...oh, I don't know. I'm stuck in some weird dream, in an unfamiliar place, with a strange guy...and I don't know what he wants. Everything is—I can't explain it. It's too bizarre."

"You're soaked to the skin."

"As are you," she pointed out.

He glanced down at himself as if to verify. Looked back up, only now he regarded her from beneath lowered lashes. His chin was set, too. That expression sent sizzling-level erotic-themed sensations shooting through her. On an unbelievable scale.

"We don't have time for this."

"For...what exactly?"

Oh, good. Her voice worked still.

"Arguing."

Arguing? That's what he called it? Elena didn't have a reply. She waved her hand for him to continue.

"You need to get into dry clothing."

"Oh. I think I'm fine...just like I am."

"I need my coat back."

Elena lifted it off her shoulders. Cold instantly slapped at her, lifting goose bumps everywhere. They even made darts out of her nipples, sensitizing them worse than before. She was shaking as she held the fur out to him, and the darn thing was so heavy, she had to use both of her arms.

Crap.

Her attire was glued to her, too. She didn't have to check. She watched a nerve work in his jaw as he glanced down at her and then he lifted his gaze to something over her head.

"You need to get into dry clothing," he repeated.

"All right. Do you have some?"

He grunted.

"Is that a yes?"

"You need to undress first."

"Oh. I think the answer to that is no. Not with you anywhere in the vicinity, anyway."

"You worry without reason."

"Really?"

"I'm not interested in ravishment."

You've got to be joking. Elena bit her tongue before the words came out. His tight leather pants weren't disguising anything. The man was aroused. She couldn't seem to ignore it, despite trying. And she had a very hard time not glancing down in that direction.

"Um. I...hope you'll understand when I reply that your answer does not inspire confidence?" she asked.

His frown deepened. He still didn't look down at her.

"You are a noblewoman. Your words betray you."

"Whatever," Elena replied.

He glanced down at her. Looked away again. "Woman. Please. I just want what's in your skirt."

Elena gasped. He instantly added more words, as if that helped.

"Wait! You mistake me. I refer to—."

He muttered something. He might as well save his breath. He had a look of distaste as he reached out and snagged the fur from her grasp. All kinds of muscle moved in his arms and chest as he did so. He slung the cape over his shoulders and walked past her on the other side of the center pole. The room wasn't wide enough to miss her. His coat was wet. It was like getting brushed with a sopping wet mop. He stopped at the door. Turned around. Elena tried to stand taller. It didn't work. She stood to his upper belly. Maybe his pecs. That was disconcerting.

"Bar the door behind me."

"You're...leaving?"

Reaction was setting in. Her voice was timid. Unsure. Tear-choked. She wished the words unsaid the moment they left her mouth.

"Go to the fire. Warm yourself. Undress. Cover with the blankets. You will be safe if you stay here."

Elena didn't reply.

"I'm going for my horse," he spoke as if she'd asked.

"Your...horse?"

"We are leaving once I return."

"We? What we? You expect me to travel with you? Just you? On horseback? In this weather? Tonight?"

He regarded her for a long moment while Elena's heartbeat just got louder and faster until it resounded through her ears. She had to concentrate to hear his next words.

"You can stay. But not until I get the fortune you have sewn into your dress."

Elena gasped. Looked down at her skirt. Lifted a portion. Dropped it. There was a distinct jingling sound. They both heard it.

That's what he'd meant?

Oh, jeez.

"You're very pretty."

"What?"

Elena looked back up at him, tried to hold his gaze. Her vision was awash with moisture. *Oh, please. Not now.* She couldn't cry now! Despite the thought, she sniffed. It wasn't her fault, though. She was completely out of her element, stuck in some inescapable weird realm, and this was rapidly turning into a nightmare. She dropped her focus to the floor between them.

"Pretty enough that Cedric may decide not to kill you... once he has your trunks. And I am gone."

Elena blinked a tear into existence. It slid down her cheek. Dripped off her chin. She watched it land on the skirt. It didn't show. The material was still too wet.

"What is your name?"

His tone was soft. That started another wave of emotion. She sucked in a breath and held it, tensing everywhere to hold back sobs. And finally, it worked.

"Well?"

"Elena," she whispered.

He grunted. "Elena. I said I'd protect you, and I will. But only if you wish it. So. Do we have an accord?"

"I'll undress while you're gone," she told the floor.

The sound of the door opening and the closing behind him was her answer.

CHAPTER SIX

ELENA TOOK A DEEP BREATH. Her life had been a mess. Now, it didn't even make sense. And that had made her cry?

Dumb.

Tears wouldn't help. They never did. Sometimes, they even hindered. Immune systems could be affected by emotion. She had to stay upbeat. Optimistic. Strong. None of that had mattered when her baby had been birthed at six months and failed to breathe. She'd sobbed for weeks, gotten ill, and then gradually the depression had faded. Her health returned. She'd gained a few desperately needed pounds. She was young. So was her husband. They could have other children.

And then, she'd found the lump.

Her mother had died because she'd tried to save her breasts. Elena had been a child, but she'd seen the horror her mother had been through. That's why Elena opted for the double mastectomy. But only after she'd freaked out. Called in sick. Hidden in her bedroom. Sobbed for two days...

Elena blinked the rugged wooden door back into focus.

She needed a drink.

Badly.

How could she be thinking about all that now? The divorce? The surgery? The baby? She didn't know how much time she had before Morrigan returned. She knew he would, though. Because this was too real. She had to be living this. She'd somehow been transported to a historical period when men thought they ruled, and women were supposed to...

She didn't even want to guess what a woman's role was. It was too frightening. There had to be another explanation.

Please, God.

Reincarnation!

That was it! But...*how?* Even if she believed in that, shouldn't she be a newborn? And shouldn't this be the future? Unless...

Her belly sank.

Could there have been an apocalypse and this *was* the future?

Something hit the side of the hovel. Elena jumped. Had Morrigan returned with his horse already?

Oh, crap. She needed to get the door barred.

The portal was about six feet from where she stood. It took an act of will to reach, however, with her skirts dragging every step. The wooden bolt creaked before it fell, slamming down into metal brackets. That bolt was about the size of a two-by-eight, although it wasn't smoothed like those in a lumber store. Looked stout, though. Elena brushed her palms together, and took a step back. The hem of her attire didn't follow. She yanked it toward her and then looked down at herself.

Wow.

This dress was borderline obscene. The fabric appeared to be made from heavy bridal satin in some dark color. The bodice edge was extremely low-cut, and had a wide ribbon trim that glittered with little colored pieces. Thousands of them. Someone had gone overboard with the prom look. The stones resembled rubies. Sapphires. Emeralds. Opals. Some little black things.

Elena touched a finger to the stones before swiveling around to face the fire. The skirt twisted, but didn't move. The fire was crackling away, sending heat, but not much light. Firelight reflected off a lot of facets, however. The trim was rigid. Slightly scratchy. Looked real. Felt it. If these were genuine gemstones...?

And...

Wait just a minute here.

She truly had breasts again! She ran her hands under each one, lifting them while her eyes widened and her mouth dropped open. They were real. And they were large. Implants had once been on her to-do list, but she'd never considered this size. She'd been worried they'd look faked.

Elena moved her fingers onto the tops of her breasts next. The caress sent shivers. Tightened her nipples into darts she could not only feel but see against the satin. And why? Because the dress was designed exactly to her dimensions... and it was molding to every nuance. Her actions also sent a tingle to her lower belly. That was erotic. Everything in the vicinity got a dose of the sensation. The backs of her legs even quivered with it.

Elena slid her hands down her ribcage next, looking for side zippers. Her waist was incredibly tiny, but that could be misleading. She'd been cinched so tightly, it was beyond ridiculous. She'd worn a corset before. She'd tried shape-wear, too. Nothing had felt this restrictive. She brushed hair out of the way to see down further. And then it hit her.

She'd brushed hair out of her way.

This just kept getting stranger and stranger.

She'd already seen the hair, but it was still a shock. It was an indecipherable dark shade, somewhere between sable brown and black. It was at least waist-length. Locks clung to her torso. More strands lifted with every arm movement. She'd never worn it this long. The two times she'd tried a wig after losing her hair she'd opted for a short style. She'd worn Lady Godiva wigs on Halloween before, however. She'd forgotten how it felt. Elena moved a hand up behind her head, checking for a wig cap. She couldn't feel one...and when she pulled at strands, she got a corresponding pinprick of pain in her scalp.

Yep.

It was real hair. It was attached to her head. This body was beyond belief. She'd had a good figure once, a little on the skinny side. Weirdly, chemo had just made her gain weight, so then she'd had the opposite problem. Now, she looked like an incarnation of an adult comic book goddess.

But, what did any of that matter? She needed to get busy. Get this dress off and be covered in a blanket before Morrigan returned. Saw her.

And reacted.

That thought sent all kinds of sensations. Liquid warmth flowed through her veins, leaving heat in its wake. She wasn't remotely cold anymore.

Oh, no. No. This could not be happening.

She was getting turned on?

Oh, Elena. Get a grip, girl.

She checked the front of her gown again, craning her neck forward and lifting breasts to see. The dress didn't fasten anywhere in the front. It would be hell to try and reach the back. Her top wasn't connected to the bottom, however. Maybe she could shed the skirt first.

She found a waistband. It was sewn supremely tightly. Elena sucked in a breath, hooked her thumbs beneath the material and shifted the skirt around. She had to do it three times before the back of her dress came into view. It brought a large mound with it, as if she carried a load of laundry below the belt area.

What in the world…?

Elena stared and then pushed on both sides. The mound shifted slightly but didn't budge. It felt like she was dealing with a lot of material packed into rows. She looked up. Stared at the fire. Dealt with something that sent shock shooting through her. It replaced the heat of a moment before.

This couldn't be what it looked like.

No.

Elena didn't know much about historical costuming. Her career was in the judicial field. But this looked like the thing called a bustle. That meant this wasn't the future. No woman would allow fashion like this.

But that meant...she'd time traveled.

Impossible.

This was bad. And it was real.

Her head spun.

Oh no, Elena. No. No!

Her legs wobbled, but she tightened her thighs and fought the weakness. Time travel was off-the-charts unbelievable. Unreal. Unacceptable. And all kinds of other words that began with the letters 'un-'. At the top of the list was unsettling. The shivers she experienced now weren't remotely pleasant.

If she was in the past, she'd be expected to assume a subordinate position. And while the thought was distasteful, the idea it had already happened was deplorable. She was under the control of a man right now, although he'd called it protection. She was in his shack. Obeying what he'd asked.

No. No. Not possible.

She needed proof. And then she needed a game-plan. Until then, she'd need to be a lot smarter. Bite her tongue. Use her wits and knowledge. Figure out what was really happening *and* how to get out of here. And that meant she had to pretend to do what Morrigan wanted.

For now.

Elena looked back down at the skirt. A row of hooks had come into view alongside the bustle-thing. The top ones were at the waistband. Those were so tight Elena had to suck in her belly and arch backward to get them unfastened. But the relief was instantaneous. She opened the hooks as far as they went and peeled the satin down. It didn't fall. It was stopped by a mass of ivory-shaded linen-looking material. She could see lumps sewn all through the material with large uneven stitches. Like random polka-dots. She reached for one. Lifted it. The dot was hard, flat, and round. It felt like a coin.

Elena ripped it free. Lifted it close. Narrowed her eyes. She hadn't been mistaken. It was a silver coin. One side was embossed with a crown at the top, above a heraldic-looking crest situated between two pillars. The edge bore some lettering she couldn't read. The coin was mint condition. Obviously uncirculated. She turned it over. The other side had the profile of a large nosed-man wearing an elaborate eighteenth-century hairstyle. More lettering was around the edge. And at the bottom was a date.

1790.

Her legs gave. She didn't even get a warning. Elena dropped into the mass of material, propped onto her belly atop the bustle. Everything was damp. Chilled. Clammy. She clutched the coin while every part of her shook. Her heart turned into a caged entity, beating rapidly inside her chest. A knot seized her throat, constricting each swallow. Her eyes were so wide, the air hurt. The sound of thumping was loud in both ears. The blows heavy-handed. Continual.

Oh, dear God.

"Unbar the door!"

Morrigan's shout was loud, even through the door. Elena turned her head. Watched and heard another heavy thump smack into the door, sending a haze of wood splinters into the scene. She watched them dance with flicks of firelight. Another huge thump hit the other side of the door.

"I warn you, Woman!"

She started toward the door, but it wasn't quick, and it wasn't graceful. The gown was even heavier in this position, like an anchor. Trapped in the gown, her legs wrapped in yards of wet material, she'd resorted to crawling…her hand outstretched. Far from the door when the bolt shattered.

CHAPTER SEVEN

MORRIGAN'S ANGER EVAPORATED THE MOMENT he saw her crumpled on the floor, one arm raised toward the door. She was pale, her eyes large and wide. He hadn't been mistaken on her beauty. Bluish light from the snow-filled night lit her face, while firelight from behind burnished her hair into a halo. She didn't appear to even see him, however. He couldn't name her expression. He'd never seen it before. But he knew she hadn't looked that way when he'd left.

Was she suffering the ill effects of near-drowning? Re-living the chaos of her rescue? Perhaps she actually believed Morrigan's threat? That he'd leave her to Cedric? Or perhaps...she was the skittish sort and had spied a rat?

This was stupid. He might as well cease pondering. It could be many things, none of which he fathomed. Women were an ever mysterious lot and he couldn't be the first man to think so.

His fire-pit was reacting to the infusion of air. Flames leapt upward, reflecting off the backdrop of hammered tin. Fire hadn't reached wood yet, but there was always a risk. Morrigan quickly lowered the trunk he carried. Beside it, he settled the pack draped across his other shoulder. He brushed snow from his hood before stepping in farther, turning about, and slowly closing the door. The wood gapped open almost immediately. He regarded it for a moment before pushing it shut again. This time, he held it closed with a knee while shoving the trunk into place before it. The seal wasn't perfect, but it worked. For now. He'd fashion another bolt when he went for firewood.

He sighed heavily. Turned back to the room. Slid from his coat next, looked up to hook it from a spike in a ceiling beam. More snow accompanied his movements, the flakes sparkling as they sifted downward and dissipated. And then he moved his gaze down to Elena. She hadn't moved. He squatted to reach her approximate level.

"What is it? What's happened?"

"It's seventeen ninety," she whispered.

He took the coin she held out to him. Excitement raced through him, sending instant warmth even through his damp clothing. He hoped it came from the coin, and not contact with her. He bit the piece for something to do. Glanced back at her.

"It's a Spanish *reale*. Small. Easy to transport. Easier to spend. Not worth a lot, unless—?"

"What?"

"You have a lot of these. Yes?" He answered it himself. "You must. You weigh more than my horse."

"You don't understand. It's seventeen-ninety."

Her reply wasn't whispered this time. He looked at the coin again. Back to her. It was difficult to keep everything muted. The coin was exciting, but there was something else happening. It occurred every time he touched his glance to hers. It elevated his heart rate and temperature. Morrigan looked back to the coin and swallowed before answering.

"Uh...true."

"You're not listening. It's seventeen ninety!"

This time, her voice rose when she spoke. That was even more perplexing. She was also moving. She rolled backward, off her bustle and sat, holding the wad of clothing atop her lap. Morrigan could see the seam of her skirt was opened.

He could see a lot more spots where coins peppered her undergarments. But the main view was of her bosom. His groin twinged warningly. He lowered a hand to the area in front of his crotch ties to hide it, and moved his gaze back to her before worse things happened. Then he cleared his throat, and managed to answer.

"That means it is a new coin."

"No! It means it's really seventeen-ninety!"

Her tone raised shivers along his arms. She sounded shocked. She was trembling, too.

"If that bothers you so, worry not. It will soon change."

"What?"

"'Tis the Yule tomorrow."

"Christmas! You're telling me it's Christmas tomorrow?"

Morrigan didn't comprehend any of this. His voice reflected it. "Some call it that," he answered.

"This can't be happening. I have to get out of here."

"No one is going anywhere, Elena."

"Please don't do the machismo crap. Not now. All right? Please?"

"Machismo crap?"

He hoped his tone didn't display complete ignorance. She was beyond mystifying. The term sounded derogatory. Was she speaking Spanish? If she started speaking it now, they'd be at an impasse. The interpreter wasn't available. Her reply was in English, reassuring him on that, but little else.

"Yeah. That's what I said. That's what I meant. *Machismo crap.*"

She emphasized the last part and spoke the two words slowly as if that helped comprehension. Morrigan didn't reply, and she must not have expected one, because she decided to explain it.

"It means the – 'you will do as I say because I am a man and you're a woman' – stuff."

She'd lowered her voice as if to mimic him through some of that, but her voice was too high-pitched. She was off by a good octave.

"But I cannot leave, either," he responded.

"Why not?"

"The weather has turned. It's snowing," he replied. "Travel is...risky. That is one of the reasons I have returned with one of your trunks and not my horse. Or didn't you take note?"

"My trunks? *Mine*?"

"That is what your servant told us."

"What servant?"

"The man Cedric killed."

"Cedric *killed* someone? As in – he actually committed murder?"

Her voice rose markedly on the words. A flush colored her skin, turning it a creamy rose shade. Her breasts were heaving with each breath. A pounding noise settled in his ears, making it difficult to hear. Her eyes were sparkling, drawing his attention. Morrigan quickly looked away over her head toward the fire. He forced his mind to notice how the flames had settled down. That was good. He no longer had to worry over setting the croft afire.

"Well? Say something already."

"To what?

"You just told me your leader killed someone! And you didn't do anything?"

Morrigan moved his gaze to her and regarded her for long moments. She had a rebellious look about her. Her chin was lifted. Her mouth set. Her eyes narrowed. She was still the loveliest thing he'd ever seen, easily the most feminine. That fact was difficult to overlook. He tried not to notice how her breasts rose and fell; equally tried ignoring the spike-shaped shadows her lashes sent onto her cheeks. She had such dark eyes! Looking into them was like staring into pools from the deepest end of a pond. This was getting difficult. Especially when another shot of interest hit his groin. Unbidden. Unwanted. And definitely untimely.

"I protected you," he finally replied.

She broke the eye contact. Moved her gaze to somewhere in the middle of his chest. Two spots of color appeared in her cheeks.

"Oh. Man. I sure wished that meant something different."

"Different?"

"I'm in your control."

That was bewildering. Morrigan frowned. "You are safe. Warm. Sheltered."

"And in your control."

"I do not understand. You would rather be elsewhere?"

"Yes. Exactly."

"But 'tis a blizzard outside."

"I never said I wanted to be outside."

Morrigan pulled his head back slightly. "You did."

"No. I didn't."

"Then, what? You would rather be at the large house...with Cedric?"

The thought sent a fire-tipped sensation through him. Morrigan's breathing altered, each inhalation came more rapidly than the last, and they were heavier. He recognized the emotion. Tried to ignore it. Anger would not help with comprehension. And the croft was not large enough to vent anything.

"Oh. Perish that thought, big guy."

"What thought?"

His voice came out gruff. She looked toward him. Her glance sent a lightning bolt of reaction. His chest got a direct hit. His rod was right behind it. Morrigan reeled backward. He nearly fell. And she smiled slightly as if she knew!

"I do not wish to be in Cedric's control, either."

"Then what...do you want?" He said it from between set teeth.

"You're making me an offer?"

"I have not offered anything," he replied.

"Oh. Sorry. You're asking instead of telling. That in itself is an offer. I deal with this all the time in my career. Never mind. You wouldn't understand."

He growled.

"Oh. Listen to that. You're making my point without me even trying."

"What?"

"I'm speaking of the man-versus-woman thing. You know...I might have to reconsider things. It might be a lot of fun to mess with men's heads in this era."

"Elena."

"Yes?"

"We are stuck in here for the time being. Together."

"You say that as if it's a hardship."

He pondered that for a moment. "No. I say it because it is true."

"Well. I have to say, it could be worse," she told him. "I mean, the view is a definite plus. Know what I mean?"

"No. I do not."

She snorted. Morrigan shook his head.

"Woman. Please. I only want—" He began, only to be interrupted.

"Oh. I know what you want. I think we all know. It's crystal clear. You want my clothing. But not because you want my body. Oh, no. You only want my fortune."

He frowned.

"Now what?"

"You said we all know. Who is 'we'?"

She laughed aloud. Morrigan fell then, landed on his buttocks. He rocked back upright, hooked his arms about his knees, and regarded her. The angered emotion leached from him. He could almost feel it.   She was the most beautiful woman he'd ever seen, but she might be crazed. Her merriment slowly subsided.

"I'm sorry. I forgot. This isn't a movie."

"Are you mad?" he asked.

Her eyebrows rose. "Mad, as in angry? Or mad...as in crazy? Because I'm neither."

"Neither?"

"I'm not angry and I'm not insane, although I am in an insane position. And I have to tell you something, hon. It's getting more insane by the moment."

She leaned forward as if bestowing a secret.

"You just called me 'hon'," he informed her. "I am... unfamiliar with the term."

"It's short for honey."

"Honey?"

"Oh. That. It's an endearment. I use it a lot. It doesn't mean anything."

"Then why say it?"

She blew a sigh toward him. His shirt was plastered to him with moisture still. Her breath should have cooled. It had the opposite effect. He got an instant sensation of warmth. And along with that came an odd tingling.

"I was wrong. This could get really old, real quick."

"What could?"

"Conversing with a person from seventeen ninety."

He grunted something she took for a reply.

"So. You want my clothes? Fine. Be my guest. I don't want them. They're cold. They're wet. And they're incredibly restrictive. I would so much rather be snuggled in a blanket over by the fire. You have no idea."

"Why aren't you?"

"Because whomever designs women's clothing needs a new

job."

"I believe there are many designers."

She regarded him solemnly, although her lips twitched. "Let me clarify. Whoever designs *fancy* women's attire should be fired. It's obviously a man. Maybe he should be castrated."

"Castrated?" Morrigan stared at her, horror lifting his brows, widening his eyes. He recoiled, shaking his head.

She laughed again. His heart pulsed oddly. His manhood had the same reaction. That was unfathomable. And it needed to stop.

"It's just an expression. I don't really mean it."

"You say many things you do not mean. And you say them... quickly."

"You're having trouble keeping up."

She didn't ask it. He wondered if that was intended as an insult. Morrigan watched her for a moment. "I did not say that," he finally replied.

She sighed again. The damnable sensation of heat spread again as her breath reached him, and this time the tingling reached his groin. Morrigan shifted to get a bit more room in his crotch.

"How about I just explain? I couldn't follow your orders to get undressed because I can't get out of this outfit by myself. The idiot who designed it made it so tight I can't even find the seams without expiring from lack of oxygen. I know a woman didn't design this. No sane woman would put other women through what amounts to torture. That means a man must have. And he doesn't understand a thing about female anatomy. Does any of that make sense?"

Morrigan regarded her for long moments. He hadn't listened to the whole of it, because his body was giving him too much trouble. He'd had women before. He'd been much pursued. But he'd never had a reaction to this extent. She talked of restriction, when it felt like he was being pinched.

Leather trousers hadn't enough room. His rod wasn't obeying. His mind wouldn't stay focused. She asked if she made sense when the world had gone senseless. How as he to answer? It was better to stay mute. But that wouldn't work. She was looking at him patiently, while awaiting his answer.

"You need...help?" he asked.

"Exactly!"

She beamed a smile at him before lifting her hair and swiveling about so her back was to him. Morrigan swallowed hard. And he knew it was audible.

CHAPTER EIGHT

U*H OH, ELENA.*
You are in trouble.

Nothing had worked.

Morrigan was the handsomest male she'd ever seen, easily the sexiest. And Elena hadn't had sex in over two years. She hadn't missed it.

Until right now.

Her body was firing shots of hormone-fueled interest all through her. They got stronger and came with increased rapidity the longer she was in his proximity. It had to be noticeable. Shivers accompanied every breath. Her nipples puckered constantly against material, rubbing. Aroused. Her voice had taken on a husky tone more than once. And worse! She'd even fluttered her eyelashes at him. This was unbelievable. And he said they were stuck? Together? In this small space. *Alone?*

Oh dear.

She'd tried to control her reaction using verbal assault. Woman-versus-man. Far from making him look like a fool, her attempts to antagonize, frustrate, and confuse only made the man sexier. The vibes emanating from him hotter. More vibrant. Sensually thick. She wouldn't have believed it, if she didn't have proof. Even now, she vibrated in place, her thighs clenching and unclenching in the midst of a ton of still-damp material, while her loins moistened and itched...and he hadn't even touched her yet!

She'd even tried relegating him to the same level as Donald. Morrigan was a male. Men were not to be trusted. All they wanted was sex. And when they didn't get that...

What was she thinking? She was the one ready to ravish him. She was exhibiting every indication of a sex-starved female on the make. And that wasn't far-off the mark.

He finally touched her neck. His fingers were cold. There was a vague tremor to his movement. The dress started releasing its grasp about her and then he stopped. Long seconds passed.

"What is it?" Elena tried for an acerbic tone. It failed. The words were barely above a whisper, a hint of sound. She was breathless with excitement. Need. Desire.

"You may need to..."

His voice stopped. Elena held her breath. The sound of each heartbeat was loud in her ears. A log fell in the fire, sending a spurt of light into the room. She cleared her throat. This time, she'd try to sound assertive. In control. Unbothered. As if she faced a courtroom full of recalcitrant potential jurors.

"Yes?" she finally offered.

That failed miserably. The word came out in a rush of expelled breath. To her own ears, she sounded feminine. Needy. And ready. She'd never possessed what could be called a 'come hither', bedroom voice. She did now.

"Uh...suck in a bit. Perhaps...arch back."

"Really?"

"'Tis...very tight."

Elena tried. That sort of position made her feel incredibly wanton. Open. Available. Her breasts were barely staying in their confines. Air reached skin that hadn't known it a moment before. She felt his touch along her back again. His knuckles pressed against her spine as the restriction about her got tighter. Her breasts bobbed with every move he was making. His tremor was audible when he spoke.

"Uh. That was a...bad choice."

"Bad choice?"

"It does not work. These hooks are—. I can't seem to—."

The sound of ripping fabric rent the air. It came with a corresponding release, not of her breasts, but she could actually take a deep breath if she wanted. Elena glanced down. The reason was obvious. Her satin bodice had gapped forward. Beneath it she could just make out a corset in an ivory shade. It had little, rose-colored demi-cups, trimmed with ivory-colored lace above it. They'd been sewn with gathers at the bottom for support. They were barely doing their job. And it was the sexiest thing she'd ever seen.

Elena returned her gaze to the fire but couldn't prevent the smile. She was stunned. She didn't just have large breasts. She was astonishing buxom!

"For...give me."

His words started at a higher pitch than his normal. That was interesting.

"For what?"

"I've ripped...your dress."

There was a distinct catch in his voice mid-sentence. The last portion came out rushed. Deeper-toned. And with some kind of unvoiced meaning. He had a great voice. Full of bass. It rumbled through the room.

"Good riddance," she finally replied in her husky breathless voice. She'd surprised him. She didn't see him stare at her. She had to envision it.

"This is a...beautiful dress."

Definite catch mid-sentence again. Same drop in tone. As if he had trouble linking words. Fought for control. That was imaginative, but the possibility sure was fun.

"It's an instrument of torture."

"You don't have...many others."

"Thank goodness."

She was talking, but could be saying anything. Her mind

was on where his fingers hovered at the opening he'd made in her dress. She didn't have to see it. She felt it! Near-contact sent incendiary signals her body had no trouble deciphering, and then acting on. And she had to do something before she lost all sense of propriety, turned around, and attacked him. She licked her lips. Took a breath that shuddered.

"So...um. Does this mean you agree with me?"

"What?"

"Designers of women's fashions should—"

He sucked in a breath as if she'd actually say '*be castrated*'. And if she hadn't been in a whorl of sexually-tinged excitement, she'd have probably giggled. None of that sounded in her voice as she finished. She still sounded like a siren of desire. A fount of yearning. A being of passion that had been given physical form.

"...find another occupation."

He grunted a reply. He did that often. It was an extremely masculine sound. It should sound like he evaded an answer. It didn't. Instead, that grunt sent sparks of excitement that seemed to hit everywhere at once. Elena swayed sideways, and caught the fall with an outstretched arm.

"Elena?"

Wow. She'd never heard her name said in that tone! He sounded like a wild creature in torment.

"Um. Yes?"

"I may...have to cut it."

"Oh. My. Yes."

The words carried every bit of her interest and excitement. She hadn't meant to say them, either. The instant silence behind her was palpable. It raised shivers. She heard a rustle of movement. Felt something against her spine that could be the insertion of his blade. Watched the front of her dress fall forward as he finished. She hadn't been mistaken. This corset was one sexy design.

She felt him shuffling. He came around front, in a crouched position. Firelight touched his blonde hair, turning it reddish again. He had his eyes downcast, his face averted. He lowered his head farther, displaying the width of his shoulders.

Oh my, Elena.

My.

She watched with bated breath as he lifted the hem of her satin skirt, put his knife beneath it and shoved upward, piercing the fabric. He yanked the knife toward him. His blade was sharp. There wasn't any sound until the hem ruptured and then the skirt immediately started spilling coins. They drained with a jingling sound, forming two piles at his sides.

It was expected, but still a surprise. Elena's gasp would have been audible, but there was the strangest aura of pressure in the room. It sucked up sound. It was a sentient presence. Wrapped about her like a silken blanket of warmth. Moisture. A strange sense of electricity accompanied it, sending a jolt of mild voltage that came in surges. Elena's loins moved now in rhythm with it.

Morrigan didn't seem affected. He didn't act like he'd heard her gasp, or sensed anything strange at all. But then he turned his head slightly. His features were set. A nerve bulged out one side of his jaw. Everything else on him looked hard. Tensed. Locked. He lifted one side of her rent skirt with a hand that visibly shook. Elena watched as he ran the knife toward her – blade up – slicing the seam apart. He reached where her skirt had originally opened and didn't have to touch anything. The dark fabric fell open and then slid off, making a chinking sound as it settled around her.

"Um. I think...I can manage...now."

Her voice was still breathless, just as excited, and carried an undertone she hoped he wouldn't recognize. It wasn't faked. That was exactly how she felt. Several ribbon ties had come into view at her waist. They were supposed to be in the back. The top one opened the rows of starched ruffles that comprised the bustle-thing. The next one belonged to a petticoat...as did three more beneath it.

Good night.

This was a ridiculous waste of fabric. And time. She wasn't a history buff, but she'd learned somewhere that women dressed like this in order to prove status. Well. One thing was certain – she wasn't a peasant. Anyone wearing this outfit had a lot of time and money and resources available. Just getting dressed would be a production. Why...if the events of her arrival were true, this wasn't even court attire. This was a traveling ensemble. She must be someone of great importance. Maybe even royal. That was almost comical. She'd heard that people claiming past lives had always been someone of great importance. Princesses. Empresses. Queens.

Damn it.

Thinking through things didn't work, either. She didn't know who or what she was, and she didn't care. She was having too much trouble trying to contain massive desire for Morrigan. And failing. He didn't say anything as he sheathed his knife. That wasn't helpful. She didn't know his expression, either. She didn't dare check. If he was feeling even a fraction of her desire...all kinds of things were imminent. Ripples of pleasure coursed her skin at the thought.

But...if he wasn't?

Oh.

The potential for embarrassment was too high. She'd rather remain in ignorance. The last of the ribbon ties came apart. She'd reached the waist of her corset. Elena worked her way through the layers, pulling each gap again, widening them so she could wriggle backwards. That way she could shimmy out of the entire mass with one move. It took a few moves, but she was out. Staring at what she'd revealed. And it wasn't the wad of coin-filled clothing that was between them.

The rose-colored demi-bra appeared to be part of a full slip. It wasn't very long, akin to wearing a silken mini-dress. She had ivory-shaded stockings that ended above her knee. They'd been knit into a ribbed pattern, attached to wide lace tops. Ribbons in the same rose shade as her chemise were woven through the lace and tied in front. Whoever had tied the bows had done a fantastic job. They would have looked good gracing a present under a Christmas tree.

What a thought.

She looked like a Christmas present. The pressure in the room was getting denser. The air imbued with heat and moisture, and all kinds of shiver-inducing light. Elena cleared her throat. Spoke.

"Um. Morrigan?"

He groaned.

And Elena looked up.

CHAPTER NINE

"GET...TO THE FIRE. COVER YOURSELF... WITH a blanket. Now."

It was an order. Difficult to consider, even harder to voice. The words came out as a guttural croak, scraped his throat. He directed them to the pile of her discarded clothing. He didn't look beyond the mass of cloth. He might not be able to control what happened. He couldn't lock his muscles any tighter.

"But—?"

By hell fire! She argued it?

He was doing his best to keep from attacking her. Stripping the little clothing she had left from her body. Finding her haven, burying himself, and discovering paradise. He didn't question it, either. He somehow knew. Every muscle on his body was pulled tight. Taking each breath was a chore. His heart was pounding so mightily, it might launch from his chest.

"You are...not safe," he managed to answer.

"I feel safe."

"I swore to protect you."

He shook while saying it. There wasn't any way to disguise it. And then she pushed the mass of coin-filled attire to one side. Morrigan blinked on the spot, experiencing all manner of astonishment as she scooted into it. Her breasts jiggled as he watched, unable to even shut his eyes. Her legs kept moving as she shuffled closer. The woman was perfect. Unbelievably womanly. She tucked her legs beneath her, leaving her creamy thighs on display, along with the sight of pink bows just above her knees. Leading his eye to...

Argh.

He barely caught the groan. A knot formed in his throat at the effort.

"Um. Okay. I mean – all right."

"Elena? Please. You must go...and. Uh. You must—." The words were almost unintelligible. Grumbled. Bestial.

"Yes?"

Her breath touched him, tingeing his existence with even more hellish fire. And then she scooted even closer! His entire body reacted, despite the hold he exerted. His frame lunged upward a fraction before he caught the motion. He pulled each muscle even tighter, proving he still could. Sucked-in air iced his teeth. But the inhaled breath warmed the longer he held it. The hammering of his heart became a torment.

She reached out with a hesitant gesture. He watched as she lifted one of his shirt ties ends, and pulled it toward her. Morrigan lost his withheld breath. Words came out with it. He was pleading. And it sounded like it.

"Go to the fire! Please! Get covered."

"Maybe I don't want to."

He growled. The obstruction in his throat shifted painfully. Bass notes pulsated through the space. The bow at his neck came undone.

"I will not take...an unwilling woman!"

There. The fear was voiced. She couldn't mistake him.

"Um. Morrigan?"

She'd dropped his tie and began twisting her fingers together, making her breasts jounce against each other. Morrigan thought he fought hellish desire already. He'd been mistaken. Somehow, he stopped the involuntary lurch his body made. Toward her. And heaven. And he actually welcomed the ache that went through his muscles at his action.

"I just want to...um. Talk about the unwilling thing."

He reeled backward slightly. His head shot up, his eyes went wide. Hope sent a blast of cool air through him. She had her head bowed and was looking at her entwined fingers. Was it possible...?

"Are you perhaps...a courtesan?"

"I don't know," she whispered.

"You do not know?"

"It sounds impossible...and it is. Honest. But...despite everything, I have to accept the fact that I'm actually here. It's the year seventeen ninety. I'm in...um...this unbelievable position. And I'm getting bombarded with feelings I thought were lost. The idea that you might feel it, too? Well. That... um...brings me to the unwilling part."

Morrigan held his breath. He didn't dare move.

"It's been so long since I felt womanly. Desired. Wanted. The combination is beyond heady...and it's running really high at the moment. Maybe because it's late. We're alone. This is a small room. You're a lot of male. The thought of—uh. Yeah. With you? It's just, um...I don't even know if I'm making sense."

Her words stopped. She looked up. Her dark eyes shone as if glossed with unshed tears. Morrigan's heart felt like it swelled at the sight while an ocean took over his hearing, filled with the sound of his pulse.

"Are you saying you are not...unwilling?"

He managed to ask it. Her lips curved into the slightest smile. She raised and lowered her eyebrows several times.

"I don't think I have ever been this turned-on," she told him.

Everything stopped. His heart. His breathing. The crackling of the fire. The sound of waves in his ears. Even time held back for the merest moment. His swallow was audible.

"The phrase...is unfamiliar to me."

"Oh. I think you'll figure it out."

And then – to his amazement – she blew him a kiss!

Morrigan didn't know who moved first. Her perfect body reached him, putting a cushion of softness against his chest. His arms wrapped about her, pulling her even closer. His heart thundered through his chest, but it was the kiss that nearly sent his head off his shoulders.

This woman knew how to kiss.

The moment their lips met, she was sucking and pulling, and moving her mouth against his, igniting all kinds of sparks. This woman was incredible. The sensations she evoked with her lips – staggering. Her mouth sent incendiary sensations. He slid his tongue between her lips. Her moans combined with his long, drawn-out groan. Their tongues tangled, their breaths commingled. And Morrigan launched backward, landing with a thud.

She writhed atop him throughout the kiss. And it went on forever. He wasn't willing to break the contact. It was addictive. He couldn't get enough. Her legs separated. She straddled him. Then she used that new position to grab the sides of his open jacket and shove at it. Morrigan sat slightly, lifting her with it, shrugging first one shoulder and then the other free of material. She was probably trying to help as she stretched out, pushing at his sleeves. It didn't feel like help. That position had her legs splayed apart, her breasts smashed against him, and her warmed cavern pressed to his lower belly, as though suctioned in place. The contact of their bodies sent incredible sensations through him. He gave in. No amount of control was left.

He struggled with the jacket, settled with rolling to one side to get an arm free. He rocked back the other direction and waved his arm, trying to free it from the sleeve. She clung to him the entire time. He felt it, but then every sensation was lost in the continued wonder of their kiss. He wasn't foregoing a moment of it. The deep sounds emitting from his throat were proof. The jacket fell, making a wadded bundle at his back. He ignored it. It didn't matter. What did were the ties up her back, lacing the corset to her. Her stays had been fastened with the same rose-shaded ribbon that adorned the rest of her undergarments. The tie was between her shoulders. He found it by touch. Pulled both ends of the ribbon, releasing the bow, and then he started unlacing and pulling the corset open, working his way to her waist.

She hadn't been docile. She'd grabbed the linen of his shirt and was pulling it upward. That moved her...downward. Matching her woman-place to where his rod strained against the crotch ties of his trousers. Her legs tightened about him as she fit against him. And then, she moved.

Morrigan jerked, and then hovered in place while whispers of the very devil himself went through his ears. She slid back down him. His head whirled. His breath caught. His fingers reached the bottom of her corset at the same moment her hands touched his bared skin.

Morrigan shot to his feet. He didn't even know how he'd managed it.

Elena was in his arms, but the move had separated their kiss. Her every breath harassed where it touched. Her corset was no longer affixed to her. He watched it fall, parting locks of her hair that tried to snag it. Dark strands clung to his shirt. His lower jaw. His arms. Tendrils outlined their embrace, somehow giving it form.

His shoulder smacked the support pole as he passed it, rocking them sideways a step. It didn't stop him. He looked down at his bench. Spent a moment considering. It was sturdy enough, but much too small.

"Where...are we going?"

Her breath was a curse. Her words only enhanced it.

"Bed."

The word was deep-toned. Rough.

"Oh, my. Yes. And hurry!"

She didn't realize what she did. She spoke the words to his throat, and then touched her tongue to him. Morrigan jumped. His head hit a rafter. The resultant drop jolted his limbs and made him clumsy. He almost dropped her. He shifted her upward onto his shoulder before anything worse happened. He held her there with one arm, while the other shoved items off his bed. All, so he could pull the pallet at its base loose. Drop it to the floor. The straw-filled burlap unfolded with the move, making a barely-padded surface. He unfurled both blankets atop it next, flapping them into place. It wasn't perfect, but it would work. It was the best he could manage with how she wriggled, consuming most of his attention.

And worse.

She hadn't worn a stitch of clothing beneath her chemise.

Firelight glowed on her spectacular hind-end. At the sight, Morrigan's knees wavered and then collapsed. He dropped with an awkward motion, but he had her on her back before his knees had time to notice. Or complain. Her hands were full of his shirt again. She wasn't using it for a handhold. She was pushing it up and out of her way. Morrigan lifted long enough to help. A seam tore somewhere in the linen. He didn't care. He yanked the shirt over his head and chucked it before slamming his hands to the bedding at either side of her, propping him from her. He couldn't get closer because she had her hands roaming about his abdomen and chest, making little mews of pleasure while her loins gyrated against him. Then she spoke.

"Oh, wow. Morrigan. Wow. You are really something. Gorgeous. Ripped. Manly. I mean, wow. Just. Wow. "

He didn't understand most of the words, but he couldn't

mistake her awed tone. He grunted and flexed muscles, preening for her.

"I can hardly wait to see the rest of my um…present."

Her hands touched his waist. Fumbled with the top of his crotch tie.

"Present?"

Morrigan didn't know how he managed to speak. He'd gone still at the first touch of her fingers to his groin. And then he vibrated in place.

"It *is* Christmas Eve, isn't it?"

She winked. He jerked. Her fingers grazed his belly as she worked at the rawhide lacing. And then it hit him. She wasn't the only one with a present. Each of her movements pushed her bosom toward the edge of her chemise. Morrigan twisted to put his weight on one arm, put a finger beneath her garment, and then he pulled it down.

Oh!

She was beyond beautiful. Even beyond perfect.

Morrigan wavered but caught any fall by tightening his abdomen. He pulled up enough so he could maintain that position. So he could use both hands. She had perfect nipples, too. Dark. Small. Morrigan massaged and enjoyed, twisting her little nipples into pinpricks that stabbed into his fingers. He barely felt it as she finally worked his ties loose. Nor did it get through to him that she'd opened his trousers. But then she wrapped him in her hands and started squeezing and the immediate lurch nearly sent him into the rafters again.

"Oh, woman. Oh! So *mass*. So *milis*. And oh, so *crodae!*" The words fled his lips in groans.

"I don't know…what that means. But the answer is yes. Yes! And another yes!"

The last yes ended on a high-pitched cry. Morrigan licked his lips. Shuddered. Somehow managed to answer. "It means beautiful. Sweet. And wild."

"Oh, yeah."

She added to her reply by stroking his rod. A riot of sensation shot down both legs. Morrigan went rigid. He stared, shock mixing with a degree of pleasure he hadn't expected, and couldn't remember experiencing. She held his gaze for what felt like an eternity while her fingers worked his member. Her body writhed beneath him. She licked her lips...

And that's when everything went truly crazed.

Morrigan grabbed her hips, shifted her into position, and she helped. It was her hand guiding him. Her upward lunge that linked them. But it was his solid thrust that burst through an obstruction to join them. Her body jerked at what had to be pain. Morrigan sucked in a breath. Held himself rigid. Tried not to move.

"You were...a maid?" he asked through clenched teeth.

"Don't stop, Morrigan. Not now. I'm begging you."

Her whisper barely filtered through his consciousness. Heated strength engulfed him. Moistness cocooned him. Concentric rings of suction were gripped about him. All of it combined into a mass of sensation. All of it was entreating him to move. And she begged him not to stop? He didn't think that was possible. It was barely controllable.

"Please?" she added, as he hesitated.

Her cavern held tightly as he eased out. Felt even tighter as he filled her again, feeling the constriction stretch. He pulled out again. Pushed back in. A third time. Fourth. Each time was akin to being stroked with fire. Hugged with near-pain. And then something altered. He wasn't imagining it, either. She started meeting his thrusts. Assisting with his move to pull out. Only to thrust back in. Pull out. Thrust.

Again and again.

A solid feeling of pressure formed at his lower back, the sensation beyond heavenly. His every move increased it. Each lunge. Every time he withdrew. The resultant thrusts back into wonder. He'd been mistaken. This was past *milis*. Sweet was too small a word to describe anything about her. And what she made him feel.

She was attuned with him now, too. Her legs gripped about him. Her thighs flexed with every motion. She used the position to make everything more intense. Stronger. Much more *crodae* – wild.

The power behind each thrust increased, each one getting a little harder. Going deeper. His every breath carried a growling sound, while hers may have begun as little sighs, but they grew in strength and volume until it was a litany of feminine-sounding appreciation.

And then it was a blissful-sounding scream that filled the croft with sound.

Her legs locked tightly about him. She grabbed his shoulders with such strength, the move lifted her. Soft breasts smashed into his chest. Non-rhythmic tremors scored her frame in a palsied fashion. Her legs locked tightly about him throughout. Her cry ended. Everything about her softened. She eased back to the nest of blankets beneath her.

And then she smiled.

He'd been mistaken. She wasn't just sweet. She was *nemdae* – absolute heaven. Her release sent fuel to his every muscle. A shot of power to his loins. His thrusts increased. Over and over. Again and again. And she started matching him again.

The pressure at his back scorched him. Heat accompanied every shove. Faster. Harder. Her sighs began again. Built. Went to keening level. She screamed again.

And Morrigan exploded.

A bolt of lightning crashed through the croft, or something similarly massive. Flames burst within the fire-pit, sending light and heat. Unbidden emotion stabbed at his eyes at the uncontainable ecstasy filling him. The release intensified. Morrigan shoved his head back, gritted his teeth, and shuddered, his body propelled through all manner of wonder. Elation. Solid bliss. Heavy, thick heartbeats accompanied each pulsation of pleasure, the sound solid. Harsh. Strong.

And then it was over.

Strength faded almost instantly. Morrigan panted. Bent his head. Looked into her eyes. His heart jerked. She had such soulful dark eyes! Deep and mysterious. Luminous right now with the gloss of tears that threaded down her cheeks. His arms trembled in warning. He collapsed on his side next to her, saving her from his weight. He hoped his weakness wasn't apparent as he lifted his head and propped it atop an arm that shook.

"Oh. Wow," she whispered.

The words carried the same awed tone she'd used before. She turned her face toward him. Her expression matched. His heart was still hammering within his chest, each breath difficult to gain, but he managed a smile.

Elena lifted a finger and used it to trace the indentations of his abdomen muscles until she reached mid-chest. Right next to his heart. Her lashes lowered. She caught her lower lip beneath her teeth. His body gave a slight jerk.

"And to think...I used to hate Christmas," she told him.

"You...did?"

He had to clear his throat mid-sentence, but his voice worked. He had strength enough for that. The rest of him was still in a state of euphoria. Adrift on a cushion of comfort. Replete. He couldn't even stop a jaw-stretching yawn.

"Never mind. It's...a long story."

She flashed a smile up at him. The move released her lip. His heart not only skipped a beat, it twisted in place. But that was fanciful. He was imagining things.

"We can talk...tomorrow. We need rest. And I think you've earned yours."

That was supremely pleasurable. But he had to say something

first. Something he'd never said before.

"Elena?" he asked.

"Yes?"

"Would you do me the honor...of accepting my hand in wedlock?"

CHAPTER TEN

THE SIZZLE OF SOMETHING FRYING woke her. The mouth-watering smell of bacon came a moment later. Elena smiled. Stretched, feeling the hard surface beneath her as her shoulders and butt arched into it. This camping stuff could get addictive. Maybe it was the fresh air. She'd rarely felt so energized. Alive.

Healthy.

And that had to have been the best dream of her life.

"Ah. You've awakened."

Elena gasped, grabbed the covering to her breasts and sat up. Her eyes went so wide the feeling of air hurt. Her mouth dropped next. The impossible sight of Morrigan was crouched just beyond the foot of the bedding. There was a metal contraption above his fire-pit. Several long-handled hooks splayed from it. Some of them held cast-iron pots. He'd been stirring something in the largest one. He had a skirt-thing wrapped about his hips. It wasn't hiding much. He was easily as gorgeous as she'd first thought, and entirely as physically ripped.

All this? And he cooked, too? Her lips twitched at the instant thought. She stifled it.

"You hungry?" he asked.

"For bacon? Oh, yeah. Anytime."

He frowned, but a second later his expression cleared. "Ah. You speak of the meat. No. No bacon this morn. This is pork fat."

"You're cooking pork fat? For...breakfast?"

Yuck.

He read her expression accurately. "This is the beginnings of a stew. It will last us some time. Days."

Days?

In here?

Alone with him?

Oh. No way.

"I made porridge."

"Porridge?" she asked.

"Aye."

What the heck was in porridge?

"You wish a mug?"

He lifted an arm over his head without looking and pulled down a really large cup. The move displayed nicely muscled pecs and washboard abs. Well-formed biceps. Her mouth went dry. Despite that, Elena tried to swallow. This was insane. But nice. No. She mustn't think that. This was bad. She should probably watch what he was doing, rather than ogle him. She moved her focus to the wall behind him. It wasn't easy.

Ah.

On the wall to the right of his fire-pit, there was an array of items. Most of them hung from hooks. A couple of pans were at the bottom. Long-handled spoons were above that. Knives. Long, two-tined forks. Some mugs toward the top. He had quite the compact kitchen in this corner. She hadn't noticed that last night.

Then again...she hadn't noticed much beyond him.

How was it possible for a guy to be this good-looking? He hadn't even combed his hair. The shoulder-length mass of it only added to his appeal. Blonde locks looked reddish with the firelight's glow behind him. It matched the slight scruff of whiskers on his jaw. He didn't have much chest hair, and that was unfair. The guy even had a distinctive happy trail. Starting right above his belly-button, and drawing the eye downward to all kinds of...

Crap.

She needed to get her mind on something else. She just didn't know how.

Morrigan scooted alongside his hearth, moving to give his attention to a smaller pot. He stirred it before lifting a spoonful of off-white-colored muck. It looked about the texture of grits mixed with lumps of something. That must be porridge. It was steaming hot. That might be why his skin glistened as he just crouched there, waiting for her, looking like a flesh-colored Grecian statue. He'd tied the kilt-thing low at his left hip. The resultant opening gave her a spectacularly good view of legs. Really muscled thighs. A lot of shadowy area above that. This was a fantasy come to life. It had to be. Morrigan was unbelievable. Making love with him had been even more so...

Damn it, Elena.

"Um. I'm more...in need of a bathroom," she said.

His eyebrows drew down, making little lines. He settled the spoon of porridge back into the pot.

"Uh...restroom facilities? Water-closet? Toilet? Oh. What am I thinking? This is seventeen ninety, isn't it? Indoor plumbing isn't around yet. And even if it was..."

Your hovel wouldn't have it.

She bit her tongue to prevent the last bit. She looked to the left of her toward the bare bench thing. It had a base of solid wood planking beneath it; probably storage. She swiveled to the right and craned her head to take in the table and stool beneath it. Then she arched backward, looking over her head at the door. The wrinkled and stained mass of fabric that had been her attire. The same material he'd cut from her body...

Damn it.

Even viewed upside down, the scene was a reminder. It sent

an itch to her lower belly. And that somehow moved to the rest of her. Her skin felt really dry. Almost scaly. She absently rubbed at an arm as she looked back at him. She rubbed the covering against the other arm. It didn't help. She still felt itchy. That was weird.

There was a definite flush on his lower cheeks. And she was being bitchy. That was uncalled for. The man *had* saved her last night, even if he didn't have backbone enough to handle Cedric and assume leadership. What was it to her? They'd just met. He didn't mean anything...nor did the twinge that went through her chest as she thought it.

So Morrigan lacked intestinal fortitude. That wasn't the primary reason she'd declined his declaration last night. No. It was because she was in a time warp.

There.

She'd given it a name. That meant she had to accept it.

Elena swallowed with a painful motion. She couldn't escape the fact of her current reality. She really had gone through a time portal. She didn't know how. She didn't know why. She didn't know if it was permanent, or how much time she had.

Wow.

She didn't know much.

"Um. It's no biggie...Morrigan." *Double crap.* Saying his name sent shivers. That was another bad sign in a world of them.

"Big...gie?" he asked, splitting the word.

"I mean...I was already camping. This is just a bit more... uh..."

Archaic.

They probably didn't have toilet tissue. She'd just have to make do. She could always rip a bit off her petticoat. She had miles of fabric she could use.

"You refer to your need to...uh..." He stopped. The flush on his lower jaw went darker. More pronounced.

Elena dropped her eyes. Now, she was blushing. "Um. Yeah. You probably have an outhouse. Yes?"

"The women have a spot they use. I can show you."

"No. Please. I think I can probably find it." *I sure hope I can.* Anything else would be too embarrassing. "I think I'll just..."

She lifted the fur he'd placed over them with last night. Before he'd pulled her close. Fallen asleep. She needed to move her thought process. This was really getting annoying. She still wore her chemise slip thing. It wasn't much cover. Her hair was going to need work. Washing. A lot of combing. Looked like the beginnings of dreadlocks. But she still had a magnificent bosom.

She pulled the fur back and held it in place beneath her arms.

"I have a shirt you might be able to use. For now."

Morrigan rose and walked past her. She didn't have a choice. She had to watch him. Elena swiveled, taking the covering with her. He lifted the pack he'd crammed things into last night, pulled out a length of material that would probably reach her ankles, and tossed it atop his shoulder.

"And I think I can fashion something for your feet."

"My feet?"

"You do not have shoes. Or boots."

Oh. Weird.

She hadn't even noticed that last night.

He pulled a ball of twine from his pack, and then two circular fur things that looked like long muffs. He certainly had packed some interesting things. Then he turned back and walked toward her. The kilt was above knee-length. It was showing off a lot of skin. He was a lot of male. And she had a one-track mind this morning. She needed to get her thoughts on something besides the gorgeous and masculine Morrigan. But everything fought her! He even slipped the fabric off his shoulder with what looked like a sensual gesture. It dropped onto the fur beside her. The ball of twine followed. Worse yet was when he followed, going to his knees before her, and altering just about everything. Elena focused on the span of neck beneath his chin. Tried to ignore the rest of him.

"I need your foot."

He held out one of the muffs. Elena slid a foot toward him. Well. Apparently she still wore the thigh-high woven stockings. Although one was twisted just above the ankle. That had probably happened some time during the amazing love-making session from last night...

Crap.

Elena!

She almost voiced it. She really needed to move her mind to something else. Anything else. He snagged her foot and moved it toward his lap. Settled it atop a thigh. It figured she'd have perfectly formed, tiny feet. Really shapely legs, too. She was the epitome of feminine glory in this incarnation... matched for some reason with a magnificent specimen of maleness. They were secluded in a one-room cabin. Warm. Safe. Private. With little to do except...

Stop it, Elena.

This wasn't her body. This wasn't her life. This wasn't even possible.

But it sure was nice.

He maneuvered the muff onto her foot. Picked up the sinew ball, found an end, and pulled at a length of it. His arms and chest moved with the motions. Elena caught the sigh, but the catch in her breath was audible. She knew he heard it because he stopped moving for a second. He had about a yard off before he pulled his knife and cut it. Pulled another bit of cording the same length. He draped them across his thighs... where the kilt had gapped again. That position showed off a lot of thigh. It added to the amount of skin he already had on display. He truly had some really nice thighs. Her glance kept roving over how the muscles flexed and moved as he shifted. Even there.

Elena swallowed. Her ears popped. This was ridiculous. But nowhere was safe to look! Every spot on Morrigan's body was drool-worthy. Displayed perfectly. Kissed with the glow of firelight. And playing havoc with her intentions.

He tucked one opening of the fur beneath her arch next, overlapping the ends. He spent a lot of time wrapping the twine about her foot before moving it up her leg. He tied it off at mid-calf. And just like that, she had a makeshift snow-boot. Elena lifted her foot and looked it over. The mass of twine crisscrossed about the bottom of her foot even made a credible sole.

Wow.

This was just pretty darn cool.

"I need your other foot."

His voice was a grumble of sound. Elena tried not to react. She really did. But shivers accompanied her movement. It wasn't her fault. Morrigan was quite the male. With a closetful of attributes, that started with last night's fantastic lovemaking session and just went from there. He was really well-built. Extremely easy on the eyes. Good with his hands. Inventive. Appeared to be an excellent provider. He even cooked.

On the negative side was his slight courage flaw, as demonstrated by his refusal to handle Cedric, but hey. No man was perfect. Donald certainly hadn't been.

She might need to rethink the marriage proposal thing.

CHAPTER ELEVEN

MORRIGAN FINISHED CHOPPING VEG-
ETABLES INTO his stewpot. Added water. Moved it to one side of the fire, so it could come to a slow boil, perfect for simmering. Next, he stirred the porridge. Added water. If he kept it hot, added more oats and wheat as needed, water when required, the porridge would also feed them for days. It was bound to be bland, however. Elena was from the New World. She might have different tastes. Morrigan kept hardened honey squares, cinnamon and other spices in a basket in the rafters. He heard a shuffling sound outside the door.

Ah.

That would be Elena returning. Morrigan filled a mug with porridge, placed a spoon in it. Stood, and was just lifting the spice basket down when the door burst open. Elena rushed in, resembling a small bear in his coat. She shoved the door closed, yanked the new bolt he'd fashioned into place, and then backed from it. She acted as if she'd been chased.

"Elena?"

She turned about. Her face was in shadow, not only from the lack of lighting near the door, but the hood of his coat overhung her face. She glistened everywhere with an accumulation of snowfall.

"I have porridge for you. Spices. Would you like it at the table?"

"Do they burn women at the stake around here?"

He blinked several times with surprise. He still couldn't see her face, but she'd sounded serious. She started fumbling with the length of twine tied about her waist. Her movements were clumsy. That's when he noticed how badly she was shaking.

"Women?" he asked.

"Yes! Women! Like...do they tie them up, put them on a pile of kindling atop a stake, and then light them afire?"

Her belt came undone. Morrigan took slow steps toward her, wondering why this felt as if he walked across an ancient slatted-wood bridge. With missing timbers. Where any step could send him plummeting to his death. And he'd been blind-folded.

He set the porridge and basket on the table when he reached it. That put him within arm's length of her.

"Innocent women have never been burned," he finally replied. "At a stake or anywhere else."

"Oh! Thank goodness."

She sagged, smacking her backside against the door. A moment later she was back upright.

"Wait a minute. What do you mean *innocent*?"

Her voice rose on the last word. She might be angry, but there was something else. Something he sensed. She sounded frightened. This was completely mystifying. His voice reflected it.

"There have been witch burnings...if that is what you ask," he replied.

"*What*?"

She screeched it. Morrigan leaned backward at the assault on his ears. She shoved the fur off, twisting and turning, and showing off a lot of woman. Then she flung the coat at him. The move sent her sideways. She nearly lost her footing. That was amusing, but he didn't show it. He caught the coat easily, despite a showering of melted snow, found the collar, and lifted it to a spike in the rafters so it would dry. She was looking up at him when he'd finished. She was also starting to breathe rapidly, shoving her breasts upward with each one. That was dangerous territory. Morrigan forced his gaze up from her bosom. She'd paled. The contrast of her dark lashes and eyes, as well as the red hue of her lips, were especially vivid.

"I do not understand, Elena. Did something happen…while you were out there?" His question was hesitant. Low-voiced. Calm. It didn't match how he felt.

"Yes. Something happened while I was out there. And I have excellent hearing, Morrigan. I always did. Excellent."

"You…heard something?"

"I found the woman place. There were three of them there."

"Women?"

"Of course, women! I smiled at them. And do you know what they did, Morrigan? Huh?"

He shook his head.

"They whispered and called me a witch! And then they made the sign of the cross on their bosoms! And now you tell me they burn people for that?"

"But, you are not one."

"Of course I'm not! I must look like it, though! I mean, look at my hair! I probably look more like a banshee!"

She was completely wrong.

She didn't remotely resemble a witch. They were hags. And she was the furthest thing from a banshee he could imagine. He'd have pegged her as a woodland sprite from folklore, perhaps a little fairy like those purported to flit about a forest on a summer night. Dancing on the mists. A man could spot them if the moon was full. The weather just right. And he was supremely lucky.

But that was fanciful. Nothing about Elena looked anything other than deadly serious.

"Oh, my God! How can this happen? I've been dumped

into a hotbed of religious superstition! Just when I'm thinking it might be really cool to be stuck in 1790! I mean, I've got a fantastic bod, no cancer in sight, and a really hot guy. I started thinking how bad can things be, anyway? And this happens?"

"I do not understand. What exactly has happened?"

"I need to leave, Morrigan! I can't stay! I just can't!"

"We cannot leave. We are snowed in."

"I don't mean that way! I know we're snowed it! I can hardly move out there! The snow is waist-deep. It filled my boots! My feet are wet and cold. I'm wet and cold. And I'm a mess. I need a bath. My hair washed. Combed out...but – what am I saying? I can't stay that long. I have to leave. Now! Using the same portal that brought me here! I just need to figure out how!"

"But...your ship sank. You were pulled from the ocean."

"I don't mean that! I mean—ah! I can't even explain what I mean!"

"Please. Elena. You speak too rapidly and your words are strange. I need to assign meaning."

"And that's *exactly* why I have to leave!"

She twisted in place. Wrung her hands. Her gaze flitted about the meager contents of his croft. Touched on him. She looked panicky. And her words didn't clarify much. If anything, things were more perplexing.

"What is?" he finally asked.

"I say incomprehensible things, Morrigan, because I'm not who you think I am! I can't guard my tongue twenty-four-seven! I'll slip up. Say strange things. And why? Because I am strange. And I just found out you burn women for being strange! You call it witchcraft! And I even fit the part! Crap. I really could use a bath."

"We were soaked to the skin just last eve."

"That's your idea of a bath? Well. Fine. You might have been soaked in rain and snow, but I sure the heck didn't! I'm crusty with brine. And what-all else. I mean look at me!"

Her bosom was heaving. Her chemise filmed her skin, highlighting every bit of her perfection. Her hair was a cloud of darkness, framing her. Her eyes sparkled with emotion. He'd been trying not to look and she required it?

Morrigan looked over her head at the top of his doorframe. "You look beautiful," he managed to answer.

"Oh! This is impossible! I can't explain. I can't even think. I am so screwed. I really need a bath. I really need to work on my hair. And – it's just a guess – but bathing is probably one of the things you people assign to a witch."

"Once we wed, no one will call you other than wife."

She looked upward. Took several lengthy breaths. When she looked back to him, her eyes glistened like the deep onyx gemstones. And then he realized why. She held back tears. The last thing he wished to do was make her cry. His heart immediately seized up inside his chest, as if a fist had grabbed it and squeezed.

"Morrigan, please? I said it last night, but I'll repeat it. You are very sweet to propose. But the answer is the same as last night. I can't marry you."

He swallowed. "I am an honorable man, Elena. I took your maidenhead."

"And I am a grown woman who knew what she was doing."

"Elena, please. We must wed. You do not understand. Your beauty will make women jealous. That is why they called you names. And now you stay with me alone in this croft. We will wed. I have arranged it for tonight. Sooner, if the priest finishes with last rites and can attend to us."

"But I can't marry you! It would complicate an already impossible situation! You can't go back and change history. I mean...what if there were children?"

"You do not wish...babes?"

He was reeling. The fist around his heart held it so tightly, every beat sent ache. And he'd failed at preventing her tears. He watched a teardrop slide down her cheek and drop off her chin. She licked at the one that followed. She was shuddering, too. And then she looked back up at him and sent the pressure inside his chest to agony-level.

"I'm sorry, Morrigan. I can't wed with you. I can't even tell you why. I can't explain anything. I'm too afraid."

"Of...me?"

"Of everything! You don't understand. Nobody does."

She swiped at her cheeks with both hands. Lifted a lock of her hair and then dropped it again. Frowned. And that's when he knew exactly what to do.

CHAPTER TWELVE

'*YOU DO NOT WISH BABES?*'

Did he really ask her that? And had she really given him reason? Losing a baby had nearly destroyed her. Sometimes, she'd wished it had. Her ex, Donald had told her to 'get over it.' He hadn't understood. Nobody did. Not the well-meaning people who'd told her she was still young, she'd have another. Even the grief counselor had felt like a waste of time. She hadn't even thought about having a baby until she'd been pregnant, and then – after the stillbirth – it became the most important thing in her life. She'd felt like an empty shell. Every day had dawned gray and ended black.

She didn't think it was possible to get over losing a baby.

All she could do was find a way to live with it.

She'd finally learned how and eagerly looked forward to checking her pregnancy tests, and then the cancer had come calling...

Crap.

She needed to stop this. It wasn't reminiscing. It was torment. And none of it bore the slightest resemblance to her current situation. If she accepted that she'd gone through a time portal and landed in a new reality, she needed to relegate what had happened to another realm. Consider it as something that happened to someone else. No. It was something that *would* happen. It wasn't the past. The entire series of events were hundreds of years in the future.

Elena stared at the last of her porridge before shoving it

into her mouth. She'd let it get cold. It was gag-inducing. She washed the bite down with a swallow of the concoction he'd called tea. It didn't smell like tea. Didn't taste like it. But the drink was warm. And wet. It could have used some cinnamon, though. And some honey.

She should have thought of it earlier. She had both items in the spice basket. Elena shuffled through the little sewn packets that looked like sachets, before picking up another honey piece. She popped it into her mouth, sucked on it, and then spun around. The top of the stool was wide. Slick. She nearly slid off before catching it with a grab at the table again.

That probably looked as silly as it felt, but she didn't have an audience. And it wasn't entirely her fault. Morrigan had tucked her feet into the blanket after he'd slit the rawhide bindings of her boots and pulled them off. He hadn't given her much room with the rest of his wrapping job at all. He handled her way too easily. She probably should have struggled, or at least balked. But she'd been battling inner demons at the time. She didn't have any fight left for him. She wasn't used to being five-foot-nothing, either. Waifish.

Heck.

She was practically ballerina-size...

Except for this bosom.

Elena looked down at where her cleavage peeked above the blanket. Shook her head. Looked back at the fireplace. The flames looked lower. Now that she considered it, the entire room felt a bit chilly. Maybe she should put another log on. It felt like Morrigan had been gone a long time, at least an hour. She didn't know when he'd return. He'd been very mysterious. He'd planted her on this stool. Told her to eat. Stay bundled. He'd be back.

She watched wordlessly as he'd donned the fur coat as if he wore something besides a kilt, shoved his feet into enormous, solid-looking boots without worrying over socks, and then he'd looked back at where she perched. It was then that he'd winked. The man was gorgeous. Looking at him caused all kinds of reaction. A wink was enough to jumpstart an engine.

If they existed.

And she hadn't been fighting tears.

Elena sucked on the honey square. It was a nice treat. But she'd need to floss and brush at some point. Floss was easy. Figuring out a toothbrush could be problematic. And it would create comment. She had a lot of pitfalls ahead. She could ignore a lot, but going without dental hygiene wasn't going to be one of them. Telling time was another thing she needed to figure out. She didn't have any method at the moment. Even if the sun had been out, there wasn't even a window in this—.

This—.

Hmm.

She needed to find another moniker for his home. She'd been calling it a hovel. Shack. Hut. But right now, it looked pretty darn nice.

Something smacked against the door. Elena jumped. Then it happened again. With the third one, she knew it was knocking. Finding an opening for her legs took time, and effort. The blanket might as well be sewn shut. She hadn't even found an edge when the door flew open, sending a blast of wintry air with it. Flames leapt behind her, highlighting Morrigan as he stepped in, turning to set a large trunk beside the one he'd brought last night. He held the door open with his butt as he brought in a large bucket full of snow. Another one followed. He moved enough that the door shut behind him, but seconds later he walked in again, this time carrying not only another bucket of snow, but what looked like a wooden cask on his shoulder.

He'd brought wine? *Well.* Getting drunk sounded like a grand idea.

"Oh. Good. You are still here."

Elena gave a half-smile, although it didn't matter. He wasn't looking. "Where would I go?"

He grunted. Set the pail down and then lowered the keg. She'd been wrong. It was about three-fifths of a keg. The edges weren't smooth, nor were they the same shade as the rest of the wood. It looked like somebody had recently taken an ax to it. Apparently, getting soused on wine was not on the menu, but something even more wondrous might be. Her heart quickened. Was that a tub? And had he brought snow to melt?

The keg didn't look large enough for a child, but she could work with it. And it sounded heavenly. She was probably glowing.

Morrigan ignored her as he removed the coat. That flexed all kinds of muscle. He didn't look toward her before turning around, either. He raised his arms to hook the fur from the rafter again. Then he pulled off his boots, one at a time. His little kilt wasn't hiding much. Elena's jaw dropped slightly. It didn't seem possible, but she must have forgotten this part. The guy was unbelievable. Gorgeous. Ripped. Manly.

Wow.

He was going to make spectacular babies.

Elena was blushing as he turned back around, her flush making everything warm. And here she'd worried over temperature.

"I've fashioned a tub for you," he told her. "It should work."

"Oh, my."

Her eyes filled with stupid tears again. She blinked rapidly until they cleared. He'd hefted two buckets and gone past her to the fire. She watched soundlessly as he settled them atop the rock hearth. Picked up a fire-poker. Worked at the fire. Lifted another log and placed it at the back. All of it showcased muscle. Might. He turned and caught her watching. He must have read her expression correctly because his eyes widened and he immediately dropped his gaze. And then two spots of color darkened his cheeks. Something shifted in the fire behind him. He jumped slightly. Elena almost giggled.

"I didn't know you were a MacGyver," she finally commented.

He glanced up. Looked back down. "I'm not. I am KilCreig."

Elena laughed delightedly. He glanced up at her before looking away again.

"I've brought more of your belongings."

"Really?"

"I cannot get them all. Even if I could, I have no way to transport, or even store them. Not here."

"Cedric would probably balk, too," Elena added. "And you'd allow it."

"Cedric has yet to awaken."

"We're stealing them while he sleeps? How...fortuitous."

She tried to keep the censure from her voice. She knew it wasn't successful as his flush deepened.

"Cedric does not sleep. His head took a bashing last night. He struck the mast."

Elena gasped. She remembered something he'd said. It had gone right over her head at the time. "Wait. You said 'last rites'. When you mentioned the priest and—."

Marriage. She finished silently.

"Aye."

"Was that for Cedric?"

"No. The interpreter. He is worse hurt. May not last the day."

"I'm sorry. Not about Cedric, but the interpreter."

She was, too. She didn't know him from Adam, but aside from Morrigan, he was the lone man who'd come to her aid against Cedric. That alone was reason to mourn.

"Cedric may not awaken."

"I don't wish him ill, all right? I'm just—the man tried to kill me. And he would have if you hadn't been there. Um. Will he recover?"

"His family hopes as much."

"He has a family?"

Morrigan nodded.

"Is that why you don't challenge him? Take over leadership?"

Morrigan grunted. That was a cute masculine affectation that could get really old, really fast. Elena regarded him solemnly for long moments.

"That is not an answer."

He took a deep breath. Lifted his head. Grabbed her attention. A solid sensation of heat blossomed throughout her chest. Spread from there, sending a very pleasant tingling with it. She could probably blame the clear, crystal blue of his eyes or the directness of his gaze. Maybe it was his stance. Hands on hips. Feet slightly apart. It could be due to the fact that he wore such a little piece of material or how the firelight behind him caressed every inch. She nearly sighed before catching it.

This is ridiculous. She needed a bath. Her teeth brushed. Decent attire. The last thing she should be thinking of was a lovemaking session. But, oh! It sounded nice.

"I am a stranger here, too, Elena. My destiny does not lie with this village. I have a different future."

"I think I heard those lines in a movie once," Elena teased.

"What?"

"Sorry. Um. I was thinking aloud. But...this explains a lot. Uh. About your character."

He straightened. Pulled in a breath. That just put more of his abs on display. That was a really nice view. And he really should put more clothing on if he didn't want females to notice.

"'Tis a good thing you speak our language...albeit strangely. This would be a bit more difficult."

"What would?"

"There was a letter of introduction enclosed with the trunks. The interpreter read it before he—uh. Well. Before. I have it now if you'd like to see it."

Elena shook her head. It was pointless. She didn't speak or read Spanish. Yet.

"How much of your past do you remember?" he quizzed.

"Uh..."

"Do you remember anything from the New World?"

"Oh. *That* past. Absolutely nothing." That was true. Her tone reflected it.

"You are a woman of great wealth. Position. And substance. Or...you were."

"Really?"

"Your name is Margarita Elena Esmeralda Juana *de* Bodquin."

He stopped as if she was supposed to say something. Elena actually grunted but stopped the smile that followed.

"You are a member of the Bodquin family. Is that familiar to you?"

"No, but I sound very important."

"He is the Viceroy of New Spain."

"New Spain?" *Where the heck was that?*

"He controls the Spanish colonies in the new world. All of them."

"*All* of them?"

Her eyes were huge. He nodded.

"Oh. My."

She didn't know what to say. Was there something she could say? Hadn't that been most of South America, all of Mexico, and part of the southern U.S.? *Holy crap.*

"Your marriage has been arranged to Jose Manino, the Count of Flobanca. These trunks were part of your trousseau."

"Is that...good?"

"He is one of the most important men in the Spanish court.

A royal minister. I have even heard of him."

"Oh."

"He is very old."

"Great. Sounds like my wedding night will be un-fun."

"Fate has changed your destiny, *Senorita*. You are not wedding the Count of Flobanca."

"I'm not?"

"Oh, no. You are not wedding with any man save me. Tonight."

He lowered his chin and regarded her. His upper lip was lifted in a snarl. A round of shivers accompanied his statement. They added immeasurably to the tingling sensation she was already suffering. She'd never seen anything to compare him with. She didn't even try.

"And...that is a problem?"

Her voice was breathless. It was true. It felt like he'd just stolen not only her ability to breathe, but every bit of available air.

"Your family may not approve of our union."

"Oh. Well. Do we really have to tell them? I mean, can't we just burn the letter? I can go back to being anonymous?"

He stiffened. That just defined more of his physique. She didn't have the vaguest idea of why, so she just blazed on with words in a conversationalist tone.

"Um. Is my water warm yet? And...perhaps? No. It's too much to hope."

She'd seen steam rising. It was doing a fantastic job of coating his body. And that was doing a perfect job of tying her tongue in a knot. The man had too much in his arsenal, and she was directly in the firing line.

She was afraid she'd be drooling if this kept up.

"What?" he asked.

"Do you have something I can use for shampoo?"

He folded his arms. It changed the perspective, but not

much. That just highlighted his arms, shoulders, and pecs. Dang. He looked massive. Masculine. And something weird. He looked defensive, like he was preparing for a blow. All at once. And she was really having difficulty thinking.

"Sorry. I meant soap. Perhaps there's something...in my trunks?"

"I do not know what is in that trunk. I only know what's in the first one."

He pointed to the area beside the door where he'd shoved the two trunks. Elena's gaze followed. The new trunk was a lot larger than the first one he'd brought.

"I'm not sure I want to know what's in it," she whispered.

"Your jewelry." He moved his gaze from hers, focused somewhere on the door. His tone had lowered, while the words were practically spat out.

"Oh."

His reaction was beyond baffling. She didn't understand why. So, Morrigan was into acquiring wealth. He wouldn't be the first man with dollar signs in his eyes. As far as she was concerned, that was a minor blip in an otherwise fantastic-sounding future. Morrigan was practically perfect. If she was writing a romance, she'd have written the rapacious part of his character out, but she wasn't balking. She had a lot on her plate this Christmas day. Starting with what looked like a sponge bath with some dunking possibilities. Dental hygiene to figure out. An outfit that wouldn't cut off circulation. All of that before marrying a bridegroom that would have stopped traffic in New York...or any other city she could think of. As far as she was concerned, this beat the heck out of life in the 21st Century.

Hands down.

She couldn't wait to get started.

CHAPTER THIRTEEN

SHE PROBABLY THOUGHT HE WANTED to wed with her because she was rich. He hadn't given her any reason to doubt it. He'd carefully slit threads and removed the *reales* from the satin skirt and layers of petticoats while she'd worked soap into her hair, rinsed it off with a dunking in the impromptu tub, and then dried it with one of the petticoats he'd taken to her after he'd emptied it. She hadn't asked for his help. He hadn't offered. Both times he'd glanced in her direction she'd studiously avoided his gaze.

That had galled.

Morrigan had set his jaw and created stacks of coins, pushed them to the back of the table, and then repeated the process until the tabletop was nearly covered. She'd carried a small fortune on her last night. The jewels in her trunks were probably worth as much as his ancestral home. There had been a silver brush and comb set in her jewelry trunk, packed along with a mirrored silver tray. All of it inlaid with costly gemstones. She'd snatched it on sight. He let her. He wished he didn't need her silver. Or that he could tell her the truth. So she wouldn't be embarrassed over a union with him – so embarrassed, she didn't even want her family to know of it.

She'd finished washing her hair, had it wrapped in a large unwieldy-looking turban, and that's when she asked him to leave. So she could bathe and dress in privacy. Morrigan hadn't demurred. Her pink-tinted chemise had been soaked into a see-through state. Being near her was tantamount to torture. She could prepare in the warmth of the croft. He'd make do with the stables.

Morrigan shoved his feet into black leather thigh-boots with a vicious gesture, stomping a few times to stretch them. They were tight. His entire outfit had the same issue. He'd grown some since he'd arrived here, with little more than his sword, a horse, and a heart full of hatred. He hadn't worn this outfit in months. The ermine-trimmed satin short cape was wrinkled. The velvet of his jacket was crushed, his muslin shirt in need of starch and a hot iron. The leather pants were stiff and unbending. It couldn't be helped. He'd kept this ensemble rolled up and secured with twine atop a roof beam. Hidden. Awaiting one thing. A victorious entry back to his castle.

And for the first time since he'd left, the thought of that event failed to spark even a hint of interest.

Morrigan had been consumed with the idea of vindication. His world filled with making certain the world knew what a murderous coward his younger half-brother had become. His only goal gaining his proper position as head of the KilCreig family.

Now?

All he wanted to do was erase the doubts in Elena's eyes. Replace them with something else. She needn't worry over his character. Morrigan Amorag KilCreig wasn't marrying her for money. Or social position. Or even for the reasons he'd stated originally. It wasn't because he was the man who had taken her virtue, and was honor-bound to correct that.

No.

He was wedding her because of what had happened when the interpreter had translated the letter to him. It didn't matter if she was strange, or that the idea of having his babes seemed to frighten and upset her. They would work through whatever they needed to. He was marrying that woman because the thought of any other man having the right to touch her had sent a fire of reaction through Morrigan's gut, a hammer strike of anger into his chest, and wash of pure red to color his vision. Such a thing had never happened to him before. Morrigan realized what it was even as he feared it. And even that didn't change what he felt. He wouldn't have believed it possible to fall in love within the span of a few hours.

If he wasn't fully in its grasp.

Right here.

Right now.

Love was a powerful emotion. It even altered the physical realm. He didn't see the bare starkness of the stable. Hear the whickering of the horses. Feel the cold. Thoughts of his brother's perfidy failed to raise any emotion. All Morrigan wanted was to be with Elena. Search her eyes. Hold her close. Experience again the sensation of pleasure only she seemed to raise. Alleviate her worries.

He couldn't wait to see her expression when she saw her bridegroom in his proper attire, either. That's why he'd brought this ensemble out of hiding. She needn't hide in shame over a union with him. Morrigan was the holder of an old and respected title. He claimed lands and a castle. He'd been accepted into the Knights of the Order of St. Patrick. That honor came with a riband to be worn across his chest. It was a striking band of satin, in a sky blue shade. Once he'd secured it in place, the riband seemed to overcome any lack from the condition of his attire. He hadn't even donned the collar of the Order of St. Patrick, yet. That piece included a jeweled star at its center, equal to any of her gems. It was draped over the top of a stall, where it twinkled if the light from his lantern caught it just right. He was almost ready. He finger-combed his hair back before securing it in a queue.

"Have you about finished, Morrigan?"

"Yes, Father."

The priest had arrived with a flagon of ale and an offer to assist. Morrigan hadn't declined either item. The ale brought welcome warmth to his innards, and the man's company helped assuage any nervousness. Besides, the priest had shuffled through thigh-high snow just to reach the stable. The lone trail to Morrigan's croft would be more difficult to negotiate, since his steps had carved it, and he'd only been here twice.

Morrigan lifted the Order of St. Patrick collar and settled it about his shoulders, then put his fur coat atop the whole. Lifted the lantern. Nodded to the priest. Tried to smile reassuringly, despite how his belly fluttered. He forced his hand not to shake. This was truly odd. He couldn't recall ever feeling this apprehensive.

Snow had finally ceased falling, other than the occasional flake. Evening light sent a bluish cast to the landscape. Everything was disguised. Crofts were identifiable by the threads of smoke coming through roof holes. Trees limbs were coated with white. And everything sparkled as his lantern light touched it. The trek to his croft was completed in silence.

He told himself he was ready as the front of his croft came into view. He still swallowed nervously, and the lantern shook in his hand. It wasn't possible to hide it. The light wavered across the doorframe, giving him away. He lifted his other hand. Made a fist. And rapped at the door.

"Yes? Who is it?"

He heard her clearly. So did the priest if his choked laughter was an indicator. Morrigan blew a sigh heavenward before looking back at the door.

"Morrigan. And Father Simon. May we come in?"

"Oh. Yes. Of course."

They heard the sound of the bolt being drawn, but then nothing happened. Morrigan regarded the door for a span before turning the handle and pushing it open. Air from their entrance stoked the fire at the back, lighting the interior easily. It lit upon Elena. She'd moved the stool, and was sitting beside the fire. She'd used the time to arrange herself. He couldn't see her clearly except as a silhouette, but she looked like a queen. It was obvious. And completely frightening.

Morrigan blew out the lantern before stepping in, holding the door for the priest. The man walked in without a hint of the edginess dogging Morrigan. He put his attention on securing the door against the elements, hanging the light from a spike. He unfastened the coat and pulled it off. Took his time hanging it beside the lantern.

And then he turned around.

CHAPTER FOURTEEN

ELENA'S EYES WENT WIDE AND her jaw dropped. She felt it. And then she was on her feet and approaching him, ruining every bit of the impression she'd spent so much time setting up! She didn't have much room in the gown she'd chosen, but it was the best of the lot. There had been three dresses in the large trunk to choose from. All wrapped in layers of linen that turned out to be undergarments. One was made from heavy black satin. It wasn't too wrinkled, and had a lot of silver thread for embellishment, but she didn't want to get wed in black. That could be a bad omen.

One was crafted from a red striped material that she didn't care for, and one had been crafted of velvet in a variety of sea-green colors. There was a silky slip included. A corset. She had to wear one. They seemed to be the lone item that would support her breasts. She would have worn the green one, but it fastened up the back with a webbing of lacing that looked daunting. The black corset was her lone choice, and once she had it laced up, it did a wonderful job of not only supporting her breasts, but putting a lot of cleavage on display...but that was helped by a goose-egg-sized pearl set in the center of a necklace she'd found in the jewelry chest.

She'd barely finished in time.

Getting her hair under control had taken hours. She'd settled on a braid. It probably looked messy at the beginning, and it weighed a lot more than she was used to, but at least the fly-aways were under control. She was going to have to figure something out for conditioner if she kept her hair this long. And something for the split end problem. But it was out of her way. And looked pretty nice.

What was she thinking?

She wasn't just nice. She was ravishingly beautiful. Pulling the hair back had highlighted high cheekbones, dark eyes with a slanted cast, a lot of eyelashes, and unbelievably perfect features. Even viewed in a mirrored tray that warped her image, Elena had been stunned. Shocked. And amazed. She hadn't believed much about actually being here in seventeen-ninety, but seeing her new image had been so over-the-top incredible, it was almost obscene.

And gratifying.

Morrigan deserved a beautiful woman.

Ah.

Morrigan.

Morrigan KilCreig.

Mister and Missus KilCreig.

Missus Elena KilCreig.

Hmm.

She'd giggled, but couldn't seem to banish the thoughts. She was wedding Morrigan! The thought thrilled. Sent goose bumps along her skin, tingling to her breasts, and a huge surge of warmth had gone everywhere else. It was so exciting. He was so manly. She was so in love.

Oh, shit.

No.

She'd stopped her preparations. Dropped the dress. Stared at the door. But still the certainty sat in her belly, sending something that alternated between a fluttering like butterflies and a sinking sensation like lead. She'd fallen in love? Oh. This was bad. But, true. And that was bad. But incredibly wonderful at the same time.

Then again...why not? She was stuck here. With him. And he wanted to marry her. *No.* The man had pretty much demanded that she marry him. And that sounded like heaven. Whatever his reason, surely between them they'd figure out how to make it work. They already had massive passion going for them.

Oh!

She couldn't wait to see him again! Watch him unwrap *this* Christmas present.

The thought sent another burst of mirth through her. So, she'd set it up. Finished fastening the row of hooks up the back of her dress and somehow swiveled it around. She really did have a fabulous bosom. The necklace was probably overkill. She hadn't been able to sit still, however. She'd packed everything back into the trunks. Washed dishes. Moved the stool. Worked at finding a pose that would highlight her.

But when he'd turned around, a surge of electricity shot right through the space between them, lifting her to her feet and completely ruining the entire effect. He had a slight smile as she gazed up at him, absolutely awestruck. He looked like something out of a royal portrait. There was a huge piece of jewelry in the center of his chest, hanging from a chain that looked like real gold. She didn't know much about gems and prices in 1790, but that thing could probably buy a nice section of Manhattan. Even in 21st century prices.

How could he need money?

"Elena?" he asked.

"Holy crap," she replied.

"Holy what?"

The black-clothed figure of a priest answered from where he stood beside Morrigan. The priest was not only dwarfed, he looked like he hailed from a different species. She hadn't even seen him.

"My bride hails from the New World, Father. She doesn't

remember anything of her past life. She speaks our language well, but some of the words she says are unknown to us. I believe what she is saying right now is that she is...impressed. Yes?"

Morrigan winked at her. Elena's knees turned to water and her thighs to mush. The support pole saved her from the embarrassment of falling, although she probably looked gawky as she swayed into it and then grabbed on.

"Um. I. Um. I. Um."

She stopped trying to say anything. His lips curved into a smile. Elena's heart lurched.

"Are you certain you wish to wed this woman, Morrigan?" the priest asked.

Morrigan's smile grew broader. He didn't reply. She was surprised he didn't grunt.

"An unknown woman?" the priest continued.

"Un...known?" Elena managed to find her voice enough to interject.

Morrigan lifted his jacket, pulled out a long paper-looking thing. He unfolded it. There was a really cool-looking design across the top. A lot of calligraphic writing.

Was that parchment?

How the heck was she supposed to know? Morrigan strode past her to the fire. Nobody said a word as he put the edge of the letter to coals. Then, he held it up so flames could consume it. When it was down to thumb-size, he dropped it into the fire. Turned around. He was grinning broadly. She didn't understand why. And then it dawned on her. *If that was her introduction...?*

"Was that what I think it was?" she asked.

He didn't move his gaze from hers, but he addressed the priest. "In answer to your question, Father Simon. Yes. I wish to wed this woman. The one we pulled from the sea. The one without a past and no relatives. The woman known only as

Elena."

He *had* just burned her introduction!

"You are certain?" the priest asked.

Elena couldn't move her gaze from Morrigan. He had such riveting blue eyes. If she wasn't already in love, that look would have done it. She was close to swooning.

"Oh, yes, Father. Positive."

"Very good. And you, Miss Elena?"

Long moments passed before she realized the priest had addressed her. But she couldn't seem to break eye contact with Morrigan. Not until he winked again. Elena gasped, held tighter to the pole and managed to swivel around to face the door. And the priest.

"Y-Y-Yes?"

Crap. She stuttered.

"Do you wish to wed this man?"

What in the heck was wrong with her? Her eyes were filling with tears. Her throat closed off. She had to settle with a nod. But then he added words that sent her head spinning.

"You understand you are wedding a man known as Morrigan, but he is really the Earl of KilCreig?"

"The Earl of...*what*?" she asked.

"Father Simon!"

Morrigan's reply sounded especially loud. There wasn't any need. The cabin was small. Reverberations from his outburst were enough to rattle the walls.

"You may be in hiding, my lord, but I know the truth."

"You know nothing!"

"I do. I have been south. To your castle."

Morrigan had a castle?

The men kept speaking with each other, sending the temperature in the room higher with each spate of words. There wasn't much break between them. Elena clung to the support pole and looked from one to the other as each spoke.

Then she realized something. This was as good as watching a stage play.

Oh. Wait.

It was déjà vu. This was exactly like her first experience when she'd been pulled into this era. When Morrigan had faced Cedric and saved her. Only this was so much better. She didn't question what was happening to her. Or if this was a dream. She knew it was reality. And she knew it wasn't going to end.

"I don't have a castle," Morrigan replied. "I have exactly what you see here."

The priest sighed loudly. "Once you regain it, you will."

"That has yet to happen."

"All you need is your uncle's assist."

"He does not answer my missives."

"He is ill. I've been to his bedside. He only awaits your arrival. And your plan."

"I need men. An army."

The priest waved a hand toward the stacks of *reales* on the table. "The Lord appears to have provided for that."

"How do you know all of this, Father?"

"I've given services at Castle KilCreig. There are many still loyal to you. They are fully aware of your innocence."

"Are they?"

"You would never have poisoned your father."

"You think not?"

His father was poisoned? Damn. This was really good stuff. Unbelievable. Then again, little had been believable ever since she'd fallen overboard in the section of the Colorado River called Satan's Gut. Been pulled from the ocean in the year 1790. Met the man of her dreams. Fallen in love.

This had to be the best Christmas on record.

Holy shit. Morrigan was an Earl? Once they wed, she wondered what would that made her. *Oh, wait, Elena.* She needed to pay attention. They were speaking again.

"I attended your stepmother for last rites. A month past."

"The marchioness has died?"

"Dowager Marchioness."

Oh. Sweet. That must be her title. She'd be a marchioness. Sounded very impressive. Then again, what did she care? Morrigan was an impressive man. She'd have wed him regardless of what he was. Peasant farmer. Penniless adventurer. Scoundrel.

"You know, I cannot divulge what transpired at last rites, but your stepmother believed she'd been poisoned. By the same hand that had killed her husband. Your half-brother."

"He poisoned his own mother?"

Whoa.

This brother sounded like an evil shit. They needed to get moving. Find an army and pay for them. Rescue everyone. First things first, though. It was Christmas day. Late. She was getting married. And then, they were going to say good-bye to Father Simon. Maybe exchange a few words. And then she was going to unwrap her husband like a present, and —

"Elena?"

She shook her head. Stared for a moment uncomprehendingly at Morrigan before answering.

"Um. Yes?"

"Father Simon wishes to know if you are ready?"

"Heck, yeah. I mean—"

Elena straightened and then cleared her throat. Tried to sound like a marchioness – whatever that was. But then she ruined it by giggling. "I mean. Yes. I am."

He grunted. And Dang! She really loved it when he did that. He held out his left arm to her, crooked at the elbow. Elena let go of the pole and settled her fingertips atop his forearm. She'd seen this done in movies. She hoped she did it right. She glanced up at him. He was smiling. Good thing he didn't wink. She'd have probably fallen. He took a step toward the door, turning her at his side so they faced the priest.

"You have a ring?" Father Simon asked.

"Ah. It had escaped my mind, Father, but I do have a family ring. A small one. It might even fit."

Morrigan wore it on the little finger of his left hand. Elena wasn't giving up her grasp. He worked the ring off, moving a lot of muscle beneath her fingertips. She nearly gave sound to a sigh of appreciation. But it didn't really matter. He was entirely sigh-worthy and she was in love...and then he showed her the ring.

Elena gasped. Her knees wavered. And her eyes went huge. And for a moment everything spun. It was identical to the spiral ring she'd purchased in the gift shop. Somewhere in Arizona. How could that be?

"What is it, *milis*?"

She remembered that word. It meant sweet. Tears were threatening again. Elena sniffed.

"I have a really bad feeling about this," she replied.

"Wedding me?"

"Oh, no. Never. But...do we have another ring I can use? Perhaps something in my...jewelry trunk?"

"You fret for naught, my love."

His eyes were so riveting. Mesmeric. And completely enthralling. She barely heard what he said, but she heard the endearment he called her. And everything went to a standstill as he finished.

"'Tis just a ring. What could possibly happen?"

"Please?"

"*Is brea liom tu.*"

"What?"

"That is Celtic. It means...I love you."

Oh my stars.

Elena was going to melt.

There couldn't be a better setting. Or a better future. Or a more wonderful Christmas. Elena kept the sobs at bay while saying her vows. Listening to his. She wasn't as successful when he kissed the spiral ring. But they were tears of happiness now. Rinsing away every hint of her past.

He slid the ring onto her finger. And absolutely nothing untoward happened. The little golden spiral sitting on her finger glowed in the firelight. Reacting with the haze of wonder that surrounded her...and the man she loved. The Native American woman from the gift shop had been right when she'd sold an identical ring to Elena. Owning this ring was her destiny. She'd simply needed to alleviate the portals of time to reach it.

She'd never believed in Christmas magic.

Well.

She did now.

ABOUT THE AUTHOR

JACKIE IVIE LIVES IN THE enormous state of Alaska with her husband and three very spoiled pets. She started her writing career writing hot highland historical romances for Kensington Publishing. There are now ten "Clans series" books, available in seven languages. Keeping her head in the clouds most of the time, Jackie now spends her time researching, developing, and writing her paranormal series – the **Vampire Assassin League**, the NEW **Chronicles of the Hunters**, and **The Portals of Time**, as well as her other historical line – the **Brocade Collection**.

Jackie loves hearing from fans, who can contact her at www.jackieivie.com or www.VampireAssassinLeague.com

Want to keep up with the assassins of the Vampire Assassin League, the dark angels of the Chronicles of the Hunter, or the time travelers of the Portals of Time series? Sign up for Jackie's newsletter at http://jackieivie.com/para/news.htm.

Want to know and discuss all things VAL? Consider joining the Assassin Street Team at http://www.facebook.com/groups/379151425455048/

www.ingramcontent.com/pod-product-compliance
Lightning Source LLC
Chambersburg PA
CBHW061537170626
46811CB00001B/12